Centralia

Family, Freedom, Faith

Centralia

Family, Freedom, Faith

Peter Sheesley

Published by Peter Sheesley
Centralia, Washington

ISBN-13: 978-0-615-64696-1
ISBN-10: 0-615-64696-4

Dedication

For my parents who gave me a childhood full of love, faith, and art. You are my heroes.

For my Aunt Jennifer who has been a friend and a spiritual, emotional, and financial patron these last few years.

For my real life brothers, Ben and John; oh mercy, I love you both so much it hurts!

A big huge thank you to editor extraordinaire, Kristen H.

For the good people of Centralia.

About the Author

L.L. Diamond is more commonly known as Leslie to her friends and Mom to her three kids. A native of Louisiana, she spent the majority of her life living within an hour of New Orleans before following her husband all over as a military wife. Louisiana, Mississippi, California, Texas, New Mexico, Nebraska, and now England have all been called home along the way.

Aside from mother and writer, Leslie considers herself a perpetual student. She has degrees in biology and studio art but will devour any subject of interest simply for the knowledge. Her most recent endeavors have included certifications to coach swimming, certifying as a fitness instructor and indoor cycling instructor, and she is currently studying to be a personal trainer. As an artist, her concentration is in graphic design, but watercolor is her medium of choice with one of her watercolors featured on the cover of her second book, *A Matter of Chance*. She is also a member of the Jane Austen Society of North America. Leslie also plays flute and piano, but much like

Contents

"'Will you come with me to the mountains? It will hurt at first, until your feet are hardened. Reality is harsh to the feet of shadows. But will you come?'" (CS Lewis, _The Great Divorce_ 39).

2010

Blue Flower

A great dark-blue tarp covers the sky at night. Outside the tarp glory and light surround. There are tiny holes all over the tarp that let bits of light and glory in. These are called stars. All of life happens underneath these stars.

It is a beautiful day outside; the sky is blue and small clouds are moving happily from northwest to southeast.

Centralia, Washington, hovers like a goddess between the mountains and the ocean. With a fleece jacket tied around her waist, Centralia patiently carries her populace. She is just. Centralia does not laugh at injury, nor does she gloat in victory: she journeys, balanced like the scales of justice, between the mountains and the sea. She is temperate and green.

Jim Moore stands on the side of the road, a pawn on an empty chess board. The soles of his tennis shoes have a white rubber rim. His sharp Moore nose makes his eyes look always attentive. He is shorter than the cars that pass but taller than the rails along the side of the road. All around him are the imaginary squares of a giant chess board, one-step moves into the afternoon. A large truck speeds past him, its draft making his loose, partially unzipped sweatshirt billow in the wind.

He walks west out of town toward 605 Galvin Road, the address written on his list . . . it's his Great Uncle, Dollar Moore's house; his Dad told him that this morning. He surveys the landscape, enjoying it. The trees are like giant brooms. As he looks at the river he feels it inside of him, as though he is the land and he is drinking the river. Where the earth rises into a mound he feels the uplifting; where it sinks into a gully he swoons with it. Patches of green grass dapple the overall yellowish color of the fields. As the clouds move down the valley toward him, he can see that some hills are in the sun and others are in the shade. His senses are especially alive this afternoon.

The school day was long and he spent nearly the entire day gazing out the window at the beautiful sunshine. The ultra-bright sun coming through the windows exaggerated the dimness of the indoor light. How could he be expected to sit there and focus on the grim pages of a book with the full force of the sun bombarding the room? That supernatural power, that blinding light, the breaking in of something pure and holy, was too profound to be abstracted and superseded by the curving ligatures and serifs of a font on the page of a book; too majestic to fit in the lesson plan. The light of the sun shone through the school day, manifest as rectangles, bars, trapezoids, rhombuses, diamonds and jewels playing on the linoleum floor and jumping onto desk legs, lying down across backpacks, tanning in the middle of the floor.

That light pursued Jim all day in school. He waited, holding back his senses with a leash, for the end of the day to come.

By the time he reaches Galvin Road and makes his left turn he forgets that he just spent eight hours of the day at his school desk on a plastic chair with his feet between its four metal posts, with the smell of glue and erasers perfuming the air.

There is an eagle standing in the wet, tall grasses about a hundred yards away. He watches it awkwardly play in a small area. It lifts ten feet off the ground, then tumbles sideways, lands, and pecks in the earth. It walks, lifts again, then falls down with wings spread to land again. The eagle behaves as though no one is watching, as unashamed as a rectangle of sunlight in the middle of a classroom floor. But instead of austerity it projects a somewhat clumsy self. The contrast of its playful awkwardness to the awesome grace of its full flight makes the moment comic. He imagines the sheer pleasure of flying on those strong wings, coasting over the earth, then over the river, as if it is all one and the same; imagines riding over pre-creation Earth like the wind of God sweeping over the waters.

Jim kicks a littered plastic juice bottle from the gravel by the side of the road into the ditch further down. He watches his feet go through the action and return to walking as though they have a mind of their own. He does the same kicking motion again, but only kicking at the air. Repeat. And again, repeat--then two steps and a step up onto the narrow concrete walkway of the first bridge. His left hand reaches out to skim along the large sage-green metal tube running along the walkway. Leaning over the rounded tube, the blood rushes to his head. He does what all boys are apt to do on bridges: he spits slowly into the water below, watching it dangle from his mouth, then release, fall, and become smaller as it nears the water's surface, then land silently and whisk away. The water looks cool and thick with mud. A log sticks out at an angle below the bridge. He looks for fish, for the flash of moving brightness a fish's back would make if it rose near the surface.

Just a few feet behind him a car speeds across the bridge. Nine years earlier Jim was an infant in a back seat, in a plastic car seat, and his Grandfather, Creek Moore, drove him in a car along this road. His Grandfather's brother, Dollar, just happened to be leaving his house to drive into town and was coming down the road in the opposite direction. The weather and the roads were clear. Dollar's T-shirt was tucked into his blue-jeans but he was not wearing his belt. It was supposed to be a quick errand.

It's amazing how many cars pass each other at high speeds in opposite directions on a narrow strip of road without colliding. Driving requires a simple faith in people. It hopes for safety despite the inevitably inadequate attention, skill, and order of a broad swath of imperfect people. Nine years ago, these two brothers approached each other on this same road with that simple faith.

Tragedy intrudes unexpectedly but not uncertainly. In fact, the certainty of tragedy keeps people from going insane. Amidst the struggles of the brain to understand, undo, or dream away tragedy, tragedy holds, silently, like an anchor. Life before the tragedy differs from life after it in this way: before a tragedy are times of uncertainty, dreaminess, potential and hope; after a tragedy there is mostly sober certainty—though it may lie heavy beneath a veneer of denial, it does not go away.

Nine years ago Creek drove his one-year-old grandson, Jim, west on Galvin Road. Dollar was approaching from the opposite direction. They did not recognize each other, and there was no warning, no angelic interlude admonishing them to pay attention. Dollar simply got distracted by a piece of lint on his dashboard. He reached out to brush the lint away. In the less than two seconds it took him to do this, his dark-green Nissan wandered across the centerline, wandered enough to collide head-on with Creek's white Subaru. They collided about 25 yards on the other side of the bridge from where Jim now stands.

Dollar's Nissan ended up on the road, spun around, the front completely crushed. Dollar survived, though his ankles were both broken. Creek's white Subaru was off the road in the grass, just over a small rise in the ground. His car looked less damaged, but his head and neck were so rattled by the crash that he died almost instantly. Creek's lifeless body leaned against the wheel. Next to him, young Jim in the car-seat, survived without any serious injuries.

This accident took Creek's life at age 59. Dollar was 57.

"Am I my brother's keeper?" God tells Cain that Abel's blood is crying out to him from the ground, and he sends Cain out of his presence.

Jim struggles to decide whether to go play frisbee with his friends from school or do his weekly volunteer visit with the elderly for the Our Family program. Some decisions only become more difficult the more you think about them. This is one of those decisions, and his mind is caught spinning around it, like a Ferris Wheel that won't stop. His decision is based on tomorrow's weather, which he can't predict. Eventually he'll just have to take a risk one way or another.

On the other side of the bridge, still undecided about whether he will make a visit for Our Family or play frisbee, Jim wanders from the road. Walking toward a bump in ground, he walks about fifteen feet until he sees a small blue flower.

At ten-years-old Jim unexpectedly walks off the side of the road to the exact same spot where he had survived the car accident nine years before. Though he was there for his Grandfather's death he doesn't remember it at all. For Jim, the world is friendly and exciting. The heavy burdens of loss, regret, revenge, do not weigh him down. As he puts the small blue flower in his shirt pocket he thinks to himself, "maybe I will give this flower to Great Uncle Dollar today."

There are two bridges on Galvin Road. They both go over rivers, and the second river, the one farther west is larger. As Jim walks across the second bridge he looks out across the water to the North and beyond it to the hills in the distance—an emerald paradise. It is as though the landscape is perpetually doing a green curtsy.

605 Galvin Road is the address written on his list of people to visit for the week. His dad had told him where the house would be, just past his friend Mike's house. It is a mile or so out of town, but not completely rural yet. The houses here have most of the decorous trimmings of those in town, but they also have their share of make-shift addendums. For example, maybe the homeowner made his own garage, or poured his own sidewalk, or constructed his own awning. There are also more tools, both discarded and functional, lying around in the yards. In town, each square foot of yard is on display. Out here there are specific areas for display but the visitor is not expected to look at the other large areas of flotsam and untrimmed grasses—they are overlooked. They are unselfconscious. Maybe these areas result from practical placement of necessities, both those currently used and those defunct. Or maybe the home owners really do appreciate the aesthetics of landscaping yet at the same time they have developed a taste for the bruised and untrimmed, the substitute and the dented, the left-over and the forgotten. Perhaps in the simple and imperfect gesture of a stack of iron fence posts by a shed, or a child's bicycle leaning against garbage cans, they are intentionally

achieving something like the monks of ancient Japanese calligraphy—a mark upon the earth that is simple, unedited, economic, and to the point. These are the homes Jim finds himself walking past until he reaches 605 Galvin Road.

Jim's dad, Thomas, told him Dollar is a recluse. When Thomas talks about Dollar his tone of voice becomes more cautious. His words are surrounded by more space and his eyes look to the side, unfocused. He doesn't talk about Dollar very often.

Over the years Great Uncle Dollar has turned in on himself, turned on himself, turned around himself, become twisted and tangled in himself. Jim has heard about the events of the car crash, how Dollar's car hit the car Jim and Grandpa Creek were in, and how his Grandpa died instantly without feeling any pain. But Jim hasn't really felt the emotions of that event—he was too young when it happened. The story is told to him, and he believes it and knows it involves him, but it doesn't stir any emotions in him. Because it is the only reality he has ever had (this car crash at one-year-old, and a dead Grandfather) it is all simply normal to him and he doesn't wonder about things being different. In the same way, visiting Dollar doesn't really mean that much to him because it is the only reality he has ever known. All he thinks to himself is, "I have a Great Uncle who I don't see very often. He is quiet and doesn't get out much; now he is on my list of people to visit this week: it will be nice to visit him and say hello."

Checking his shirt pocket to see if the flower he picked is still there, he remembers why that bump in the field seemed familiar. That is where his parents sometimes stop along the road, pointing off the side of the road, to tell him about the accident he was in when he was a baby.

Getting up from his recliner to answer the door, Dollar looks older than his 67 years. Most of his hair is gone though some on the sides is messy and longer than it should be. He wears a sweater-vest in which his shoulders seem to have disappeared. The most prominent feature of Dollar is his nose. Over the years it increases in size so that now his nostrils are long enough you could slip a quarter into each one. His hands and feet move like flippers--not tools of precision. As his frame decreases in size and his shoulders diminish, his nose, hands, and feet become proportionally larger. In his posture now there is an ape-like form, as his head shifts forward and his arms with their ponderous hands begin swinging lower and lower. He wears a pair of tan slacks that are beset by small stains—none so large to merit new pants, but collectively forming an impression of thriftiness at best, griminess at worst. For shoes, Dollar wears old black walking sneakers. They are totally black with frayed stitching and lettering also in black, and they are somehow puffy in their effect on the eyes. His face is the roof of a cave. There are hidden crevices and surprising protrusions. You have the feeling of going back through time the longer you look into it.

Dollar is a creature of habit. Though today's visitor is expected because the organization called ahead to remind him, for Dollar only the habits that are a part of each and every day are truly welcomed. He likes his slippers to be found in the same place every morning when he wakes. They should be parked next to each other under the corner of bed closest to the door, facing in. The morning paper should be found within an approximate five-foot circle near the foot of the front porch. Since retiring from the mill, he wakes at 6:30 each morning, makes a pot of coffee, and cooks a fried egg. The first hour of the day is spent reading the newspaper. The second hour is spent shaving, showering, and dressing. The third hour is spent wandering around the house, yard, and garage looking for things that are out of place or need to be fixed. The next several hours consist of trips to the hardware store and the grocery store. Then the late afternoon and evening are spent in front of the television. Occasionally some of the guys from work will stop by to say hello—about once a week. Most of his life is solitary, predictable. He likes it that way.

Opening the door to Jim, Dollar fails to recognize him at first. "How can I help you son?"

"Mr. Moore, I'm Jim Moore, I'm here for Our Family."

"Yes. That is now, isn't it. Come in Jim. Would you like some soda?" His interaction is spare, like a chain-link fence around a schoolyard. An infomercial about sink-cleaning products plays quietly from the living room TV.

Dollar's yellowed fingernails pick at and pull a few ice cubes from a tray, dropping them into a small glass that is smoothed and frosted with age. Small within the doorway to the kitchen, Jim watches with his backpack still over his shoulder. Dollar opens the refrigerator, leaning over to look in. On the door of the refrigerator there is a row of eight or so matching cans of Coke. His large hand grips one of them by its top, and knowingly flips open the lid, pours, and without saying anything turns and walks out of the kitchen into the living room. Jim follows him, follows the glass of Coke to a flimsy looking coffee table and the end of a soft, worn couch. After sitting in a La-Z-Boy chair to the side of Jim, Dollar uses the remote to turn off the volume, but leaves the picture on the TV.

Jim sits on the front of the couch, sipping his drink at regular intervals. Dollar sits back in his La-Z-Boy with arms folded across his beltline. They watch the infomercial without volume. The black and white figures gesture and smile like Martians in a fish tank. The salesman and objects in the TV look like they are from a different world. Without volume, the action and expressions are commical.

"How's your Dad's school year going?" Dollar asks as though he's talking to a newspaper held between his hands, as though the conversation is a column in a newspaper he's about to read.

"Fine," Jim says, not really thinking about his Dad, or his Dad's job as a high school history teacher—but thinking mostly about what the proper response to this question should be, and settling on the safest and shortest option for the occasion, "Fine."

There is silence for a couple of minutes as they gaze toward the TV. "Did you hear they caught the red-hat robber?" Dollar asks. To him this seems a sure talking point. Everyone in town has been following the story of a bank robber who wears a red knit hat and robbed three banks in the last week. He's not a sophisticated robber, with his knit hat and large earings, but the local law enforcement isn't that sophisticated either. They are a good match for each other. Most of the banks in the area don't hold much cash anyway. People in town are afraid because the robber fired his pistol in one of the banks, putting a hole in the ceiling. Dollar hopes Jim will be excited to talk about the robber.

"Oh." Jim answers, faking some enthusiasm. He has heard of the robber but doesn't really think much about it. He doesn't go into banks and his world at school and home seem totally disconnected from the world of the red-hat robber. He's still too young to care about a community novelty like this.

Half of Jim's Coke is gone. He moves his thumb up and down the side of the glass to wipe away condensation. They sit in front of the silent TV where a woman smiles and holds out her hand toward the camera. The view changes to a close-up of her hand with a large diamond ring set in thick band. Her skin is very tan and when the picture goes back to her smiling face her teeth glimmer white from behind the dark, waxy apple of her lips. Her face looks like a mask. Jim looks away, to the left of the TV, toward the front of the house and a small window with a curtain pulled in front of it. There are no lights on in the living room, so the TV and the two windows—one to the front and one through the door in the back room—are the brightest parts of the room.

"I'll show you my new irrigation system" Dollar says with marked pride. Jim doesn't respond. They sit for about another minute looking at the TV. Then Dollar slowly rises from his seat and walks to the back room. Jim instinctively follows, leaving his empty Coke glass with three melting ice cubes on the coffee table.

The backyard is a square about 30 yards deep and 30 yards wide, with a chain-link fence keeping foreign things out. Along the two sides are the neighbors' yards, both more full than Dollar's, with trees, bushes, birdfeeders, flowers. Along the back are a few feet of scrub bushes, then a scrappy forest that leads into a marsh.

The symmetry of Dollar's backyard is perfect. Along each side and the back are three evenly spaced beds about three-feet-deep and eight-feet-long, tilled into fresh dirt, each with its own chicken-wire fence. Running along the front of these beds, and all the way around the three sides of the yard is a six-inch-wide and six-inch-deep moat lined with black plastic sheeting. The sheeting is held in place with toothpicks punched into the ground at its sides. This miniature moat makes three sides of a square that sits three-feet inside the outer fence. Between the moat and the fence are the empty garden beds. At the front of the small moat are one-foot-tall wooden stakes spaced about six-feet-apart, with a white string tied to their tops, running along the three fenced sides of the yard. In the four corners of the yard are four used plastic soda bottles duct-taped to stakes and raised about a foot off the ground.

Each bottle is filled with a yellowish liquid and there are no tops on the bottles. Other than the slightly browned grass, nothing grows in the backyard.

Dollar and Jim stand at the back of the house. They both face the back of the yard and Dollar's toes reach just over the cement walkway onto the grass. It's a warm day for early spring. What began as a fully cloudy day has become sunny with only spots of clouds. Dollar talks without moving or pointing, "Beautiful, isn't she? Whole thing only cost me forty bucks. My friend Nick told me the ancient Mayans never gardened without an irrigation system. I can circulate fifty gallons of fresh water an hour, if I want. By the way, that's corn syrup in the bottles. Nick said the Mayans made a concentrated liquid from their best corn to keep pests away and get blessings from the gods . . . blessings from the gods . . . watch this . . ."

Dollar walks over to the near corner where a garden hose is coiled and connected to the spigot in the back of the house. He slowly bends to put the end of it in the trough and turns on the water. They stand without speaking, watching. Jim hears the sound of water moving through the hose, the sound of a lawnmower a few houses away, cars on the road, and a dog barking intermittently. Dollar stands over the hose where it fills the trough. Jim is still near the back door watching patiently. After about five minutes the trough fills with water.

Jim is mystified by the whole thing. It looks like there is an order and a system, a structure and a method, but he can't really put the pieces of it together. He's not sure how the water gets into the gardening beds, what the string does, or if the corn syrup is really doing anything at all. He sees a spot near the back right corner where water is spilling out and beginning to pool in the grass.

"It's almost perfect, almost finished" Dollar says. Then he

turns off the hose and walks back inside the house. Jim follows. Dollar speaks without turning toward Jim, "Looks like it's been about half-an-hour, our time's up. Thanks for stopping in."

"Okay Mr. Moore. Have a good night." Jim picks up his backpack, walks through the entryway and out the front door. He hears Dollar clear his throat and shut the door behind him.

As Jim leaves Dollar's house he remembers the flower in his front pocket, the flower that was the only blue flower in the field, the flower he picked from the ground on the hump in the field, picked from the spot where ten years ago Creek was killed and Jim was spared in a collision with Dollar's car; that flower was taken from a moment of chaos and entropy, taken from under the cold, unfeeling, mindless grinding wheel of fate. He leaves the little blue flower on the peeling wooden railing of Dollar's front porch.

Far beyond Jim's childhood perception is the distant perspective to see that his being there to visit Dollar with Our Family is a result of his Grandfather Creek founding the Our Family program.

Jim walks back in the same direction he came. The day becomes so clear he can see Mt. Ranier. It surprises him, as it often does when it comes out from hiding on the horizon, behind the clouds. He turns right, off Galvin onto Eshom. He looks at all the different ways people have of dressing up their front yards. When he gets to his house, his dad is already home from work. Jim's mom, Ellen, gives him a hug as he comes in the front door. Thomas has made one of his experimental meat-loafs for dinner. Jim isn't thrilled about the meatloaf but he does think it's funny when his dad tries to convince them of how great the meatloaf is before they eat. Jim's brother and sister giggle with him as Thomas says, "Tonight, my friends, I have prepared a succulent savory scintillating feast of the finest flavors for your most discerning delight and delectation. In this humble loaf are three vegetables, two meats, five spices, and six mystery ingredients. May your bellies be happy and your tongues satisfied. And if you must, there's plenty of ketchup to wash it down!"

In his bed, young Jim Moore dreams of flying. It starts out as simple walking, but he feels a breeze pick up and move against his body. By clearing his mind and leaning into the breeze he notices that he walks a few inches off the ground. Before long he leans more and can stop moving his legs, and he coasts forward, a few feet off the ground. Some of the people walking around outside look at him with confused expressions. Then a stronger breeze comes and he rises up higher; catching turns in the wind, and with a gust he is several hundred feet in the air, exhilarated by the feeling of flying. He looks down to see squares of grassy land laid out like a quilt below. The quilt ends at a river to his right and at distant mountains to his left. Here and there are patches of dark green that are fir tree forests.

1956

Stick

54 years earlier, in the town of Centralia, in 1956, Dollar
Moore is twelve years old. He is home alone. His parents and
older brothers, Creek and Lorne, just left for one of Lorne's basketball banquets at the high school. The four of them fit loosely into
the family's Ford Country Squire station wagon. They talk about
Lorne's basketball team as they ride to the high school. Dollar has
had a cold for two days and his Mom recommended he take a
bath while they are out for the evening. His nose is totally stuffy
and his neck is becoming sore. He slowly lowers his body into the
hot water. Most of his body is under the water, but his head, the
top of his chest and his knees remain dry.

Dollar day-dreams. He is a giant.

His stomach moves with each breath. As he breathes in it
rises up above the surface; as he breathes out it is slowly sub-
merged in water—first his belly-button fills, then the whole thing
falls below the surface. He begins taking smaller breaths, nar-

rowing the range on either side of the filling navel, so that just the slightest breath in or out will raise his navel island above the water, or submerge it . . . about twenty breaths in and out. It is a cautious breathing, timid, and always on the verge of bursting out of control.

In his Earth Science class the other day, Dollar learned about the various temperature ranges and atmospheres on all the planets in our solar system. He thinks of the narrow and fragile state of conditions necessary to sustain life on Earth. The range is small like the breaths he takes, and it seems to be always on the verge of a larger inhale or exhale, a catastrophic collapse or expansion, a release of the vital tension we live within—in one direction or another.

Dollar loses track of time as he lies with his eyes closed in the warm bath.

The rest of the family returns. That night, in the twin bed across the room from Dollar, Creek dreams vividly. It probably has something to do with his lawn mowing chores. In the dream Creek is lying on his back in the grass. A shovel, and various leaves and sticks, lie on top of him. Turning his head to one side he sees the lawnmower, wet with gasoline and with handles in flames. The gas cap is loose and it is clear that if he doesn't get over there to twist it shut the whole thing will explode. He turns his head to the other side and sees the tail of a small snake. Looking past this tail, there is a larger snake moving quietly toward him, about eight feet away. He tries to get up but the weight of the shovel and sticks is too much. He can roll over and start crawling toward the lawnmower, but at just the moment when he reaches out to tighten the cap, he is on his back again under the shovel, too far from the lawnmower, and the snakes are closer. It is a frightening dream.

In the morning they sit at the breakfast table eating cereal. The Moore family lives in a modest house, with one truly wonderful feature: the view. It's located up on a hill, on River Heights Rd., Northwest of downtown. From the windows in the back of the house they can look out and see a large valley, and opposite the valley, Mt. Ranier.

Surely, growing up with such a grand view of such a massive mountain effects a family. It is a common anchor plunged into the seas of their imaginations. They share this distant lofty vision that can only be contemplated in its entirety from afar where it is most intangible. Throughout their lives and the lives of their children they will move variously toward and away from the mountain. Most of the time they don't even think of it. Some days it is obscured by clouds, some days it is clear. They will play in the woods; they will drive on highways with no view of the mountain; they will at times completely forget about it and be surprised to see it again: the mountain that sat through so many breakfasts with them as children will remain stable and stationary, as their lives spin and rocket in unknown directions, as they flame up, bloom flowering trails of light, and burn out, like fireworks.

Lorne is the oldest of the three boys. In order, they are Lorne, Creek, and Dollar; ages eighteen, fourteen, and twelve. Saturday morning at the breakfast table everyone is home. Dad makes pancakes.

The rhythm of safety and predictability is lovingly cemented into their lives. Jacob has been a literature professor at the local community college for twenty years. Mom returns from the grocery store.

Susan stands at the kitchen counter unpacking the paper bags of groceries. In this moment their world is like a photograph—all of the important information is fondly named.

Lorne will be starting college next year at Washington State's Business School. With his calm, persistent temperament, and outgoing personality, there is no reason to believe he will do anything but succeed. At six-feet and two-inches Lorne is the tallest of the boys. If a piece of wood is soaked in water and then placed between strong enough vices it can be bent without breaking, and when it dries it will keep its bent shape. Wonderfully, the forces shaping Lorne's life have not served the purpose of bending him, but of keeping him straight. And now, as he is leaving his teen years, it is fairly certain he will remain unbent. He is like a good tool that can be relied on and is sure to work without failing or complaint.

He is one to be trusted, solid like a window sill, or a stable ground of rock and clay with no history of upheaval. He stands from the table, his body moving like a deer in the kitchen. Notes of music are heard from the street vendor peddling knives outside. Everywhere there is harmony. The windows are open slightly to let in the late spring air. True and good paths of thought have developed themselves in his brain so that anything entering it falls into one of these paths, and no matter how it started, it tends to become true and good. He is not totally blameless though. Like any high school kid he has made some silly decisions. But Lorne is the closest thing this town has seen in quite a while to a person of limitless potential.

Creek and Dollar play tic-tac-toe in the air, imagining the game board and pointing to squares to place their invisible X's and O's. They both have soccer practice to go to later in the day. Their lives are full of games. It seems they never stop playing games. They go from a sport competition, to a competitive schoolroom, to board games, to random word games with each other in-between times. As far as they know, life is one long competition, one long test in which to prove oneself.

Creek is older and bigger. At this age he's a little bit on the hefty side—not quite as tall as his older brother Lorne, but nearly the same weight. He's the most handsome of the three brothers, having his father's sharp eyebrows and eyes that sit pleasantly under the brow and over the cheekbone, and his mother's refined nose that looks as though it was conceived by a 18th century French sculptor in marble. Jacob and Susan have unconsciously taken a hands-off approach to Creek. Being the middle child, they unwittingly trust the brothers on either side will bolster him from harm. Creek draws an X in the center of the imaginary board, then gestures diagonally from the top left to the bottom right to show his three X's in a row—his victory. He makes a quick exhaling sound to let Dollar know it was an easy win. Dollar writhes with desire for a rematch.

Creek gets up from the table and picking up his empty cereal bowl walks over to the counter where the groceries are. Shuffling through the bags of groceries that are not yet put away, he finds a new box of Life cereal and has it open and his bowl filled in no time. He begins to eat this bowl of cereal standing at the counter.

"Dollar's team doesn't have any good defenders." Creek says with his mouth full, as if there were already a conversation about Dollar's team taking place.

Dollar happens to be a defender on his team but his immediate response is not angry, "your team had more goals against it than mine last week."

Creek realizes he's been stumped so he changes the topic. "I heard Dollar's math teacher tackled a kid in the hallway yesterday."

This was the big rumor at school all yesterday afternoon. In fact Dollar was in the hallway and saw the event taking place.

Don Rasmussen, nicknamed Raspberry—one of the more aggressive, larger, and angrier students—was chasing another student through the hallway, making pig noises at him. The math teacher (who had been a football lineman in college) heard the noise, stepped into the hallway and quickly stiff-armed the heavyset Raspberry. Upon striking the adult, tree-trunk like arm, Raspberry spun half-way around, into some lockers then fell to the floor with a loud slapping sound. By the time he hit the floor, the math teacher had already returned to his classroom.

Raspberry didn't really know what had hit him. When he got up he had forgotten who he was chasing and was instead focused on saying, "What are you looking at!" to the unfortunate few who happened to be watching nearby. Raspberry's face was raspberry red. It was Dollar's friend, Kevin, who was initially being chased. Kevin came out from around the corner, taking small and quiet steps. Kevin and Dollar walked quickly to their next class.

"He didn't tackle him," Dollar says to Creek, "he got in his way so that he'd stop chasing Kevin." The teacher was one of Dollar's favorite teachers, so it was natural for him to see him as innocent. And this bully had been making Kevin's life miserable for the whole school year. This was not the first time Dollar was relieved to see Kevin walk away from an embarrassing attack from a bully.

Each of the different breeds of dog has its own personality. True, each individual dog has a unique personality, but they mostly adhere to the general traits of the breed to which they belong. If you were to go to a dog park in a small city (one of those fenced in areas where dogs are free to interact and play) you might see several different breeds in action. As you watch the dogs you'll probably notice that you can associate the way the dog behaves with its basic physical characteristics. For example, a small Bulldog, with its snub nose, will barrel its way into other groups. A skinny Weimaraner will nervously dart around the periphery like a comet. A Labrador Retriever will calmly move amongst the others as though it is a friendly diplomat, interacting without malice, observing, playing, and responding to all others with respect whether they are aggressive, disgruntled, passive, or playful.

The quickest way to describe Dollar, as a kid, is to say that he is like a Labrador Retriever. It is nearly impossible to make him truly angry. Almost always, his first instinct toward other people is a gesture of cooperation or kindness.

Creek and Dollar are on their way to eat lunch at MacDonalds. Their dad has just given each of them Chicago Cubs baseball hats. Creek carefully bends the bill of his hat into a gentle curve and wears it low on his forehead, the cool way to wear it. Dollar is somewhat oblivious to the style, hasn't bent his bill, and wears it his high on his forehead. Creek doesn't have time to teach Dollar the cool way to wear it, as they have just received the hats—and he isn't really paying much attention to Dollar anyway. In this state, they walk to MacDonalds for lunch one Saturday, and sit down to hamburgers and fries. There is a group of four boys a few years older than them sitting two tables over to the side. These four boys look like they have just come from a basketball game, in mesh shorts and sweaty t-shirts.

The four boys notice Dollar's un-cool baseball hat, and start giggling and adjusting their hats to look like his, to make fun of him. One of the boys has a large red zit on the tip of his nose. Creek immediately notices they're making fun of Dollar and starts feeling uncomfortable and angry. When Dollar notices they are paying attention to him, he looks over at the four boys and gives them a very natural smile, then looks back at Creek and continues eating his lunch without a single ounce of anger. Creek looks over at the boys; they're still wearing their hats like Dollar and smiling extra-wide at each other to mock Dollar. Dollar and Creek finish their food and walk out. As they leave, Creek takes Dollar's hat off, carefully gives the bill a gentle bend, and puts it back, low on Dollar's head.

At soccer practice Dollar looks across the trim green grass toward the edge of a nearby forest and smells the spring air. There is a grouping of tall pines, and beyond them a hill covered in green trees. He thinks the curves of telephone wires between poles along the side of the park resemble the path of flight of some of the smaller birds in the air; and some of those birds sit on telephone wires . . . is that where they get the idea to fly like that? Dollar takes a deep breath in through his nose. He rocks back and forward on his toes, enjoying the way the soccer cleats sink into the semi-wet field. His head appears slightly large on his skinny young frame. He looks to his side and sees that Kevin has taken a crouching defensive stance.

The whistle blows loudly, "Mr. Moore! Would you rather be baking a cake! Take five laps, now!" Coach Datley is not known for his patience. He is a short, skinny, Lebanese man. He once played in European soccer leagues and is now living out his dreams of soccer greatness by coaching a kid's team in the Pacific Northwest. He often forgets where he is and imagines he's coaching a team making a run for the world cup, screaming out things like "Oh almighty God!" and "My eyes are red from you!" when he is upset with his team. As the rest of the kids get into their defensive stances he blows the whistle once sharply for them to shuffle backwards to the left, and then again for them to shuffle right, and so on and so forth. By about the sixth tweet of the whistle half of the boys are shuffling in one direction, and half in the other. "Oh almighty God! (he tweets the whistle) Left, left, left!"

he yells hitting the palm of his right hand against his forehead. He looks across the field to see that Dollar has paused in his run around the field to pet a dog who's owner is throwing a tennis ball nearby. "Moore! My eyes are red from you! Make ten laps!"

As Dollar finishes his tenth lap, Coach Datley blows the whistle signaling the end of practice, saying "Huddle up!" The team comes together in a circle in the middle of the field. "Okay boys, we play the Badgers next weekend, they run a modified tiger front line, so we're going to have to be in good shape to keep up with them. Go home, don't forget to eat your protein, and be here for practice at four pm on Monday." As the kids walk from the field to the parking lot, Coach Datley is left standing in the field looking like a lost and bedraggled business man in his button-down shirt and polyester slacks. The shirt is tucked in at the front, but has come untucked in the back.

Kevin and Dollar get into the station wagon with Dollar's mom who waits to give them a ride home. Dollar sits with his mom in the front, and Kevin is in the back seat. "How was practice guys?" says Mom.

"Okay. We ran a lot" says Kevin.

Dollar looks back at Kevin, then at his mom, and says resolutely, "I'm sorry Kevin, but I'm not going to play soccer anymore this season."

"Dollar, Honey, are you sure? You're good at soccer, and you have friends on the team."

"Mom, it's no fun the way Coach is having us practice and play."

"Alright honey, I understand. We'll find something for you to do that you enjoy more."

For Dollar making the choice to stop playing on the soccer team is not difficult and he doesn't overthink it. He finds himself naturally tapping into the life-giving, low-running, gravity-bound, short riverbed of experience that is his life. He allows himself to be carried along with the current of reality. Without knowing it Dollar takes a Taoist desion making approach to life. Sure, he's a twelve-year-old Protestant boy, but his uncanny ability to evade the temptations of self-aggrandizement likens him more to a smiling old monk in a robe with a shiny bald head. Dollar thinks to himself, "I don't need to spend my time getting yelled at and not having fun, all for a game. I'll stop playing on this soccer team and I'll find something fun to do instead."

That same morning, Creek's soccer team practices on the other side of the park. Creek's soccer coach is more rabid than Dollar's. He is a forty-five-year-old man who acts like a ten-year-old bully. Coach Motto. He's about five-feet six-inches tall, has a potbelly, and always wears baggy nylon running pants and a white T-shirt. On both his left and right hands are two large gold-like rings that match the thick gold-like chain around his neck. He resembles the one donut in the box of a dozen that nobody sensible will dare to eat—it is cream-filled, powdered, frosted blue, with chocolate drizzled over bits of crumbled butterfinger bar. His fake tan lasts throughout the year. His cologne can be smelled anywhere within a ten foot radius. There are rumors that he has a hot-tub and work-out room in his basement. His comb-over hair is whispy, only slightly covering his bare shiny dome of a head like a cat's stringy toy. Coach Motto is known to grab kids by the top of the ear and move them around the field like helpless little leashed dogs. He drives a dark-blue 1958 Studebaker with tinted windows and big, white, tail-fins, and he's always the first to arrive at practice and the last to leave. He usually smokes a cigar as the kids leave and he carries the cones and soccer balls to the trunk of his car.

On this Saturday morning practice Coach Motto has the boys sit in a semi-circle and gives a talk that includes such topics as; how much tougher soccer players are than baseball players, complaints about the bad coffee he got at the gas station on the way to the field, the different ways to get a raccoon out of your attic, and his problem with hemorrhoids.

After the talk, the boys are riled up, though confusedly so, and they begin with push-ups, sit-ups, and sprints across the field. At the end of practice they play a fifteen-minute scrimmage. Creek plays midfield. By an unlucky series of plays Creek runs the full length of the field several times in order to be in position. After the eighth time up and down the field he is a bit slow to get to his spot. Coach Motto blows his whistle, stopping play, and yells from the sideline "Moore, I don't ever want to catch you lolli-gagging like that toward the ball again. What do think this is, ballet class? Get down and give me twenty!" While the rest of the field watches, Creek does twenty push-ups, sweat running into his eyes, breathing hard. Fortunately for the next several plays the ball moves to the other side of the field, giving Creek a bit of recovery time.

As he runs up the field, keeping his eyes on the ball on the other side of the field, Creek's mind is in a million places. His sharp nose belies the bursting cacophony of thoughts just behind it. He is spiraling in and spiraling out. His emotions are like a bull that has just been released into the ring, like the bull rider who is a noodle in a boiling pot of water, like the clown running around the bull ready to leap into the crowd. His emotions are wild.

Looking down at his legs and feet he sees muscles, bones, and cleats, but they are unknown. As he looks up and around the field the unknown grows around him making him feel like an alien, making him want to fight for his right to occupy a spot here in this world. He moves toward the soccer ball; the soccer ball moves toward him. Another boy meets the ball and Creek at exactly the same moment. Creek's thick body and hips lower, collide with, and lift the other boy off the ground, throwing him onto his side in the grass. Taking possession of the ball Creek begins to dribble it up the field. "That'a boy Creek!" growls coach Motto.

When he looks up Creek sees himself. It is as if the other players are wearing masks that make them look like him, Creek. Even the field is Creek—he is running, kicking the ball, along his own giant back. Looking up he sees his own name written in the clouds. Oddly, though the world he sees (in this moment) is made of himself, it is also distant and remote, as though he has awakened confused in a far-off land, as though he is falling and reaching out toward the air to grab a hold of something, anything. To the rest of the players on the field he looks like a dedicated player who has just stolen the ball, but in his mind he is scrambling to bail water from a sinking boat. He is a baseball that has been fouled-off and is spinning wildly up and behind the batter into the stands.

Creek's arms pump like pistons on a locomotive. His body moves like a hermit crab keeping the ball in front of him, protecting it, ready to shift sideways in an instant. His skin tans easily, so that even in the spring he has already taken on an olive hue that makes his eyes look more silvery than their winter brown appearance. His fine, but thick, dark hair is trimmed short. There is desperation in the rhythm of his movement. It is vice-presidential, the understudy sweating beneath hot theater lights, plastic fruit in the bottom drawer.

The opposite team's defender catches him unaware from the side, taking the ball and leaving him empty. Spinning around,

Creek sees that the ball is already twenty yards away. Gasping for breath, he turns to pursue his loss. Full of anger at himself he is running even faster now, but the ball is out of reach. It has passed into his own team's defense, and is kicked low and hard into the net of his team's goal. "That'a way Mick! See what happens when you don't keep your head up Moore!" comes the commentary from coach on the sideline. Guilt settles comfortably around Creek's shoulders.

This is Creek's favorite sport; he loves this game: he tells himself that he will get it right next time.

Saturday afternoon Creek walks home from practice, walks past the elementary school. There is an old half-eaten carrot on the sidewalk. He walks alone, but he hears a quiet voice in his mind telling him he's not walking fast enough. "And what is that carrot doing there? Did you put that there, is that your litter, boy?" says the voice in his head. Not hearing or seeing anyone else, Creek feels imaginary footprints behind him. They are heavy and crisp feeling, like a grammar teacher wearing a black dress, horn rimmed glasses, and high-heels. He walks faster, ignores the carrot on the ground, watches the grass on the edges of the sidewalk occasionally creep into the cement. He runs and the sound of his cleats on the sidewalk drown out the imaginary sound of footsteps behind him. He wins the race and feels good about himself.

Saturday afternoon Dollar is at home in the TV room. He has created a world in the corner of the room with an electric train set. There is an old wooden coffee table and several mis-matched pillows arranged to establish the terrain of this world. Dollar has the train tracks running around the leg of the coffee table and under a bridge of pillows. Included in the train set are a variety of old toys, miniature trees, people, cars, and a few buildings. These have been placed throughout the scene. Additionally, he creates some futuristic buildings from construction paper. It is a crowded world, and the train nearly knocks something over every time it goes around its loop.

Like grass growing over the edge of a sidewalk is the hungry movement of the train around the tracks. It's an old train though, and Dollar has to give it a push every few times around to keep it running.

Elle Crane is a friend of Dollar's. She lives on the other side of the street, three houses toward the school. This Saturday afternoon she stops by the house to say hello and see what Dollar is up to. Dollar shows her the scene he has created around the train-tracks.

Like Dollar, Elle is twelve-years-old. Like many young friendships between boys and girls, there is a remarkable innocence in their interaction. There does seem to be just a sweet hint of the mysterious sexual attraction that will in later years push its way into center stage, but for now it is without the encumbering, biting, egoism of that latent protagonist. Dollar and Elle are friends who enjoy spending time together. Even baby lion cubs instinctively play, driven by some natural desire perhaps in the mitochondria of their cells. Elle and Dollar know theirs is a special relationship and feel a certain playful loyalty to each other.

Elle looks like a young deer, if you can imagine a young girl looking both beautiful and like a young deer. Her eyes are wide and big, with matching cheek-bones; like a deer's eyes they are always aware. Her hair is blond, and looks like the gold Rumpelstiltskin spins from straw. She is not an overly talkative girl. Her glasses and her thin frame make her look like a prodigious astrophysicist. When Elle smiles, the outside corners of her eyes angle upwards and her front teeth show themselves like a set of handbells playing Pachelbel's Canon.

Dollar explains to Elle the world he has created from his toys and train. From beneath his Cubs hat, he says, "There are two levels. The top level is in charge. These people control the people below who are their servants. The top people tell them what work needs to be done and make sure that it gets done. The train goes around to move the food they need to work and to move the products they make. Then all of the things they make go up this elevator (he points to a red construction-paper tube). The top people use as much as they want, then send whatever they don't want back down this tube (he points to a blue construction-paper tube). The top people all follow the orders of this man (he points to a small, isolated figure standing above all the others on a small cardboard box). It's like a pyramid."

"You shall present your offering from it, as an offering by fire to the Lord, the fat that covers the entrails, and all the fat that is around the entrails; the two kidneys with the fat that is on them at the loins, and the appendage of the liver, which you shall remove with the kidneys. Then the priest shall turn these into smoke on the altar as a food offering by fire for a pleasing odor" (Leviticus 3:17).

"Who are these people?" asks Elle.

"The people on the bottom are called the Weeglets. They worship a Bald Eagle. Every day they take whatever the top people have given them in the blue tube, they divide it in half, and throw one half over this cliff" (he looks at the edge of one of the nearby chairs with a pillow leaning up against it). Pointing at the pillow, Dollar says, "They walk up this hill with the stuff in bags on over their shoulders, when they get to the top they line up and one by one throw the bags over the cliff, where the great Bald Eagle is perched on the side of the cliff, out of view over the edge. They walk back down the hill without talking, single file, with their arms out like wings. Each one repeats in his mind this phrase, breathing in, 'Great Eagle, soaring King,' and breathing out, 'save us from this tyranny.'"

"What about the people on top?" asks Elle, "Do they worship the Great Eagle?"

"No, they just keep making themselves happy with the things the Weeglets make for them. They don't need the Great Eagle's help for anything."

"Are they really happy?" she asks, looking at the miniature figures positioned in an evenly spaced circle, facing away from each other, with the single elevated figure sitting on a small box in the center.

"Sometimes they are happy; sometimes they are lonely; sometimes they are jealous of their leader, and they each want to become him," says Dollar as he tilts his head to the side, scratches his forehead, then walks over to a bookshelf by the TV.

On the top of the bookshelf is a ceramic, fully painted, one-foot-tall bald eagle with its arms stretched out and its beak and eyes pointing downward—as if it just identified its prey. His parents put it there and told the boys that it's not a toy; it's expensive and breakable. There is a shiny coat of clear varnish on the ceramic bird making it look wet. Dollar points at the bird and he and Elle stand looking at it. Though it is now part of the world Dollar has set up it still retains its otherness. The eagle looks so powerful up above the rest of the room. It is much bigger than any of the other figures, who are below and several feet away in Dollar's imaginary world. In Dollar's mind it is circling that small world, watching it. In Elle's mind the eagle is listening to the people walking down the hill, breathing in and out, "Great Eagle, soaring King, save us from this tyranny." The ceramic eagle is absolutely still, but for Dollar and Elle it is alive.

Lorne sits on the couch in front of the TV. He's the biggest person in the room, but also the most recumbent. The position of his body is totally relaxed and vulnerable, somewhere between sitting and lying on his back, with his chin against his chest. He's been flipping through the channels and comes to rest on a show about wild animals. There is an image of vultures picking at some sort of carcass. The camera is close so that you can see the birds grabbing hold of stringy stuff and clumps. It all looks slippery. With his plate balanced on his chest, Lorne eats his lunch, peanut butter on toast, an apple, and some oatmeal cookies with milk.

Lorne watches the black and white television. Dollar and Elle stand looking up at the eagle. Creek walks into the room holding his soccer cleats in his hand.

Creek starts talking immediately upon entering the room, "Oh, has Dollar made another pretend world? What is it this time Dollar, Eagleville, the land where all the people think they can fly? Why don't you stop playing make-believe and come out to the river with me and Robby?" Dollar doesn't answer. Elle has quietly backed away from Creek, putting Dollar between her and Creek.

"Whoa, check that out," says Lorne from the couch. Lorne still looks totally relaxed. He drinks a Coke with ice from a glass in his right hand. He points at the TV with his left hand that holds the remote, without turning his head away from the TV. The screen shows a young deer walk down to a river and get snagged by a crocodile. The scene is replayed in slow motion. The deer walks about a foot from the edge of the water, then turns its head to look around. Then the deer moves a few feet to the side, so it is now closer to the water and parallel to the edge. What looks like a clump of mud in the water by the deer's rear feet suddenly surges out of the water and bites at the rear left leg of the deer. It clamps down on, and tugs the leg, but the leg kicks itself free. For a moment—though the deer is free and the crocodile is within snapping distance—neither moves. It is as though the deer is stunned and still held by the force of the surprise and fear, like a nightmare where you want to run but your legs don't work. And the crocodile seems to know that the deer is captive, and seems to know exactly how long it has to wait before making its second attack. This time the jaws of the crocodile snap closed much higher on the deer's leg, and the deer is no longer stunned, but struggling with its front legs to scramble up the bank. The crocodile weighs about four times as much as the deer and the weight of its neck and head bring the deer's whole body crumpling to the ground. In a few more seconds both the deer and crocodile are gone under water, and there is a trail scraped into the mud of the bank from the deer being dragged into the river.

All four kids watch this replayed on the TV. It is shown about four times in slow motion. Lorne turns to Creek and says teasingly, "Maybe you'll see one of those down at the river. Keep your toes away from the edge." There is a smile on Lorne's face as he puts the remote and drink down and makes a snapping motion with both of his long arms toward Creek. Creek swings his cleats playfully at Lorne's hands.

Then surprisingly, Elle says, "We'll see you out there in a few minutes," looking at Dollar the whole time she's talking.

Behind the Moore's house is a 50-yard-deep backyard that slopes down to the edge of a brambly forest on the side of the hill. Running through this forest and down the hill is a small brook that the kids call a river. At its fullest, the brook is about four feet across and two feet deep. There are occasional spots where it broadens into pools, and narrows in channels, but it is fairly easy to find a spot to step over it during most of the year.

Robby and Creek stand on the opposite sides of the brook at a narrow spot that is about a foot wide. They have found large sticks and swing them at each other, sword fighting. Robby is also on Creek's soccer team and lives down the road. Robby's house has an in-ground pool in the backyard. Everything about Robby is perfect. He looks like a young James Dean with handsome cheek-bones, and soft blonde hair. Robby looks like his older brother, Tommy, who looks like their dad, Mike. Mike is a successful general contractor who does a lot of business in town. The family belongs to the country club, and they're all good at golf. In fact both Robby and Tommy are good at every sport. To top it all off they are both very popular at school. They are bred to have suc-cessful junior high and high school lives.

The red marks on Creek's arm are from Robby playfully striking him. They are collecting between his wrist and forearm, mostly at the same angle. Creek keeps making the same mistake by swinging down hard with his right arm and stick, and turning to his right, so that Robby can dodge to his left and strike Creek's right arm. They are both having fun, but Creek is starting to get frustrated by his habitual mistake, as Robby repeatedly says, "too slow!" just before his stick lands on Creek's arm with a sting.

Meandering through the trees, following a vaguely estab-lished trail toward the brook are Dollar and Elle. Elle is whistling the tune she is learning in her piano lessons. She moves her arms through the air as if conducting the trees as she whistles. Dollar doesn't recognize the tune so she tells him it's something by Cho-pin. "That's nice, and slow," says Dollar. He is blowing bubbles from a plastic stick with a circle on its end, dipping into the bottle and creating streams of bubbles to their sides as they walk.

When Dollar and Elle reach Creek and Robby at the river, Robby is showing Creek how to spin the stick around in his hands. He makes the stick do a figure eight in one hand then passes it to the other hand to continue the motion on that side. "Cool!" says Dollar, "Let me try!" The older boys ignore his request, and Creek says, "Blow some bubbles for us."

Dollar blows some bubbles at them and they swing at the bubbles with their sticks, popping them. Creek and Robby really get into it, spinning and running as they swing and chase wandering bubbles. There is a bubble about six feet in front of Dollar just above his head's height. Creek spins between the bubble and Dollar, and with his back to Dollar swings powerfully across his body and up at the bubble. From Dollar's perspective the moment of Creek's follow-through striking him in the face happens simultaneously with the pop of the bubble, as if the stick traveled the 9 feet of its arc in no time at all.

At what seems to be the exact same moment as the bubble disappearing into nothing, Dollar feels a loud darkness in his head, sees a flash of black, and realizes that he's lying on the ground. Now there is pain beneath his left eye and the left side of the bridge of his nose. He gently reaches his hand to his face touching the skin, then looks at it, surprised by how rich the color of his blood is.

"Oh shit!" says Creek, turning around to see his brother on the ground with a bloody face, "are you alright?" Dollar sits up but doesn't answer. The blood runs down his face and starts to drip off his chin. "Come on let's get to the house," says Robby, calmly taking control of the situation. Robby takes deliberate steps toward Creek and looks him in the eyes saying, "Creek you run ahead and tell your mom and dad what happened. It looks like you missed his eye." Robby steps toward Dollar, "Dollar can you see out of both eyes?"

"Yes," says Dollar, as he gets up and they start walking to the house. Dollar has his left hand, with blood on it, propped out to his side as he walks. He tries to not touch his face, as Robby has instructed him. Creek runs ahead. In the back of the group is Elle; she tells Dollar that he's going to be alright and that it doesn't look too bad.

When they arrive back at the house Dollar's dad is ready with a wet rag, some bandages and an ice pack. Without asking what happened he brings Dollar into the kitchen, sits him down on a chair and starts cleaning off his face gently. "You guys go back outside, he's going to be okay," he says to the other kids so he has some space to work. Jacob stands over Dollar and uses both hands to gently maneuver Dollar's head, and clean out the cut with the rag. Fortunately the cut is not too deep and he says, "Dollar I don't think you need stitches, but it looks like this really hurt. Your nose has already started to swell and turn blue. I'm going to put this bandage on, then I want you to lie down on the couch in front of the TV, and hold this ice pack over your nose. I'll look at it again in about half-an-hour."

As Dollar walks into the TV room he glances up at the eagle on top of the bookshelf. He lies down on the couch with the ice pack on his nose, and closes his eyes.

Lying on the couch Dollar dreams.

Sometimes you can lie in bed at night unable to sleep because of a tiny itch on an ankle. On the other hand sleep can happen quickly and deeply in the midst of serious pain and commotion. Dollar has fallen asleep quickly despite the throbbing pain below his eye and in his nose. His head rolls toward the back of the couch, resting on the icepack and a pillow. His dream is peaceful. He is lying on his back in a park watching the clouds. The rich, blue dome above him is continually changed by clouds moving across it. It is like a giant Etch-A-Sketch filled with clouds and then erased time and time again. Some of the higher and thinner clouds look like sound waves. The waves emerge from a larger clump near the horizon, then spread into a rhythmic pattern above him. In the dream Dollar understands this as God singing. Patterns slowly and evenly develop and transform into unique shapes then disperse into thousands of tiny puffs. The clouds are God's song moving silently and beautifully around the world, always changing, sometimes resting, sometimes building into storms.

"Dollar, Dollar, how are you feeling?" His dad leans over him with a hand gently on his shoulder.

"I'm alright, I was dreaming about clouds. It still hurts. Where is everyone?"

"Elle went home. The boys are in their rooms. Mom and I are going to the get some pizza to bring home for dinner. I wanted to make sure you're okay before we go. Will you be alright for a little bit until we get back with the pizza?"

"Yeah, I'm okay. Can you hand me the remote?"

As Dollar sits up a little and untwists his clothes, Jacob gets him the remote and gives him a new ice pack, looking closely at Dollar's nose then going to put the old ice pack in the freezer.

While their parent's are getting the pizza, Creek and Lorne come back into the TV room with Dollar. Creek takes the remote (connected by a wire to the Zenith TV) out of Dollar's hand and sits where Dollar's feet are, making Dollar bend his knees to shorten his body. Lorne is flipping the pages of a National Geographic magazine, sitting in the La-Z-Boy chair. Creek says to Dollar, "Hey, how are you feeling? Good thing Robby was there to help us make it back to the house." Dollar doesn't answer, instead he drifts back to sleep.

While Dollar takes a nap, we move into the future like people riding a bus. Some people dream that death and the afterlife come to them at first as a bus ride. When they reach into their pockets and can't find money for a fare, they are then relieved to wake up, not having been able to pay the fare for passage out of life. Imagine the four years, between Dollar's falling asleep and his waking up from a different nap, like a bus ride. This is not a bus ride into the afterlife but a bus ride forward in time. Some people on the bus are wearing headphones, trying to temporarily escape into a different world. Others are reading, playing games, or in conversation.

Dollar recognizes many of the important people in his life on the bus. Lorne is there, sitting next to a very attractive young woman; they are deep in conversation. Creek is near the back of the bus. His head pops up and he throws a ball of paper across the isle at another kid, who quickly returns the favor. A few seats behind him, Dollar recognizes Elle sitting next to another girl. They are smiling and talking to each other. Elle has a unique way of making eye contact that is at once inquisitive and comforting. Turning her head first, then her eyes, she meets the dreamer's daze. In front of them are his parents and some other adults. Most of them look like they're sleeping, and a few of them are reading. There are a lot of people he doesn't recognize on the bus. Next to him is his friend from school, Kevin. Looking out the window, Dollar doesn't recognize the landscape. He notices that the trees and telephone poles closest to the bus are moving past them very quickly. Trees and hills that are farther away are moving past slowly. And the very distant mountains and clouds don't seem to be moving at all.

1960

Test Tube

Dollar wakes up on the same couch in the same room, four years after being accidentally hit below the eye with a stick by his older brother Creek. He is sixteen years old. His feet now lie on top of the armrest, and there is a small scar below his eye. The eagle is still on top of the bookshelf. Lorne has gone to college. Creek is a senior in high school. The small train-set world Dollar set up in the corner of the room four years ago is gone.

Three textbooks, surrounded by at least as many notebooks and folders, and are on the coffee table in front of him. Seeing the biology textbook, Dollar remembers that tomorrow the biology class is going to the zoo. They've spent about a month learning about the zoo's special holdings, like the Crowned Crane, the Kudu, and the Royal Python. He's also excited about the birdhouse, where they have several bald eagles.

When the class arrives at the zoo, they are shuffled through the front gate as the teachers count the number of kids going through. They move slowly, appearing to be much more interested in each other than in the zoo around them. Most of the kids have formed groups of three or four. There are a few doubles and singles near the front of the class. None of the students will keep up with the teacher at the front. This is not because the teacher is walking fast, but because this is a universal, unwritten rule of class transportation dynamics. Dollar is near the front, walking with Kevin. They are talking about which zoo animal they would most want to see while hiking in the wild.

Kevin has been talking about monkeys for the last month, "I saw this show on TV . . . it would be great to be walking in the jungle and see a pack of squirrel monkeys. It's so fun watching them run, spin, flip, and play with each other. Watching the way they move is like watching the movement of otters under water. It's like they can move their body in any direction they want." Kevin makes quick movements with his hands and spins around.

"Yeah, I like the monkeys," says Dollar, raising his left arm, scratching his armpit, and making a monkey face at Kevin, "but I'm most excited about the bird house."

"Of course, the EEeeagles!" Kevin makes a screeching noise that is supposed to be an eagle sound with the "E" at the beginning of the word.

Dollar smiles, and says, "If I was walking in a field, I would want to see an eagle swoop down just above me and land in front of me. I would ask him to be my pet. They feed them rats in the zoo, but I would give him fresh fish every day. And I'd take him out to a field to fly. Once he bonded with me, he'd stay with me for life. They're very faithful animals."

"Maybe he'd teach you the secret to flying," jokes Kevin.

Miss Goodrich, the biology teacher, is one of Dollar's favorites. She isn't the most popular teacher, because she keeps a strict class and often issues detentions to students who aren't paying attention, but her classes are interesting. She is tall and buxom, with rusty orange hair that hangs straight to her shoulders, except for a neat line of bangs just above her eyes. Her dark green skirt has an orange plaid pattern on it. Though strict, she does have fun when the kids are participating and seem to be interested in the topic. Her smile is most noticeable in her eyes; they lock into one's eyes, and almost seem to make a humming noise, like a wet finger circling a wine glass. When you answer one of her questions correctly, or with an interesting question in return, she rewards you with that smile, and it makes you feel like there is nowhere else you'd rather be. Miss Goodrich is walking past the Kevin and Dollar as they are talking about the eagles.

"Gentlemen, did you know they have a pair of eagles here that are 15 and 20 years old?," asks Miss Goodrich.

"Oh yeah, I can't wait," Dollar, does his best to rein in his excitement.

"Well, next is the monkey house, then we go to the birdhouses," she answers.

"ooo oooo oo aa aaa," Kevin makes monkey noises as he smiles at Dollar.

Miss Goodrich addresses the class with her melodious voice, "Alright class, this is the monkey house. Now say it with me, Kings Play Chess On Fine Grained Sand; Kingdom, Phylum, Class, Order, Family, Genus, Species (most of the class repeats the words in time with her). Remember when we talked about the Animal Kingdom? They have nuclei, eat for energy, can move, have different types of cells, have sexual reproduction, and have flexible cell walls; and then there is the Chordate Phylum—with symmetry down the middle, a head torso and tail, and a spinal column;

and the Mammal Class—with fur, or hair, and milk; and then the Primate Order—with larger brains, use of vision as the primary sense, and opposable thumbs (here she holds up both hands and wiggles her thumbs in and out, smiling). After that, within the primates, the humans and some primates begin to separate into different families, the humans stay in the Homonid Family with the orangutans, gorillas, chimpanzees, and bonobos—and each of these animals is its own species. So we should all feel comfortable in here; these animals are the most like us," she says, slowly winking her left eye, "you might want to find the one animal in here that you think most resembles you," she grins, and the class responds with moderate appreciation of her humor—some of the kids smiling and others are acting like they didn't hear a word she said.

They stand in the entryway to a giant space of fabricated jungle. This entryway is a place of transition from the crisp cool air of spring outside, to the humid and warm air inside. Miss Goodrich gives her final instructions to the class before they enter, "We'll spend about fifteen minutes walking through the first room, and then ten minutes in the last two rooms. You can go at your own pace, but try to stay within view of me. Please keep your voices down, and as the sign says (pointing to a sign to her left with bold red lettering), 'Do Not Provoke the Animals.'" She adds, "Remember that gorillas are about 50 times stronger than people, and could easily pull your arm off." With that she pushes the door behind her open with her backside, keeping her front toward the class, slowly turning as the class enters the jungle. There is a smile on her face when all of the kids are inside. She is always amused by how much younger the kids act on field trips to the zoo.

On an elevated concrete walkway, they walk along the side of a huge room that feels as large as a basketball gym—a basketball gym that has been abandoned for hundreds of years and is filled with vines, trees, a river, and rocky cliffs. The pathway winds slightly to the sides and up and down creating different points of view. There is a heavy black net, hanging from the ceiling, between the pathway and the primates swinging in the trees and running along the ground. Kevin and Dollar look down at an orangutan who slowly walks along the bank of the river below them. "He's got Miss Goodrich's hair," Kevin whispers jokingly to Dollar.

Ahead of them on the path, Elle leans forward and points across the room, "Whoa! Look you guys, a gorilla!" Her excitement can be seen in her feet jumping up and down, though her arms still hold onto the railing. Kevin and Dollar scoot up to her and look across at the lumbering gorilla. His silver back makes him look dignified. The gorilla faces them from about thirty feet away. For a moment, the three of them are transported to a prehistoric world where people live in jungles, in awe of other animals.

After they've gone through the large room, the class gathers in one of the smaller rooms in the back where the monkeys are on display in rooms along the walkway. They stand in front of a display full of Squirrel Monkeys. A thin black net about a foot behind the railing, with inch-square holes, is the only thing separating them from the approximately thirty hyper little monkeys in the display. Chaos. Monkeys flip, swing, jump, scratch, itch, bite, stretch. It looks like an unsupervised, overcrowded jungle gym at recess in the spring—after the kids have been fed soda and candy bars. "Remember kids, don't provoke the animals," chimes Miss Goodrich with her musical voice as they gather toward the railing in front of the display. From Miss Goodrich's point of view the kids' heads are silhouetted against the bright display the monkeys occupy.

Kevin reaches out his hand and sticks his small index finger through the net. It's hard to say why he does it. Kevin is really just like any other person, or monkey: curious and self-destructive. It's not the first time he's acted this way. When the class went to the art museum, he followed a similar impulse: One of the things that is popular in the class is called "gleeking." Gleeking is flicking into the air a small amount of very clear, wet saliva from the bottom of you mouth with your tongue. It is silent, and you barely move your mouth to do it, just open it a bit. When they went to the art museum Kevin walked up to several of the portraits and silently, undetected, stood nose to nose with the immortalized dignitaries in paint, and gleeked on their faces. He did not get caught, though his conscience occasionally reminds him of his misdemeanor. And now he is here in the monkey house, unable to resist the urge to stick his finger through the net, into the turbulent world of riotous monkeys. He's really not a bad kid. But it's as if he has lost control of his hand and his will power.

Within about one second of poking through the net, a monkey jumps up from below and nibbles on his finger tip. Kevin's scream draws the attention of the whole class, including Miss Goodrich. Her eyes grow big and are void of the humming sound they make when she smiles. His classmates instinctively back away from Kevin, so that he stands apart, holding his finger by his waist and looking down at it, ashamed. Though the monkeys still dart around screeching, the room has become very quiet. The class waits nervously for Miss Goodrich's reaction to Kevin.

"Oh, Kevin, honey, are you okay? Did it break the skin?" says Miss Goodrich squatting down beside him and taking his hand in her soft hands, with pink painted fingernails.

"I don't think so," he answers quietly without looking up at her. His finger is red, but there isn't any blood or loose skin.

"Alright class, let's move on now, out that door over there, and we'll head over to the bird house." There is a relieved sound to Miss Goodrich's voice. As they are filing out Miss Goodrich tells Kevin to wait with her by the door where there is a machine that makes plastic monkeys. She drops in a quarter and she and Kevin stand in front of the machine listening to it warm up and sniffing the unique smell of melting plastic in a monkey house. She stands next to him with her left arm around his shoulders. Through the glass in the front of the machine they can see the two halves of the metal mold press together. A nozzle drops down and plastic flows into the top of the mold. It turns upside-down and some plastic trickles out the bottom of the metal mold, which then separates revealing a blue plastic monkey that drops into a chute at the bottom of the machine. With her left hand gently resting on the center of Kevin's back, Miss Goodrich takes the monkey from the chute with her right hand and hands it to Kevin. "Maybe this will cheer you up," she says.

Kevin and Dollar walk behind the rest of the class, from the monkey house toward the birdhouse. Miss Goodrich passes them and is up near the front of the group. Noticing the blue plastic monkey Kevin is holding close to his chest with one arm like a football, Dollar asks if he can hold it. "Miss Goodrich gave it to me and I don't want it to break, so be very careful." Kevin gently hands the monkey to Dollar.

The monkey has one arm up over its head, and the opposite knee is bent, as if it is swinging from a branch or vine. Holding it in his hands, turning it over, Dollar wonders why Miss Goodrich rewarded Kevin with this gift that everyone else would eventually see and maybe become jealous of. Why would she give him something instead of punishing him, when he had so blatantly been bad and broken the rules and put himself in danger? He hands the monkey back to Kevin, and notices Kevin's relieved expression when he gets his gift back undamaged. In Kevin's expression Dollar can see a difference. Somehow this monkey as a gift—as a reward for doing something wrong—has changed Kevin's attitude.

At the same time, Dollar does not feel jealous of Kevin. In fact, he's happy for him. Dollar does wish that he too had a plastic animal, but even more, he's happy to see Kevin focused on this reward instead of continuing to rethink the monkey bite. He is genuinely happy for Kevin. As they walk behind the rest of the class they take turns pretending they are the monkey swinging through the forest. Kevin's laughter is excited as he watches Dollar act like a monkey. Moving ahead of Kevin, Dollar raises his right hand and left knee, then jumps and switches to his left hand and right knee, screeching "ooo ooo aa ooo a." He grins and looks back at Kevin who cradles the monkey in his left hand, raises his right and jumps forward toward Dollar.

Elle comes skipping back to them from the group ahead, "You guys, Miss Goodrich said they are going to have a trainer in the birdhouse showing us how the eagles fly. Dollar aren't you excited?"

"Really? That's awesome!" Dollar comes to a stand-still as he processes the news Elle has brought. This is exciting because he has never seen a bald eagle's open wingspan close up. He's heard about how long it can be, but it's hard to imagine when the wings are folded and the bird is still. The three of them catch up with the rest of the class at the entrance to the birdhouse.

"Above all other birds it is the soaring eagle, with its size and weight, that gives the most abiding impression of power and purpose in the air. It advances

solidly like a great ship cleaving the swells and thrusting aside the smaller waves. It sails directly where lesser birds are rocked and tilted by the air currents" (Edwin Way Teale, "Bird of Freedom," Atlantic Monthly, 1957).

Upon entering the birdhouse, the class is directed through a set of double doors on the right into a large indoor theater. They sit on benches in front of a stage with large black draped cages on both the left and the right sides. There is a projection screen behind the stage that reads, "Falconer Cyril: The Bald Eagle." As the lights dim, the picture on the screen changes to the silhouette of an eagle in flight—it looks huge. They are quiet, in anticipation.

Walking onto the stage in matching khaki pants and shirt is a chubby man, about 5'6", with pale skin and long, straight-brown hair tied into a pony tail that hangs down the middle of his back. His first words seem to come from his long, pointed goatee, "Good afternoon boys and girls, I'm the Falconer Cyril," they are quick and nasally words, and the class is immediately quieted by their strange sound. "What you see on the screen behind me is the outline of a full-size female Northern Bald Eagle in flight. Her wingspan is seven-and-a-half feet long. This is about a foot longer than a full-grown male. Underneath the covering, in the cage to your left (he smoothly and dramatically gestures toward it with his a fully outstretched arm) is a twenty-year-old female bald eagle, and to your right (another theatrical gesture) is a fifteen-year-old male. I'm leaving them covered now because they are shy birds and I want them totally focused when the time comes. These two were rescued in Haines, Alaska, about a thirty-six-hour drive up the West Coast from here." He snickers, "Now don't start imagining that you'll have a bald eagle caged in your backyard. It's actually illegal to keep bald eagles in captivity in the US without a permit, and permits are usually only given for educational purposes—with injured birds that would not survive in the wild," he snickers again with a short exhale and inhale. "Our old lady, Sarah, was found badly burnt because she had touched two parallel power wires at the same time with her broad wings and was shocked. And our patriarch, our male eagle, Abraham, had broken his left wing by crashing into the front of a semi-truck. Fortunately we have been able to rehabilitate them both." Cyril's hand moves to his chin, with his forefinger below his nose, "Many of the more common eagle deaths, related to environmental toxins, are unstoppable once the bird has consumed the bad fish or the lead bullet in a hunter's unclaimed prey." He points a chubby hand, with a thin curved index finger, out at the audience, "Remember, you can do something to save the eagle's lives, by being kind to the environment."

Falconer Cyril has been standing at the front of the stage. At this point he walks back a few feet to sit on a stool in the middle of the stage. He sits in the shadow between the two large black draped cages. He continues speaking from the darkness, "Now Abraham and Sarah, sadly, left their mates behind in Alaska. Eagles do mate for life, but it is also nice to know that they will replace their mate if he or she is lost—so their old mates are probably not alone anymore. And Abraham and Sarah have each other now too, though it is very rare for eagles to mate in captivity—meaning we're probably not going to see any eaglets coming from these two."

"And now, I present to you, Sarah and Abraham." With this Cyril walks over to each cage and pulls the drapery off with one sweeping motion. All of their eyes become wide and each person in the audience is absolutely still as the eagles are revealed in the cages. Cyril is once again visible in the lights aimed at the eagles.

The birds' bodies are each about a yard tall and full looking, with majestic white heads culminating in sharp, hooked beaks.

"Beautiful creatures, are they not?" says the beaky voice of Cyril. "Each one, though the size of a thirty pound dog, weighs only about ten pounds. One of the reasons they are so light is that their bones are hollow, weighing only half-a-pound all together. In fact, you've probably heard the saying 'light as a feather.' Well, surprise! All together, the eagle's feathers weigh twice as much as their bones. Even so, they can pick up and fly away with a fish weighing up to four pounds. Imagine how hard it would be for you to pick up someone who is almost half your weight, and then jump even a few inches off the ground. These are truly powerful birds."

Cyril walks to the side of the stage and pulls two T shaped platforms to the middle. Each platform is about three feet high, and he positions them near the front of the stage on either side of himself. He walks back to Sarah's cage, opens the door, reaches in and takes hold of her with two hands, pulling her close to his body like a precious vase and walking her over to one of the platforms. He does the same with Abraham. As he sets each bird on its platform he attaches a chord about ten feet long to one of its feet and anchors it to the bird's platform.

With a slow cadence Cyril says, "Now please do not make any loud noises; we do not want to startle the birds, for their own safety, as well as for ours. There are a few reasons why eagles make for difficult hunting birds," he says, sitting back down on a stool between the birds. His head is now eye-to-eye with the eagles, and only about two feet away from their sharp bills and piercing eyes. He continues, "For one, they are not easy to train; in general they don't take well to being captive. Secondly, they are dangerous hunters because they can attack animals larger than a rabbit or duck. For example, they have been known to fight foxes and small wolves—and for people living in small villages this also put at risk their own children who might play out in the yard. So let's keep the noise down. We do not want to frighten them." The class is looking up at the falconer and two eagles in awe. Many of the kids feel at this moment like rabbits beneath the gaze of the mighty hunting eagles.

Cyril and the two eagles are perched above the frozen class. Cyril has magnificently transformed from the roly-poly oddity he was at first, to a captivating, statuesque dignitary. Lowering his tone, he speaks in a hushed and serious voice to the class, "Have you ever looked into the eyes of a llama? No? Well, if you visit the llamas today, you should take the opportunity to meet their stares. When your eyes lock onto those of a llama, you find yourself swimming in a world of insanity. There is a frantic confusion in their look, one that is bouncing around the insides of their heads incessantly. They may be standing still, but in their minds they are having a terrible acid trip. They desperately avoid becoming conspicuous, attempting to hide in that strange body and long neck, like a watermelon hiding in a basket of fish." The class is still silent, somewhat scared and confused.

Cyril continues in his lowered voice, "When you look into the eyes of an eagle, it is a different thing altogether. There is a complete clarity and unity of purpose. You lose possession of your own stare as it becomes the noble bird's. You may loose track of time and your hunger certainly goes away. It is not uncommon to feel lighter, like you too could rise into the air with one flap of your wings. The eagle's stare is penetrating, but empowering, like a glass of cold water." He turns toward his right where the eagle, Sarah, is perched. Lifting up his right hand slowly, he makes eye contact with her. Her beak is pointed directly at him and motionless, though her body is facing forward. Both of their bodies face forward and their heads are in profile, facing each other. Cyril's right hand is inches away from the feathers of her chest. He has stopped speaking and is now moving his hand slowly, petting her feathered chest with gentle downward motions of the back of his forefinger.

As his arm is lowered to his side, he maintains eye contact and begins to speak again, "I see in her eyes a map of the world; I see the Earth spinning like a light-blue marble in a crisp universe; I see a single mouse running across a huge field on a rainy day; the sky is made of soup; the wind is pushing like a wave; there is a readiness in her soul; focus is not her goal, but a state of being out of which she occasionally yearns for distraction, for frivolity, for the looser bindings of anxiety and tumult."

Slowly standing, Cyril looks down at the audience, "And now, our grand finale. You see, boys and girls, the Eagle is more comfortable in the air than on the ground. Its whole body is made for flight, and for attack—its sharp talons and beak are like arrow-heads at a high speed. The Eagle is made for freedom, is a rising spirit, a being whose every fiber is yearning to travel up toward the sun. For Sarah and Abraham, being here in captivity is bet-ter than the alternative in which they would have slowly died by the debilitation of their injuries in the wild. However, they still need to be reminded of who they are, and their spirits need to be awakened and enlivened to some degree each day." He walks behind his stool and picks up a full two-liter plastic bottle of A&W root beer. The class is mesmerized by his theatricality as he is now shaking the bottle up and down vigorously. It is placed between the two birds on the stool.

"Now after the birds are in the air—and NOT before then—I want you to clap loudly, like the sound of a waterfall," he says to the silent and motionless class. The plastic bottle sits full of potential energy between the two magnificent birds, with Cyril standing behind it. He leans forward quickly and twists the cap off the bottle, shooting a stream of foam about two feet straight up. Both birds simultaneously open their great wings, instantly appearing three times larger than they were, and moving the air powerfully with their wings. They lift about six feet into the air. Looking upward, Cyril raises his arms between them, then brings his hands together and begins clapping. The whole class joins him. As the group of seated students claps, the two birds slowly flap their wings, maintaining a hovering position, with their gazes fixed on each other. The bottle is only slowly foaming now, and the birds return to their perches.

"Thank you for visiting us today. Please enjoy the rest of your zoo visit. Remember the day you saw the spirited Eagle's flight," Cyril makes his closing remark, then puts the eagles back in their cages and covers them as the full lights in the room slowly turn back on.

The class exits the birdhouse and gathers around Miss Goodrich outside. She addresses them with a twinkle in her eye, "Well, that Falconer Cyril certainly was a hoot, wasn't he? You're going to have half-an-hour of free-time now before the bus leaves. I want everyone to make sure they are in a group of at least three people, and then you can go to any exhibit or part of the zoo you want. Just remember that you need to meet right back here in half-an-hour."

The class breaks up into groups and Miss Goodrich, in her long plaid skirt and wooly green sweater, walks over to the group formed by Dollar, Kevin, and Elle. She says, with her arms crossed, "So, Dollar you've seen your eagles, and Kevin you've seen your monkeys, now Elle, where are you going to convince these guys to go with you in this half-hour?"

Dollar and Kevin both turn to look at Elle. She replies shyly from behind her glasses, looking up at Miss Goodrich only after she has spoken, "I really want to see the dolphins."

"Yeah, I wanna see the sharks and eels," Kevin opens his mouth and bares his teeth at Dollar.

"Well then, off you go, you three, to the end of that path there, and on the left," Miss Goodrich hums with her eyes wide, something like smiling. The three kids head down the path; Elle skips, Dollar and Kevin alternately run, for about 200 yards. Miss Goodrich picks up the plastic monkey Kevin accidentaly left behind.

The aquarium hall is dark inside, except for rectangles of glass filled with the blue light of water. On the left side, in the center is a very large wall of glass going from floor to ceiling and about twenty feet long. They are able to walk right up to the glass. Standing in front of it, they feels as though they are in the water. They can't tell how thick the glass is; it seems impossible that glass so clear could be supporting the weight of so much water, yet they trust it.

Three dolphins swim around the tank counter-clockwise, left to right from where the kids stand. The dolphins appear at the left edge of the glass, swim along the whole glass, and disappear again on the right. For a few minutes, as the dolphins pass by, Dollar and Kevin trace their swimming path with their hands on the glass. They tire of this game and go to the other side of the room where there are colorful saltwater fish, leaving Elle by herself in front of the large rectangle of blue light.

She stands still, with her nose about a foot away from the glass. One of the dolphins, while making its left to right pass, slows down in front of Elle and does a roll to its right, spinning like a spiral-thrown football, then continues on its path. The next dolphin approaches and does a forward roll in a large, graceful circle as it passes. When the third dolphin comes to Elle it stops and turns, pointing directly at her, about the same distance away from the glass as she is. Elle raises her hand, pressing it to the glass above her head. The dolphin swims forward and presses its nose against the glass where her hand is. She slides her hand down the glass—and the dolphin follows. She moves her hand to the left, and then right, and again the dolphin follows. Elle leans forward and rests her forehead against the glass. The dolphin points its nose down and presses the top of its head against the glass where her forehead is.

When Elle tells Dollar and Kevin about her interaction with the dolphin they are impressed, but don't know if they should really believe her. She does have quite an imagination, and has been known to confuse her dreamy imaginings with reality. She doesn't mind their disbelief though. She doesn't need them to believe her. Her experience with the dolphin was real and made her feel special regardless of what the boys think.

On the same day Dollar's class is at the Zoo, Creek's biology class is doing an experiment with fruit flies at school. The flies are called drosophila, and they are perfect for testing genetic mutations: they are cheap, small, and reprocuce quickly. They also make the room smell like a pungent mixture of a bowling alley and dog kennel.

Creek's two good friends in the class have already paired with each other as lab partners, and Creek is left with Raspberry (Don Rasmussen) as his partner. Raspberry is still tall and heavy, and has avoided acquiring any of the niceties of hygeine. He is both class bully and class outcast, two roles that are not always carried at once, with such distinction, by such a qualified candidate. Raspberry's reddish blonde hair is not curly, but clumpy, because it hasn't been washed in several days. The very top of the collar of his white t-shirt curls in like a shell and is yellowing towards its edge. When Raspberry gets up from his desk, or moves from any one place to another, he invariably bumps into something due to his overflowing girth. Most of the kids at school wear tennis shoes, however, Raspberry wears worn-out work boots with untied laces. He is a boy born into challenges difficult enough for any man. It is early in his path through life and he already has many disadvantages. Raspberry's pale skin is most obvious on his calves that stand out against the darker, dirty tinge of his yellowing socks, and on the sides of his nostrils where blackheads have established base camps.

Creek and Raspberry are sitting next to each other on stools at a black, stone lab-table. When Raspberry shifts his arms they leave shapes of sweat on the tabletop. He is frequently distracted by this, and draws back into the shapes with his fingers. The students are preparing test-tubes for the flies to live and mate in. They are supposed to be putting a small piece of bread crumb in the bottom of each of ten tubes, capping them, and taking them up to the teacher. Mr. Alberwiecz, a quietly eccentric teacher with an Eastern European accent, has instructed them to be especially careful to only allow bread in the tube, or the experiment, "vill be tay-n-ted." Raspberry picks up the last tube, faces the back of the room so neither Creek nor Mr. A can see him, and spits his gum into the tube, caps it, and places it with the others. Raspberry grabs the rack of finished tubes from Creek and bumps his way to the front of the room with them.

Mr. A, with his head down, sees a large pale hand with dirty fingernails pushing a rack of tubes toward him. He looks up at

Don Rasmussen, looks back down at the tubes and says, "vait hee-er." Picking up each tube he holds it in front of him, between himself and Don, as if Don's face is the only backdrop before which the tube can be clearly seen. Creek is watching from across the room, not knowing what sort of mess could erupt from Raspberry at any moment. Mr. Alberwiecz lifts the tube with chewing gum between his right eye and Raspberry's face. From across the room Creek can see that the tube does not contain bread, but instead a little pink wad of gum. "Meester Res-mew-seen," Mr. Alberwiecz slowly and quietly begins, still holding the tube and looking straight through it into Don's face, "you vill be in charaj," he takes the contaminated tube and slowly lowers it into the side pocket of his coat without breaking eye contact, "ov ower lab tesss-t."

Creek then watches in disbelief as Mr. A takes Raspberry over to the rack containing all of the test tubes and explains to him how to order them and place them in their storage shelf. How is it possible that Mr. A has chosen Raspberry to hold this role of honor and responsibility? Doesn't he know that Raspberry blatantly disobeyed his instructions and tried to ruin the experiment? How can he put him in such a position of trust and risk the whole class's experiment being ruined?

The bell signaling the end of the period rings and Mr. A says, "Classs, eye-vill see-yu too-mar-ol." All of the class leaves except an indignant Creek who walks with an uncommon sense of purpose up to Mr. A's desk. "Yesss Matt-ew?"

"How could you put Raspberry in charge of the experiment? Didn't you see that he tried to contaminate the tube? It's not fair. He doesn't deserve to be in charge. I've been carefully following instructions all year and he's missed a lot of classes."

"Vell, Matt-ew, Meester Res-mew-seen will mayik a goot lab-oar-tory die-rect-ar. You vill mayik a goot exp-eer-i-mint," and he looks Creek directly in the eyes, "do not vorry, I know who de-seerves."

Creek's face grows red as he struggles to keep his thoughts to himself . . . It's not fair! I should be in charge. This experiment is boring anyway!

In the hallway Creek is looking at the floor as he walks quickly to his locker. It seems as though the world around him has separated itself from him, like he is suddenly closed off from the other kids in the hallway. All he can think about is how unfair it is that Raspberry got off without any punishment. Creek has felt un-appreciated in his classes all year. He doesn't get the best grades, but there always seems to be a reason outside of him causing him to make mistakes. Whether it is having a bad lab partner, or be-ing tired from soccer practice, or being distracted by the cute girl sitting in front of him, or feeling like the teacher doesn't like him, there always seems to be something that gets in his way.

In his right hand he spins the dial of his lock with his thumb. This number-spinning has been performed so many times that he doesn't think consciously of the numbers as he does it. When the dial gets to the right number, he says the number silently in his mind. After opening the lock he wonders if he'll ever forget the combination, or get it wrong. He has at least four lock combina-tions to remember—gym lock, bike lock, soccer lock, school lock. There is a pulse of fear regarding this that sits on the back of his neck. How easy it would be to get these mixed up; the numbers seem to come out of thin air from habit as he's spinning the dial, like a pianist playing a memorized song. But this fear is small, mostly subconscious, and quickly ignored.

Standing in front of his open locker, he looks for his math book and blue math folder among the folders and textbooks neatly shelved at the bottom. He feels a distance between himself and the locker now. It is as though he can't reach the locker no matter how hard he tries, even though it is only a foot away. The books at the height of his ankles feel like they are 100 feet below him at the bottom of a well. There is the slight pain of a headache in his temples. Creek recalls how before the first class period he saw the girl he is in love with, Christy, walking with her friend. He said hello to her, but she must not have seen or heard him because she didn't look at him or reply. Now, in his mind, he can hear her voice distinctly calling out to him from the stairwell behind him. When he turns around to look at the stairs, the voice is gone and no one is there.

Creek is a senior now and will be going to college next year, but he doesn't really think about what this will mean for him. His body has filled out in the last few years, so that now the sharp features of his face are matched by broad shoulders and muscular arms. June College, a nearby liberal arts college has offered him a scholarship to play soccer. It's most likely that he'll go there, because he doesn't want to go to the community college and his family can't afford to send him to a more expensive school—he didn't apply to any of the more expensive schools anyway.

Feeling a bump against his shoulder, Creek looks up to see his soccer friend Bryce, who says, "Hey, you coming to math class? There's a quiz today."

"Hi Bryce. Yeah I'm coming." Creek grabs the books he needs and shuts his locker as Bryce stands there waiting for him.

Bryce asks, "Did you see that commercial with the kid with a baseball bat and the cat on the TV?" Creek shakes his head, no. "It's hilarious. There's this cat on top of this TV in a garage, and this kid comes out with a baseball bat and start smashing in the TV, but the cat won't let go of the TV. It's holding onto the TV and hissing at the kid with the bat. The kid finally stops hitting the TV; the cat rolls over onto its side and lies on the heap of scrap that's left, like it's going to sleep. Then the kid goes over and plugs the TV in, there's a spark, and the cat jumps off the TV and out of the picture!"

"What's the commercial for?" asks Creek.

"I forget," Bryce answers as he adjusts the way his shirt is tucked in at the sides.

In math class Creek is unable to focus. Three thoughts are ricocheting off the inside of his head; trapped like pin-balls they won't stop sounding their presence. First he is thinking of Christy, who he is in love with though she doesn't return the sentiment. Everything about her makes him excited; her voice is soft and fast, her hair is long and blonde, her body is curvy like a rural road. Maybe she'll be at the school dance on Saturday night. Maybe he'll have the guts to dance with her. What Creek feels for her is love as he knows it. But really it is a craving; it is a hunger to fill his need for affirmation. He doesn't realize it—he only feels the hunger—but in essence, what he really wants to do is wear her like a costume. He wants to be seen as her boyfriend so she is a trophy showing his accomplishment.

That being said, there is some basic animal attraction in the mix as well, outside of the more complex psychological component. He is a young man in high-school and therefore much of his energy is in fact used just to keep his hormones in check, to keep him from pouncing on any female within reach at any hour of the day. As he sits in math class his mind is playing through all of his interactions with her in the past week, trying to figure out whether they helped his cause or hurt it. His mind shows him snapshots of her face and body.

When thoughts of Christy are quieted his thoughts shift

quickly to the interaction he's just had with the biology teacher. He still gets angry as he thinks of Raspberry, but then he feels guilty when he thinks of the way he talked to the teacher. Part of him wonders if he should go find Mr. A and apologize for what he said. Another part of him still feels like it's totally unfair and unreasonable. Guilt and anger arm-wrestle in his heart.

The third thought that fills his mind is college. Daydreams about what it will be like to play on a college soccer team, to live away from home, to go to parties, to choose a career path, flit and flutter through his consciousness. They are vague daydreams, because they are based only on comments from his older brother Lorne and TV shows about being in college.

So while the teacher is introducing concepts of calculus, Creek is maintaining the posture of a good student, pen in hand and eyes on the chalkboard, but he is not even close to understanding what is being taught.

Next to Creek's math classroom there is a smaller classroom in a corner of the building. It is different than other rooms because it wasn't initially intended to be a classroom but probably a very large utility closet. There are two high windows on the wall across from the door and half of the room has a sloping ceiling from an adjacent stair-well. This is Mr. Swordsmith's room. Writing class is meeting.

Swordsmith has taught at this high school for over twenty years. He always wears a wool sports-coat over a dress shirt—the top two buttons left open. At fifty-years-old his body is fit and his frame strong, though not thick like a weightlifter's. Hair has disappeared from the top of his head and turned gray at his temples giving him a distinguished look just after a haircut and the look of a shaggy orchestra conductor when it is time for another haircut. In two corners of the room are a dentist's chair and a barber's chair, with a couch between them, and then another couch along the wall to the right of the door. Opposite the couch is a row of writing desks, and in the left corner is Swordsmith's space consisting of a roll top desk (with a wooden slat cover that pulls down and locks), a small typewriter desk, and his swiveling chair. The students can sit in the couches, desks, or barber and dentist chairs, forming a circle, during class. On the walls patterned rugs from various exotic countries are hung, and in the center of the room is a coffee table with a goldfish bowl.

On the day following their fieldtrip to the zoo, Elle has her sophomore honors writing class in this idiosyncratic classroom. Swordsmith spins around to face the center of the room and the rest of the class, "Alright, my friends, it is time to reap the fruits of your labor for the last two weeks. We are going to read aloud each person's story. Everyone will get a copy of the story to write comments on, both as we read it and also as you re-read it tonight at home—as homework. All of the comments will be collected and discussed, and then the author will have a chance to edit the story before handing it in."

The assignment they have been working on is to rewrite a fairy-tale, making it take place in the present. Elle sits on one of the couches. Her legs cross easily in blue-jeans and her posture is upright, accentuating her straight, blonde hair as it falls to her shoulders. From behind her glasses she waits eagerly to hear who's story will be distributed and read first.

"Today we will start with Miss Crane's re-writing of Rumpel-stilskin, which she has titled, 'Bangley Beady Boo.' Once every-one has a copy, you may start reading Elle."

Elle is both nervous and excited. She has always loved read-ing stories aloud and hearing them read by her mom, but she's also not sure if her story is going to interest the class. In her excitement she can feel her temples pulsing.

Elle gathers her focus, takes a breath, and begins to read her story, holding it in both hands above her lap. Her voice is quiet, but clear.

"Bangley Beady Boo . . . In the ancient city of Seattle there is a man named Ralph Wemble who owns a corner store called Ralph's Goods. He is a poor man and lives very modestly above his store with his only daughter, Lisa. Despite their economic trouble, Lisa is a beautiful young woman; beneath her threadbare clothes the wealth of her beauty is radiant: she has caused more than one traffic accident walking downtown in the spring.

"One day Ralph has to go to the courthouse to file paperwork for his business. While he is in the courthouse the mayor of the city just happens to be passing through, followed by a crew of television reporters. The handsome young mayor is a very powerful man. The powerful mayor's eyes fall on Ralph and he walks up to Ralph with the television reporters in tow, saying, '. . . for example, this man here, surely our current economic slump has impacted him, yet he persists and is hopeful for the future. Aren't you sir?'

"Ralph is taken aback. He feels insulted because the mayor has looked right into him and used what he's found for his own publicity. And Ralph is insulted because the mayor has just assumed Ralph is struggling—however correct the assumption may be. So Ralph, as he is occasionally known to do, responds with a quick barb, 'Well, fortunately, my beautiful daughter can grow money from trees.'

"The reporters are getting all of this on video tape, and the mayor, feeling challenged, answers Ralph by calling his bluff, 'Well then, your daughter will come work in my garden. She starts tomorrow. My driver will pick her up at sunrise.' Ralph walks away discouraged and worried that his big mouth has gotten him into trouble again. He doesn't want to hand his daughter over to this powerful man."

Elle pauses and adjusts her posture, then continues, "The following day Lisa is brought to one of the mayor's courtyard gardens to receive instructions from the mayor himself. She is beautiful in her simple clothes, like some of the flowers there in the garden. The mayor is dressed in a suit, ready for a busy day, with his dark hair gelled close to his skin. He says, 'Young lady, you see those three baskets, in one week they will be filled with crisp paper money that you have grown from these trees. If they are not, your father will lose his business and be forced to leave this city, and you will work with my maids for the rest of your life.' The mayor turns his back on her and walks out without giving her time for any sort of response.

"Lisa sits on the floor by the baskets with her head in her hands weeping. She doesn't know what to do.

"On the second day she is walking in a mist among the trees, when she hears the gate at the back of the courtyard open, and sees a man who looks homeless enter the garden. The man walks up to her and says with a lowered head, from within the shadow of his hood, 'I can make these trees grow money, but I will want something in return. What will you give me?'

"Lisa looks down at the watch her father gave her for her 16th birthday and reluctantly offers it to the mysterious man. Accepting the watch, the man then slowly shuffles over to the base of a tree and reaches a dirty hand into a greasy pocket. The hand comes out in a fist, and the man extends the fist, turning it over and opening it above the tree's roots. A fine black powder falls around the base of the tree. The man proceeds to several other trees, repeating the same action.

"The next day Lisa doesn't see the mysterious man at all, but notices what look like rose buds on the trees where he had sprinkled the black dust. By the fourth day she sees that those buds have turned into little, compact, green spirals about half-an-inch wide and an inch long. On the sixth day the buds have bloomed like green flowers—flowers that are actually one-hundred-dollar bills. Each flower is a neatly spiraling one-hundred-dollar bill, like a calla lily made of money. It is morning of the seventh day and Lisa wakes up to see that all of the money-flowers have fallen to the ground. She jumps up and starts filling the three baskets with the money. There is just enough money to fill all three baskets.

"At noon on that seventh day the haughty mayor comes to visit Lisa in the courtyard garden. He is amazed to see the baskets full of one-hundred-dollar bills. After an initial moment of amazement, he declares, 'Well done young lady. You will now go to my front yard, gated-garden, where I have ten baskets that you will fill with money in one week's time. If they are not filled, your father will lose his business and be forced out of town, and you will work for my maids for the rest of your life.'

"Lisa is scared. She can tell he is powerful enough to make what he says come true. She doesn't want to be this man's slave for the rest of her life. It's a terrible enough experience to be trapped in his garden with an impossible task to accomplish. But she thinks of her father, whom she loves dearly and doesn't want to be separated from; she thinks of all the work he has put into his business: the will to succeed reenergizes her.

"The front yard, gated-garden, is larger than the courtyard garden. When the gate locks closed behind her she sees ten baskets, larger than the previous baskets, stacked along the path to the right. The whole first day she sits on the ground in front of the baskets imagining her fate if she cannot fill the baskets. At the same time she listens hopefully for the footsteps of that dark, mysterious hooded man."

Elle looks up from her story to see that all of the class is sitting still and paying attention to her. She is happy to see that their pens are down, that they are not furiously marking edits all over their copies of her story. Mr. Swordsmith is leaning back in his swivel chair, smiling. Elle continues with her story:

"On the second day Lisa wakes, startled by the hooded man standing silently over her. She quickly pleads, 'I need your help.'

"He answers, 'I can help you, but what will you give me?'

"Lisa's left hand reaches to touch the small gold heart-shaped locket hanging at the central meeting of her delicate collarbones. Inside the locket is a picture of her mother, who died when she was five-years-old. 'I'll give you my necklace, the only thing I have left to give.'

"From within the shadows of his hood the man answers in a low, gravelly voice, 'Very well.' He proceeds to walk among the misty trees of the front yard, reaching into his pocket and sprinkling the black dust around the bases of the trees.

"When the sixth day of that week arrives, at least a dozen of the trees have fully bloomed with one-hundred-dollar bills. On the seventh day Lisa wakes up early to see that all of the bills have fallen to the ground, and she quickly gets to work on her hands and knees collecting the bills into the ten baskets, filling all of them.

"The handsome young mayor arrives at noon, with two aides by his side, and immediately smiles upon seeing the ten baskets full of money. His eyes then fall upon Lisa, and he ravenously realizes just how rich he might become. As he looks at her beautiful, tired face, he thinks—although I am expected to choose my wife from among the wealthy families of the city, who could be more wealthy, or more beautiful than this young woman. Lisa sees the new way he looks at her and begins blushing, and looks down at the brick path between them.

"He says to her 'I have one more task for you to accomplish. In my backyard is a swimming pool. I will have it emptied of water. You have one week to fill it to the brim with money. If you fail, your father will loose his business and be banished from the city, and you will work for my lowest maids. If you succeed, I will make you my wife, we will have children, you and your father will live with me in my mansion, and I will make you the happiest woman in the whole city of Seattle.'

"Lisa is not really excited about becoming the handsome young mayor's wife, but she is even less excited about her father being run out of town and herself being a servant to the maids. It seems that neither outcome will give her freedom, although she thinks, perhaps there is more freedom as a wife than as a servant to the maids. As she ponders her conundrum, she becomes less certain of what the best outcome would be. She is taken to the huge backyard, where the large swimming pool is being drained of its water.

"When night falls, she lies down and sleeps on the concrete by the side of the empty pool.

"In the morning when she wakes, the strange, hooded man stands over her, directly in front of the rising sun. 'Looks like you've a lot of work to do,' he says to her.

"'Who are you? Why do you keep helping me? What is your name?' she asks with her half-awake voice.

"'That's for me to know, and you to find out,' is his quick and gruff reply.

"'I have to fill this pool with money by the end of the week, or I'll never see my father again and I'll be a servant in the mayor's mansion,' she says in desperation.

"'And what if you do fill the pool?' asks the mysterious hooded man.

"'Well, then I become the mayor's wife, my father lives with
us in the mansion, we have children, and I'll be the happiest
woman in the city.'

"'How do you know you'll be the happiest woman in the
city?' asks the man.

"'That's just what the mayor said, but I'm not really sure it's
true. I think I might be just as much a servant as his wife, twenty-
four hours-a-day, as if I were a servant to the maids, twelve hours-
a-day. But as his wife at least I'd see my father a lot.'

"'Young lady, that's your decision to make, perhaps if you
weren't so pretty, or so young, or so attached to your father, you
wouldn't be in this predicament,' he annunciates each syllable of
the word pre-dic-a-ment, as if with each part he was swallowing a
spoonful of medicine. 'What I can do for you, is fill this pool with
money. But, it's going to cost you dearly. When you have your
firstborn child, I will come for it within two weeks of its birth, it
will be mine.'

"Lisa has an unhappy decision to make. It seems to her there
is no way out, no good decision for her. She must choose the
lesser of the evils. She cannot bear the thought of never seeing her
father again; nor can she bear the thought of being a servant to
the maids. Giving up her first child seems unbearable in an abstract way, but lacks the sting of experienced reality to her. 'Okay,'
she says in despair, 'Help me.'

"At the end of the week, the pool is full of money, the mayor
is pleased, a wedding is held, and the father moves in. On the first
night of their marriage the mayor asks Lisa how she was able to
accomplish the money production feats. She tells him about the

hooded man and the promise that she made. When the mayor hears, he is terrified because he has heard tales of this hooded man who respects neither money nor power and always takes what he has won.

"Life in the mansion is mostly boring for Lisa, though it is nice to see her father have time for reading and exercise. Everything changes when she becomes pregnant. She is once again excited about life and for the first time she feels genuine love for her husband, the handsome young mayor. Thirteen days after the birth of their first child, Lisa is holding him in her lap on a bench in the backyard. She has completely forgotten about the promise she made to the hooded man, but it is he who sneaks up from behind her, sits down right next to her and whispers gravely in her ear, 'The time has come. The child is mine.'

"Lisa is petrified with terror. As the weight of her ill-considered promise falls to the pit of her stomach, she begins to sob. Her sobbing becomes lopsided wailing when the hooded man pulls the baby from her arms.

"In an extremely rare moment of empathy the hooded man pauses, just before running off with the baby. He says to Lisa, 'Very well, even I can feel your pain, silly girl. I will give you one week to guess my name. If by some miracle you are able to guess it, then you can keep your child and I'll leave you alone. Otherwise . . .' he doesn't finish the sentence, but merely pats the baby's belly with a dirty hand. 'I will come every day at noon for you to make guesses for 15 minutes. And I'll hold onto this little biscuit for now. And if you tell anyone about our deal, or about my visits, I'll have the boy for stew.' He walks off into the wooded part of the backyard with the boy in his arms.

"After more sobbing, Lisa goes to the kitchen, takes a loaf of bread and wraps it in the baby's blankets so no one will suspect he is missing.

"The next day Lisa is sure to be in the backyard at noon, and has prepared a list of names alphabetically. When the hooded man arrives she wastes no time, but quickly begins, 'Is your first name Alfred, Alphonse, Abner, Alex, Aiden, . . . ?'

"'No, no, no, non, no, non, nope . . .' the hooded man seems to take pleasure in his negative replies.

"'Is it Benjamin, Brad, Billy, Bob, Bo, Blake, . . . ?'

"'Nuh-uh, nope, na, no . . .'

"'Maybe Charles, Chris, Calvin, Craig, Celery, Carl, . . . ?'

"'No, not, nil, zilch, naw . . .'

"They continue like this through the alphabet finishing the 'z's' just as the fifteen minutes has run out. 'It's been a pleasure, my dear, and so far you are no where near! We'll sing another tune tomorrow at noon. Toodle-ooo,' and the hooded man with a new sense of vigor limps back into the woods.

"At noon on the following day Lisa is waiting for the hooded man with her head full of middle names. She proceeds through the alphabet with middle names as she had previously with first names. And once again the hooded man's replies are all lively rejections. There is one moment when Lisa has some hope, she says 'Petey.'

"And the hooded man pauses for a moment before exclaiming, 'That's wrong!' But none of her other P-words make any impression. At the end of the fifteen minutes she is despairing with guessing his name.

"On the third day she attempts to guess last names. This seems an impossible task as she can't even tell what nationality the man might be to help put her in the right ballpark of names. The fifteen minutes ends once again with her being frustrated and him walking joyfully into the woods. This time as he walks away she asks, 'How is my baby?'

"'Pretty as a pea!', he replies without turning to face her.

"The fourth, fifth, and sixth days are basically repeats of days one, two, and three. Lisa is emotionally exhausted and discouraged. In her despair she takes a risk and tells one of the maids her situation. The maid tells her she will walk through the city and see what she can find out.

"That evening as the maid is walking one of the main streets, she hears an odd song coming from one of the alleys. Looking down the alley she sees a hooded man sitting, playing a guitar to a small basket at his feet, and singing, 'I am Bangley Beady Boo, and I love you, I am Bangley Beady Boo, tomorrow you'll love me too, Oh Bangley, you wise old fool.'

"The maid sneaks away quietly, returning home to tell Lisa what she has discovered. On the seventh day when the hooded man arrives for the final fifteen minutes of testing Lisa, he notices that the rings under Lisa's eyes are gone—in fact she looks almost . . . happy?! He says to her, 'May I ask why you are in such a positive mood?'

"Lisa answers, looking straight into the shadow beneath his hood, 'I slept well last night, I dreamt my baby was back in my arms.'

"'Well, I suppose you'll want to remember that dream--forever,' he retort is gruff.

"'I suppose,' she answers lightly. 'Are you ready for my final guesses?'

"'Yes, yes, let's get on with it, soon enough I'll be carrying this basket back into the woods forever.'

"Lisa begins, 'Is your full name, Thomas Wilfred Amberson?'

"'NO!'

"'Is it Carl Gustav Erikson?'

"'Not at all!'

"'How about Sean Michael O'Toole?'

"'No, no, no,' he seems to be relaxing because of her misses.

"'Then it must be Bangley Beady Boo!'

"He staggers backward; he jumps up and down, landing with both feet stomping; he pulls back his hood and pounds his fists against his shaggy head: he screams and runs headlong at a tree. His brow strikes the tree-trunk and splits open like a melon, and he falls flat on his back immediately dead. She quickly calls her conspirator maid to drag the body back into the woods.

"Lisa names her baby Sean Michael. In time the young mayor learns from Lisa how to treat people with kindness and goodness. Also, in time she finds she is in fact in love with her husband, the handsome young mayor. Her father loves to babysit Sean Michael. Indeed, she is the happiest woman in the whole city of Seattle."

Elle looks up from her story. Mr. Swordsmith is still smiling. The class gives her a healthy applause for about five seconds. She is mildly embarrassed as most of the class is looking at her, and she looks down at the story in her hands.

The bell signaling the end of class rings and Mr. Swordsmith announces, "Please re-read Elle's story tonight for homework, and make any additional written comments. We'll start tomorrow with a short discussion of Elle's story and then we'll hear Thomas's story. As Elle is walking out of class Mr. Swordsmith stops her, "Elle, wait here for a minute please, I'd like to talk to you." Swordsmith and Elle move over to his desk where he sits down in his swivel chair and she sits in a folding chair across from him. "I enjoyed listening to your story. I think you have a gift for writing. Do you enjoy it?"

Elle answers, "It was really fun. I like stories with unusual characters, like the hooded man."

"Well, I just wanted to encourage you to keep writing, and think about writing for the school newspaper next year, and maybe the arts journal too."

"Thanks Mr. Swordsmith, that sounds like a good idea."

"Yes, and also, why do you think these tales have really gruesome elements, like the hooded man splitting his head against a tree?"

"I think they exaggerate both good and bad things; it makes them more of an adventure."

Swordsmith puts his hand to his chin and slowly rubs his chin between his thumb and first finger, "I suppose you are right about that. Thank you Elle; I'll see you tomorrow."

"Have a good day," Elle walks out the door and into a hallway swimming with students.

In this stream of people we move forward in time again. During our transition Elle daydreams about riding a raft through a hallway of rafting students. The hallway has filled with water and they are all bumping off each other and paddling to get where they need to be. From her raft Elle turns to see Swordsmith standing in the doorway of his classroom, as if on shore, as if unaffected by the stream of time. Elle sees her friend Cathy in a raft headed straight at her. They bump into each other and laugh. Up ahead there is someone who looks like Dollar, but she can't tell for sure because it is only the back of his head that she sees.

1962

Boots

Two years later. Elle is in that same hallway, about to enter a senior composition class with Mr. Swordsmith. Dollar is also in the class. He looks up and smiles as she walks into the room. She walks past him and playfully steps lightly on his foot.

Creek is a sophomore at June College, and is starting on the soccer team. It's the first game of the season.

A sharp pain shoots into the top of Creek's left foot. The defender pressess with all his weight through his right toes, on top of Creek's left toes. His cleats sink into Creek's foot, but Creek will not be distracted. The whistle blows and the corner kick is an instant from execution. It is like popcorn on a stovetop. Once it begins the fullness of completion is unstoppable; it is like a large stone rolling down a hill; the kick, like a firework shooting up into the sky—and Creek cannot allow this meager distraction at his extremity to be a hitch in its realization.

The instant he hears his teammate's foot hitting the soccer ball Creek sprints toward the center of the goal box and curves-in toward the goal. Another teammate runs straight at him and crosses behind him, using him as a screen. They are the two "warheads" in the play. The kicker wants the ball to be a line-drive and head high at the center of the box, ten-feet in front of the goal. There is no margin of error for distance from the goal because the two "warheads" have timed their runs to get to that spot at the same moment as the ball.

But there is some margin of error in the height of the ball; it can be about a foot too high, or a foot too low. If it is at all low, then Creek is the active attacker and will throw his head at the ball, with the back of the net as his target. If the ball is at all high, then Creek will fake at the ball and the teammate behind him will strike the ball with his head, aiming for the goal. This is a good play because no one, not even the team executing the play, knows exactly what will happen. They are prepared for both possibilities though, so they have an advantage over the defense. By instilling the play with an unpredictable element, they have greatly increased the possible outcomes; by anticipating these possibilities they have a distinct edge over the defense—assuming the kick is in place.

The ball is exactly where it should be and slightly low—the popcorn is at the height of its popping—Creek lunges forward with his head in front—a defender also makes a move for the ball. It all happens so quickly. Fearless. When one person is fearless, great strides can be made toward achieving what would otherwise seem impossible. When two people are fearless, and cooperating, they inspire others to join them. When two opposing forces are fearless, the net result is often destructive. As Creek's head strikes the ball, in his peripheral vision he can also see the defender's head impacting the ball at the exact same instant. Creek's head moves forward and down when it hits the ball; the defender's, sideways and up: it is just enough to throw the ball off course, causing it to whiz past the goalie's outstretched glove, outside the goal-post and net, missing the goal inches to the right. That's not the worst of it though.

The soccer ball is not heavy enough to stop the motion of their heads after they strike it. So both heads continue forward until they are stopped by their relatively equal and opposite forces. Because both players made a fair play on the ball, no penalty is called, but a different sort of penalty is evident in their bodies lying motionless on the grass.

Being a small college, there aren't more than a few hundred fans in the stands. However, the silence of so many people as they stand watching and waiting is haunting. The two young men remain motionless on the grass for at least ten seconds as the other players either squat to watch the trainers who have run onto the field, or slowly walk away forming two distant huddles. At about the same time both players begin to slowly move. Before letting them get up, the trainers check to make sure neither has sustained a neck injury. Both of them seem to be okay, able to wiggle all their extremities, remember their names, and count the fingers on a hand. They are slowly walked to the corner of the field and into a school van that the trainer will drive to the local hospital.

Creek's girlfriend, Mary, is in the stands and follows the van to the hospital. She drives a white Chrysler Imperial with a white decal of a butterfly in the top-center of the rear window. Mary's sorority friends stay in the stands to watch the rest of the game.

She has long brown hair that is naturally curly, but she has it straightened and then curled in just the right spots. It's hard to describe the many different angles and lengths of hair in her

complex hairstyle: she gets it done by students at the school's sa-
lon training academy. Along with having her hair styled, she also
keeps the French manicure of her fingernails up to date. Mary's
make-up is thorough, and falls about three-quarters toward the
heavy side on the light-to-heavy spectrum of make-up application.
She is particularly attached to lipstick with a glossy sheen. Today
she wears a matching pink sweat suit with individual white stripes
along the sides. Her daytime outfits are normally athletic, or blue
jeans and fitting solid blouses. When going out at night she usually wears a dark skirt and a solid sleeveless blouse. She lays out in
the sun every chance she gets, to keep her skin tan. Even on this
somber drive to the hospital she listens to pop music on the radio.

When Mary arrives at the hospital, Creek has already been
discharged and waits for her in the lobby.

"Hey Mare, thanks for coming," Creek speaks more slowly
than usual.

"I parked in a fifteen minute spot, so let's go," she grabs his
hand and pulls him, as a mother pulls a child through a grocery
store.

"The nurse told me the other guy is having complications,"
Creek mutters with a slight pulling resistance in his hand.

"Well that's what he gets for knocking heads with you,"
Mary keeps her body's momentum moving toward the exit as she
speaks, also digging in her purse for her keys.

In fact the other guy's complications are much worse than
anyone at the hospital could have anticipated. In the several days
before the match he had been feeling tired and noticing small
red spots on his legs, and a few larger bruises in random spots
on his body where he vaguely remembered being bumped. He
knew they had an important soccer game coming up, so he didn't
want to see the school nurse until after the game because he

didn't want to lose any playing time. On the two-hour van ride to Creek's school he slept. He had developed idiopathic thrombocytopenic purpura—a low platelet count due to his body producing abnormal antibodies that destroy his platelets. The cause of the body's production of these abnormal antibodies is unknown. With a low platelet count his blood had lost its ability to clot. By the time the van carrying him from the soccer game arrived at the hospital his brain had filled with enough blood to cause him to pass out.

As the doctors race against time, their chances of saving him become less and less. Within forty-five minutes of arriving at the hospital the young man is pronounced dead. There is only one other non-hospital staff person there at the hospital with him, the home team's trainer. He doesn't even know the young man's name. Creek and Mary are already on the road, on the way back to her sorority house.

The dead boy's mother and father sometimes attended his home games, but rarely go to away games. On this day they are not even aware that their son has a soccer game. The news reaches them by telephone from the hospital.

The news reaches the rest of his soccer team through the home team's trainer, in the locker room after the game has finished. Creek finds out by phone, at Mary's, when one of his teammates calls him after the game.

Doubt about his own life's meaning insinuates itself into Creek's consciousness unpredictably through this accidental death. As Creek lies on his back on Mary's bed, still wearing his sweaty soccer jersey, he can feel the point of impact throbbing on his forehead—the murder weapon is still warm. According to ancient Jewish law he would now be required to flee to a city of refuge, until the avengers of the other young man's life had passed away. Fortunately the Washington State and United States of America's laws are more lenient in the case of accidental deaths. He is left to struggle alone against his own conscience. Though he has absolutely no reason to feel guilty, though he had no premeditated thoughts of murder, nor any thoughts of murder at any time, he still feels the mysterious undercurrents of guilt in his subconscious. This is no insanity inducing guilt like that possessing the protagonist Raskolnikov in Dostoevsky's "Crime and Punishment." Rather it is a quiet and irrational interweaving of disparate intentions. Those secret sins deep in Creek's past have attached themselves in strange ways to his guilt over the accident of the soccer game. And so a thin fog of despair begins to encroach upon his disposition. With it Creek feels the deep emptiness of a lack of counterbalancing meaning in his own life. It is all vaguely senseless to him. Why should he, an agent of death, get to go on enjoying life?

Mary is at her desk, on the phone with a friend providing updates on the events of the day. As Mary leans forward, Creek can see the tan skin of her lower back between the top and pants of her pink sweatsuit. The sight of her underwear peeking out over the top of her sweatpants makes his transition from guilt to desire quick.

Creek and Mary have been having sex for a few months. She'd had a couple of other partners in high school, but for Creek this is a first. He still feels embarrassed when he buys condoms at the pharmacy. His parents had always told him that he should save sex for marriage, but he figures that he is in college now, and he is certainly old enough to be having sex. Her philosophy is that it's just a natural part of being in a relationship.

Mary keeps the room tidy. Her taste in decorating comes straight out of whatever magazine is having a sale. It's a twin bed with rose-colored sheets and a white comforter. Creek closes his eyes, half asleep. Mary turns on some quiet music and moves to sit on the bed looking down at Creek. Her hand is on his leg as she says, "Baby I'm so glad you're okay, I'm going to kiss you and make you all better."

There are two kinds of sex. It can be intense like the battle of Gettysburg, or it can be intense like a re-enactment of the battle of Gettysburg—obviously there is a big difference between the two. Mary has only experienced the re-enactment type and her imagination has become stuck in this mode. She approaches sex like she is acting out the part of a woman having sex. As much as she may try to make it appear real, she is very much aware of doing the things that a person having sex should do. What she doesn't realize, and may never realize, is the difference between a re-enactment and the real thing has to do with what is at stake. And in fact, sex is much like war; the stakes are yourself, your heart, and your life. When the stakes aren't real, the sex isn't real.

Though she emotionally shuts out most of the stakes, there is one aspect of sex that she cannot avoid: procreation is inherent to the act. The physical reality is unavoidably a mirror of the true emotional one. These stakes are high, and she is terrified by the possibility of becoming pregnant.

While they are having sex in the afternoon, with the comforter pulled off the back of her bed, there are a few minutes when Creek appears tired and simply rests inside of her. They then resume until he is able to act his part with enough conviction to become adequately excited. After he has finished, after they have laid together for a few minutes in stillness, they separate and he is shocked to discover no condom on himself. He stammers, "Where's the condom?"

She answers, "I know you had one on." Then she finds it

inside herself. There is no more speaking as they both lie on their backs in the fear and unknowing. His hands are over his closed eyes. She is staring at the ceiling.

Dollar and Elle are good friends, and that is the extent of their relationship. After school they are standing across from each other at the net. It is spring break. Though neither of them is really a tennis player, they have been getting together at the courts in the spring for years. It really is the element of play they most enjoy. Volleys back and forth. Watching them would remind a person of watching a dog chase a ball in a park; there is a sense of focus and contentedness in their game. Even though they aren't especially good, they are having a great time. The person who misses a shot will usually laugh—not because they aren't trying, but because it is fun to try and even fun to miss. The court is behind the school and next to a park.

They take a break and sit on the bench next to the court. Behind the school building they can see hills and a sky with gently spaced cumulous clouds allowing gaps of blue and sunshine. Dollar says, "Fir trees like banjos and hills like bluegrass bands."

After about twenty seconds Elle answers, "A glade, a blue tree, a green ocean, a steel gray mind."

Dollar smiles at her, thinks for about a minute and says, "The Earth is a pearl, the universe a shell, at the bottom of the ocean sheathed in boundlessness, we dwell."

She says, "I like that." Then she points to a dead bird behind the bench with her racquet, "I don't like that!" They can see evidence in the bird of a violent death. It is ripped open near its neck and there is a dark line coming out of the wound and a spot of dried blood in the grass.

Dollar gets up and approaches the bird with a stick he found on the ground. He puts the end of the stick into the wound and picks up the bird, and walks it over to the base of a fir tree dropping it at the base. Coming back to where Elle is sitting on the bench he says, "Well, I guess it's time to be getting home. We're having dinner at 5:30 and then I'm going to a movie with my dad tonight."

A week later they are back in school. They wait for Mr. Swordsmith's Senior Composition class to begin. Dollar has never really been much into writing. He loves to read, but aside from a class paper here and there, he's never found writing interesting before—before taking Mr. Swordsmith's class. With the inspiration of Mr. Swordsmith, Dollar is beginning to see how writing can be a way to figure out what is really going on in between things—in the same way a radio picks up sound waves and makes them audible. The classroom hasn't really changed in the two years since Elle's Sophomore story of Bangley Beady Boo. Dollar is sitting in the Dentist's chair. His friend Kevin is pretending to be a dentist, saying, "Alright young man, open wide and say ahhhh." Dollar has his mouth open and is trying to simultaneously open wide and smile, with a trust abandoned to Kevin's playfully sinister dentist. Kevin continues in a voice like a vampire, "Very vell, zis vill only hurt vor vivteen or tventy min-u-ets, vor dis time, it vill be very painvil." Kevin crosses his eyes, pretends he lowering a very large drill toward Dollar's mouth and makes a loud drilling sound. They both start laughing.

The bell rings signaling the beginning of class and Mr. Swordsmith walks in from the hallway. "Hello class. Ahh, I see Dollar has been having trouble with his teeth again. Well at least we know he is in the trustworthy hands of a reliable Dentist. Okay, everyone, please put away your pens and notebooks; clear you desks and clear your minds. I'm going to introduce you to a new form of writing today and your focus is imperative."

The class has quieted and Swordsmith stands in front of his desk with the class around him in a circle. He has the look of a shaggy orchestra conductor, as it has been at least two months since his last haircut. He begins his lecture, "Some of you have probably experienced a condition called writer's block, where you just can't seem to come up with ideas for your writing. I propose to you that what you are really experiencing is a lapse in your creative energy. Like all people, you have a natural creative energy that flows through you all of the time, even when you sleep. The trick to overcoming 'writer's block' is to revive the natural creative gift each of you undoubtedly has. If you are a human being, your brain is constantly seeking to make sense of the world. The wonderful thing is that different people will notice different things in the world, they will have different ways of understanding things, and they will make sense of the world differently. Yet we are also capable of appreciating the ways other people see. When we read someone else's writing, we are discovering how that person understands the world. Generally this is a pleasurable and enlightening experience."

At this point Mr. Swordsmith sits down into his swivel chair. He breathes in slowly then exhales and gestures with his left hand. "Most of you are fairly consistent when it comes to appreciating others' ways of seeing the world; you don't have much trouble finding value in the books you read. The trouble comes when you try to tap into your own unique perspective. There are all sorts of reasons why this is a difficult thing to do. Fear. You might be afraid that your perspective won't be interesting or valuable. Distraction. You might have trouble maintaining the focus of your perspective because you are constantly being drawn to other people's ways of seeing, or to a fake way of seeing that people have created to make them feel safe—like being part of a gang, or being a rebel who is in fact just trying to fit in with the other rebels. Discipline. There is an element of finding your own voice that will require discipline. You cannot dwell in your world, if you are unable to discern which rabbit trails to follow, and on the other hand have the discipline to NOT go down those trails that you know are irrelevant. Part of the skill of thinking well is deciding what not to think about. You may have to tell yourself not to turn on the television once every minute for the first five minutes that you sit down, but after a while this will become easier. On the other hand you may be the type who will get true inspiration from having the television on: this is for you to discover."

Mr. Swordsmith gets up, goes to his desk, and picks up a violin bow and a folded yellow paper from his desk. He walks to the center of the room and places the bow and paper on the coffee table next to the fish bowl. I call this assignment 'Harmony Gardening.' The idea is to begin with two objects or ideas that seem unconnected. You will then place those two things next to each other in your mind and observe how they interact. Try to pick up on the vibrations that occur between the two. Pay attention to what one has to say about the other. Enter the space between the two and begin to tease out the meaning. Allow your mind to freely interact with them. The gardening happens when new ideas begin to grow out of the harmony between the two—thus the name 'Harmony Gardening.' This is creativity. It is taking what the world is so readily supplying and remaking from it; it is recycling. None of us can create from nothing. But we can pay attention to the ways our minds are connecting things, understanding things, and exploring things."

Swordsmith picks up the bow and the papers, "Here is a bow from a violin made around 1700, during the baroque period of music. And this piece of paper is a copy of the Bill of Rights, added to the Constitution of the United States by amendment in 1789. The first amendment in the Bill of Rights guarantees free-dom of religion, speech, press, assembly, and petition. I'm going to give you an example of the Harmony Gardening type of writing by reading to you a short essay I wrote with these two ideas as my inspiration. We'll talk more about how to get from start to finish with this essay, but for now I want you to enjoy the new thoughts grown from the interaction between these two things."

He places the bow and paper down the coffee table, walks back to his desk, picks up a notebook, and sits down in his chair holding the notebook in his lap. He begins reading:

"Boldly, the imperfect jewel of baroque art and music ex-plored new territory by way of the sensuous. At the heart-strings of listeners the Bach sonata pulled. Moving, opulent, decadent—this unashamedly fleshy sound explored new territories of form. The more musicians explored, the more they were enchanted by these new sounds. Having given life to the opera, the movement was a direct appeal to a lush Dionysian experience. Marks on a pa-per. Consider the impact. The musical score coordinates sounds; the written word, ideas. Thin black marks of ink on a page move people; the pen directs the sword.

"On the surface of a paper rest the ink markings protecting

our freedom. Dignified in its stillness, the Bill of Rights stands as a rock amidst crashing waves. It is the indelible ink on paper that keeps these freedoms from shifting: dissolving. If Handel's "Messiah" is timeless, if Pachelbel's "Cannon in D" is enduring, if Bach's "Brandenburg Concertos" abide, then the words of the Bill of Rights reflect a similar intransigence. The apotheosis of a generation's wisdom is recorded on the page: freedom is rendered in words. Freedom of speech and religion, freedom of press and petition, freedom to bear arms and not unwillingly house soldiers, freedom from search and seizure, freedom of due process and trial by jury, freedom from cruel and unusual punishment, make the Bill of Rights invaluable.

"The most intangible treasures—passionate harmonies, enlivening freedoms—are guarded by humble scratches of ink on paper. We may never comprehend how this paradox maintains its power. What other creature in the animal kingdom, guided toward the profound by its own meek smudges, can we study to help us understand our own phenomenal leaps? In this mystery, riddle, enigma, our uniquely human creativity is unveiled. We find meaning in the tension between the concrete and the abstract—meaning between the marked page and the beating heart."

Swordsmith gets up from his chair and without speaking walks over to a record player near his desk and lowers the needle to the spinning disk. For over five minutes the class sits listening to Bach's Brandenburg Concerto, No. 2 in F Major, I. Allegro. As their hearts follow the graceful trumpet flourishes and the string echoes, in their minds they picture the black notes flying across the page of a musical score. When this movement has ended on the tape Swordsmith picks up the piece of paper from the coffee table in the center of the room and reads the first amendment of the Bill of Rights. "Congress shall make no law respecting an establishment of religion, or prohibiting the free exercise thereof; or abridging the freedom of speech, or of the press; or the right of the people peaceably to assemble, and to petition the Government for a redress of grievances."

He addresses the class, "So hopefully you now see how exploring the dynamic between two seemingly unrelated ideas can bring out worthwhile creative revelations in writing. This will be your assignment for the next week. I want you to choose two objects or ideas. Begin by exploring their meanings individually with several paragraphs of writing. Then you will start brainstorming about how they might relate to each other with another paragraph. After this preparatory work, you will begin writing a paragraph about the relationship. From these paragraphs you will pare down your essay to twenty sentences. I will be monitoring your progress and helping you at each stage along the way. Bring your ideas to class tomorrow and we will begin. You are dismissed: go into the world with hungry, open minds."

After school Dollar and Elle walk home together. At this point both of them plan on attending the community college after high school. Dollar will enter a two-year forestry program. Elle will get an associates degree in Library Science. They both plan on continuing to live at home while they're in school, mainly because they are both trying to save money.

They talk about what they might possibly write for composition class. Dollar thinks of writing about bald eagles and gardening. He describes the idea to Elle, "I want to write about the birds that are flying so high in the air and then the garden that is rooted in the ground. I think there must be some connection between the two but I really don't see it yet. I think Swordsmith said that if you intuit a connection but can't really put your finger on it, it is probably a good pair to work with."

Elle answers, "Yeah, you're right, and I think that is a good idea. It does seem like there is something to be investigated there. I'm thinking of doing mine on squares and circles. It might be interesting to explore the similarities of such basic and different shapes. It seems like it might become a very broad ranging topic even though they are such simple forms."

"Yep, that does sound good. You're so good at exploring deep thoughts. I wonder if you'll end up liking one more than the other."

She says, "Yeah, I wonder too. So, do you think you'll go out to see Creek this weekend?"

"Oh, that's right, I'm going on Friday afternoon and coming back Saturday night. He has a game on Saturday morning, so that should be fun, and I think we're going to some dance party his teammate is having on Friday night," he answers.

"Ooooh dance party!" she shoves his shoulder playfully, "Are you going to hang out with his girlfriend and her friends? They're particularly pretty and peculiarly perfumy!"

"Yeah, yeah. I'm not so excited about them and their talk about trendy musicians. I don't usually understand what they're talking about, but I laugh, and sometimes that in itself can be a little bit of fun. But, their extra dark tans are kind of creepy."

The next day in composition class Dollar begins his brain-storming about bald eagles and gardening. He sits in the dentist's chair writing with a black ballpoint pen in a blue spiral notebook:

"The bald eagle. Power and grace come to mind with this bird. It is huge when you are near it, but distant and light in the sky. It is like a B-17 bomber, muscular and acrobatic. Hunting with its sharp beak, the eagle is a fisherman. It is an old, wise fisherman living in the remote hills with his old wise wife. He goes out to hunt each day and has become comfortable with his routine as the thrill of the capture is enmeshed within hours of waiting. When he is in the sky his mind is working through the rivers and lakes, scanning for fish. When he is diving into the water to make a kill, his mind rests as though he were sitting and watching the sky. When he is sitting and watching the sky, he is soaring in his mind. He has mastered the art of antithesis in his inner and outer being so that in the most intense moments he is calm, and in the most restive states his mind is exploring voraciously. This eagle has no music to distract him, no books, no words, no movies. His sole experience is the immediate impact of his environment. He has nothing to contemplate from the past and no concerns for the future, beyond his own full stomach. He is not bound by the Earth. Nor is he bound by the weight of human consciousness. Instead the eagle darts like the wind wherever the wind will go.

"A garden. Gardens are rooted and earthy. They have boundaries. A fence, a wooden wall, a rock path, these dividers separate the garden from the surrounding Not Garden. And the Not Garden and the Garden occupy different spaces of intention in the mind of the gardener. They have different functions. Inside the walls of the Garden, space is functional. The arrangement of plants is intentional and static for the duration of the plant's lives. Outside the wall of the Garden there is movement. The space outside is one from which to observe the space inside. In some ways it is thus subservient. These spaces relate to each other as do light and dark. One allows for the other. Without the space outside, there would be no neutral area from which to move and observe. Without the space inside, there would be no jewel to observe and support—like a left hand and a right hand, both are needed to clap. Plants grow from the earth, striving upward in every sense of the word. Not only do they move up literally toward the sky, they also transform from simple muddy seeds to flowering, colorful, delicious vegetables. They transform from dirt into a nutrient-rich, sustaining food. The Garden is a place of growth and transformation. It is seasonal; it is cyclical. It requires fastidious caretaking from a knowledgeable gardener to thrive. He must be willing to prune—to kill—in order that what remains might thrive. He must have a plan for his plants and check on them frequently to coax them into conformity with his plan. The weeds will need to be plucked and the lettuce will need water, and the fences will need to be high enough to keep the rabbits out.

"With the eagle there is a nobility of breathing space; with the garden, a fecundity of soil. Can we tie a rope between the noble and the fecund? To be noble is to be free of embarrassing faults and flaws, such as a limp or a lisp or a loan. To be fecund is to possess a richness of character that fosters growth. To be noble AND fecund, would mean becoming godlike--having a righteous degree of remove and a potent power to bring life into the world. So the rope between the two would be taut and strong, like a power line holding a large electrical current. And this rope would have both destructive and life-giving power. A soaring bird and a garden are complementary. The bird can look into the garden and might even decide to land within the garden momentarily. But the bird does not live in the garden. It is a force in transit. On the other hand, the garden needs the sky and sun to grow. It moves into the air and exchanges oxygen for carbon dioxide. The garden makes green. It stores. It loves the bird, and welcomes it to roost, but it does not fly away with the bird to the top of a tree. It is a source. To be a force AND a source, this is godly; this is beyond the endurance and intentions of people. Yet it does enter our imagination, in a rope tied between the eagle and the garden, like a lightening rod, clearing the mind and filling it with humble awe in the presence of magnificence."

While Dollar is writing his draft about eagles and gardens, Elle is sitting at the end of the couch next to the dentist's chair. She is writing on graph paper in a black binder, with a blue pen. She is writing her rough draft about circles and squares:

"A circle is perfect in roundness. It rolls along a flat line without changing shape, so that an observer would not know if it was rolling or sliding, because there is no wobble in the rim of the wheel. A circle on the top of a glass makes a bright humming sound when a wetted finger is dragged along its diameter. We swing a circle around our hips when we hula-hoop. A circle is both indestructible and fragile. With a dent it is no longer a circle; without a dent, there is no single point of friction to attack. The iris is a circle, the eyeball is a circle spun in place like a top. The earth is a sphere with an equatorial circle for a belt. If we figure out what we want, we draw a circle around it. I stand inside a circle and I am home. A circle is a welcoming womb; it is a feminine tank: bulging egg. Black holes are circles without borders. They are destructive because they defy definition; they break the rules. A black hole is a circle that has no diameter and no radius, but is perfectly round; yet, still hungry. To tame a black hole I would estimate its edge and trace it with a compass, being very careful not to lose the edge or cut my hand, like replacing a bicycle inner tube. With a tamed black hole I could go anywhere because the power of the circle is in its timelessness. There is no beginning and no end, and the now is always reoccurring. All circles believe every circle in the world is the same size. When one circle approaches another, there is no comparison or competition. One simply says to the other, 'Oh, so good to see you. We really are each other. Have a good morning now.'

"Squares are obstinate beasts. Most squares think they are made of stainless steel. A falling square can crush a man; flatten him against the pavement. In fact, "pavement" is made from squares of tar. The strength of a city is based on a square. Of all its enemies, the square is most afraid of water. They have spent so much time together—one holding the other. Yet, they are enemies because they have never reconciled their differences. If the square is making the argument that having four corners is the ultimate state of being, water always disagrees. Water will vary its argument on corners, sometimes believing in none, and at other times feeling that everything should be a corner. Then there is the discussion of impact, on which the two of them continually disagree. 'Hardness, always hardness,' is the square's take on impact. On the other hand, water believes in a more flexible impact. Then Square becomes a cube by flexing his muscles and does a cannonball into water, making quite a splash. Sometimes a square will look at his corners from inside and feel they are less than 90 degrees, like they are pinching and pointing. Then, sometimes from the outside the square will imagine the corners are billowing out and flattening. But this is all in the square's imagination: the corners are always exactly 90 degrees. In its most terrifying nightmares the square sees itself with fellow squares, family members. As the square moves around them he counts their corners. Each time he counts he comes up with the numbers three or five, but never four. He tries and tries, but is never able to count four. Then he asks the other squares, 'How many corners do you have?' They always answer, 'Four, of course.' But then when he counts them, he gets three or five. He runs away. Finally he rests in front of a mirror and begins to count his own corners. No matter how hard he concentrates, he always counts either three or five corners on himself. It is horrifying.

"There is a interesting way in which a circle can fit inside a square, or a square can fit inside a circle. If the square is on the outside, one is drawn to microcosmic thoughts. We dive into the crack between the floorboards, and shrinking in size, we see smaller and smaller details revealing the truth that our journey inwards is endless. If the circle is on the outside, with the corners of the square just touching the inside of its circumference, one is expanded into macrocosmic thoughts. We journey outward, becoming larger and larger until we see all things in a single small drop, like rain. The circle is movement and the square is awareness of self. When the circle and square overlap, sharing an equal average radius, consciousness is cancelled and existence is caught between the thunderclap and the lightning bolt. Squares can roll too—just not on flat ground: the ground needs to be scalloped like cartoon teeth. Every square has a secret yearning to be circular. They acknowledge this yearning to different degrees. Some have hidden it deep within themselves. Every circle imagines that one day it will act with the conviction of a square. Circles have a common jealousy of squares. In fact, circles get very jealous of many things. The circular shape tends toward jealousy."

After school on Friday Dollar drives to June College to visit Creek. He arrives at Creek's dorm room around 7pm. When Creek comes down to meet him in the lobby of the building it is clear that Creek has already had a few drinks. He is more friendly than usual, and he thinks most of what he's saying is slightly funnier than it really is. They walk down the hall to Creek's dorm room where his roommate, Dan, sits on the floor with his back against the bed, playing a card game by himself. He has a silver can of beer at his side and the deck of cards in both hands. When Dollar and Creek walk in he pauses his game, takes a drink from his can, and leans over to the mini-fridge in the corner. Pulling out an unopened can he says, "Who needs a cold one?" Dollar shyly shakes his head no.

"He says he doesn't like how it tastes, but maybe by the end of the night we'll have changed his mind," Creek says as he simultaneously puts his left hand on Dollar's right shoulder giving it a couple light shoves and takes the beer from Dan with his other hand. "Dollar, don't worry, I know I've got a game tomorrow—it's all under control. Mary and two of her friends are picking us up in about half-an-hour." Creek sits across from Dan to play cards, "Let's start a new one Dan, I'm gonna show you how this is done."

"Last Friday you had a six-pack all to yourself, and played your best soccer game yet on Saturday morning," Dan says as he shuffles the cards to start the game over.

Creek answers, "It's not a big deal. I think almost everyone on the team had a few drinks at that party." Dollar sits on the bottom bunk bed while Creek and Dan play the card game.

On their way to the party Mary's friend Samantha drives; Dollar rides in the passenger seat; Creek and Mary are in the backseat. Every couple of minutes Creek pinches Mary's side making her shriek and then laugh and try to pinch him back. The music is turned up loud enough that it would really be impossible to have a conversation. For the most part Dollar is okay with that. He has met Samantha before, but hasn't talked to her much. Mainly he tolerates the playfully overaggressive flirting she and Mary's other friends were doing with him. Their attention is sort of fun at first, but then gets a bit old. It feels fake, like he's just pretending with them—pretending to be a shy and innocent younger man. And maybe that is what he truly is, but he knows that if he were to respond in kind, it would stop the charade; they would treat him like a real person, instead of like a toy for their amusement. Nevertheless, their charade Dollar tolerates. Syrupy, effusive, acerbic—the smell of Samantha's perfume puts Dollar in a cloud of helplessness.

The houses they drive past—old, peeling, overgrown—resemble the mouth of a person who has refused to go to the dentist for years. This neighborhood was once family owned and maintained, but in the last twenty-five years almost all of the houses have become rentals for students. Roof failure or foundation faults or plumbing collapse, it is only a matter of time before these once noble homes breathe their last. Neglect. A bit of care, given monthly or yearly to these houses, might have saved them from their destined "tear-down" status. But the owners are living month by month themselves. And they have to deal with the more pressing matters of just getting the students to pay the rent and not burn the places down.

They drive through a section of the street with cars parked on both sides for almost the whole block, and find a spot to park near the corner. As soon as Samantha turns the car's engine off they can hear the bass reverberating from the party 100 yards away. All sorts of interesting sounds float through the air to them from the party, such as laughter and yelling, screen doors and car doors, drum beats and bottles. There is no moon and the stars are covered by clouds. Dark-night fir trees dominate the air. To Dollar the air, as they walk down the sidewalk, smells mildly like soap—it is a good clean smell. They walk up the front stairs and across a quiet porch occupied by several half-awake kids and the smell of pot.

Inside, swimming through the people, they swim to the back, holding their breaths and eyeing each other like swimmers. From the kitchen at the back of the house, they move to the back porch.

Creek sees a few guys from his soccer team and leaves Dollar with Mary and Samantha to go talk to them; Creek sinks into the crowd of guys standing around the keg. Dollar is no king of small-talk. The more he tries to engage in conversation, the more awkward he feels. That none of the three are interested in chatting becomes more and more painfully obvious. Using their cups to cover their mouths, the girls slowly sip their beer.

One of the forwards from Creek's soccer team walks up to them, "Hey ladies. Mary, you're looking fine tonight!" He licks his fingertip and touches it to Mary's shoulder making a sizzling sound.

"You finding enough trouble to keep you busy tonight?" Mary smiles as she grabs his shoulder pushing him away, but at the end of her push holding onto him, pulling him just slightly back.

He looks at Samantha and says with a grin, "Sam, you wanna come help me find my belt? I think I left it upstairs."

"Maybe later big boy," she raises her eyebrows then looks down into her cup.

"Alright, I can see you'all are just warming up to this party, I'll catch you later," he gives Dollar a shove with his elbow and winks at him, then walks away.

There is a slightly discontented look now on Mary's face; she stares into the empty space of ground in front of her. Leaning and shutting her eyes, then opening them again, she says, "I've only had one drink, but I don't feel good."

"Well, give it fifteen minutes, and if it doesn't get better, I'll take you home," Samantha says.

Fifteen minutes later Mary talks alone with Creek on the side of the yard. From where Dollar stands it's clear that Mary wants to go home, but Creek is not ready to leave. Mary walks away from Creek, walks over to Samantha, and taking her by the arm they walk into the house and out the front door. Creek comes over, telling Dollar, "They're leaving because Mary's not feeling good, we'll just walk home later."

Dollar watches Creek giving many high-fives and flirting with many girls. He is impressed by how popular Creek has become. How being part of a sports team can make one popular impresses Dollar. Popularity is magnetic and when you start with a good-sized group of athletic young men the magnetism is strong. If being on a sports team can make you popular then surely popularity is superficial, Dollar thinks. Yet, Dollar is glad to see Creek having fun and making friends.

On his way to the bathroom in the house Dollar has to pass through a tight crowd of people. The loudness of all the talking, the loudness of the music, the loudness of so many warm bodies packed into a small space, all create a sense of spatial confusion for Dollar. Unexpectedly, to his left, it is as though the wall has suddenly jumped out at him—the back of a huge figure has turned directly into him. This body is a foot taller than him and probably three times as thick, and it seemed to come out of nowhere. As the enormous body turns quickly toward the direction of Dollar, neither has time to move or stop his momentum. The first thing to hit Dollar in the chest is the cup of beer held by the thick arm of the thick man. The full beer spills onto the front of Dollar's shirt. A deep voice comes from the football lineman, "What the hell! What's your problem." No reply from Dollar. Stunned. All his words, scattered behind the couches in his mind, escape him. "Hey, I'm talking to you. What the hell do you think you're doing! Go get me another beer!" By this point the room they are in has become quiet and people take a few steps back, forming a circle around them. The football lineman misreads Dollar's silence as a challenge—he's used to being around more aggressive people. Dollar is functionally paralyzed for the moment. This is not a good combination.

As painfully long seconds pass (like a western showdown time seems to have slowed) one of Creek's soccer buddies goes quickly to the back porch to let him know the situation. The heavy feet of the lineman start to move toward Dollar, who's hands are ineffectually wiping at the spilled beer on his shirt as his eyes stare helplessly into the lineman's.

Creek comes in the back door and with much nerve breaks the silence, "umm, Banger, that's my younger brother, it was a mistake, he's sorry."

"Who the hell are you?" Banger's head turns toward Creek, giving Dollar a moment of relief.

Creek feels the weight of the massive body, though all Banger has done is turn his head towards him. "I'm Creek. I'm on the soccer team."

"Fine. Go get me a new beer." Banger's large arm lifts to hand Creek the plastic cup. Paradoxically, there is simultaneous mass-relief and disappointment in the room as people resume . . . well, they resume slurring words and laughing at each other's half-heard stories.

After bringing Banger a fresh beer, Creek and Dollar decide to call it a night and walk back to Creek's dorm room.

In the morning Creek leaves the dorm room early to go prepare for his game. Unable to sleep, in the soft light of morning with the curtain still closed, Dollar sits on the floor and tries his hand at some card games. He plays quietly while Creek's roommate sleeps.

Later, at the soccer game Dollar notices that he is sitting about five rows behind Banger. Trying not to think about last night, he watches both the game and the interractions of the football players surrounding Banger. They are the loudest group in the stands.

That afternoon Dollar says goodbye to Creek, "Good game this morning . . . I hope she feels better soon."

"Alright. Sorry the party was cut short last night. I don't know what's going on with Mary, she says she's not feeling well, but she doesn't want me to come over and she doesn't want to talk on the phone. Chicks, man, who can make sense of them? Hey, don't make things too easy on Mom and Dad at home. See ya." Creek slaps the roof of the car twice quickly as Dollar pulls out of his parking spot.

The next day (Sunday) Elle brings her six-year-old cousin, Mindy, over to Dollar's house to visit with him and his parents. Mindy lives with her Mom in a very small, old house near down-town. Her Dad left before she was born. Then her Mom had a boyfriend who was really mean to Mindy, was belligerent and emotionally insensitive, who talked to Mindy like she was a dog. He would lock her in the closet for a couple of hours when he had to leave. Needless to say, Mindy has some behavioral issues and is quite shy. Usually Elle will babysit Mindy about once a week to give her Aunt some time alone.

Dollar's parents, Mindy, Dollar, and Elle are all in the kitchen talking about the various flowers and herbs Dollar's mom has growing in the window-sills and in pots located throughout the kitchen. It is a clear day and Mt. Ranier is visible out the back window.

Dollar's mom says, "Well, Dad and I are going back out to work in the yard, but Dollar, why don't you read Mindy your fa-vorite book from when you were a kid?" She smiles at Mindy, then looks at Elle, who is nodding her head and smiling.

"Ohh, yeah, the one about the baby eagle. Do you know where it is Mrs. Moore?"

"I think it's on the bookshelf in the TV room, honey. You guys have fun!"

Dollar, Elle, and Mindy go into the TV room and start looking for the book on the shelf. "It's thin and tall, and probably down low. It's called, 'Fly Eagle!,' and has a picture of a baby eagle on the front," Dollar says. After a few seconds Dollar locates the book and the three of them sit on the couch, Dollar in the middle.

He opens to the first page where there is a picture of an eagle's nest on the branch of a tree, with five small heads sticking out of the top of the nest. He looks at Mindy, "Do you see the baby eaglets?" She nods her head shyly. Dollar begins reading, turning the pages to new pictures with every few sentences:

"Baby bald eagles are extremely hungry, all the time!" He reads the first page.

"Ernie the eagle was born smaller than all his brothers and sisters. In the morning Mommy would go out hunting for food. While she was gone, and the others moved around the nest, Ernie got pushed down toward the bottom." The illustration on the second page is mostly dark with two little eyes shining in the darkness.

"When Mommy returned with food, Ernie never got as much food as his brothers and sisters because he was so small and low in the nest.

"Ernie would pray to the Great Eagle in the Sky to help him fly away so he wouldn't get pushed around the nest anymore.

"One day Ernie got tired of being pushed around the nest and decided he had to take action. He thought to himself, I've been praying to the Great Eagle in the Sky for big enough wings to fly, but nothing has changed. I'm going to make myself wings like

Mommy's.

"So while all his brothers and sisters were pushing around, Ernie stayed at the bottom and made himself wings from twigs and leaves. He tied the leaves to sticks, then tied the sticks to his little wings. He worked very hard for three days. When Mommy came home with food he stayed at the bottom of the nest so she wouldn't see him. He got very hungry, but was devoted to his project.

"On the third morning the sky was moving fast when Mommy left to hunt for food. Ernie prayed to the Great Eagle in the Sky, 'Great Eagle in the Sky, today I'm going to fly with these wings I've made. I hope you are okay with that.'

"Ernie carefully climbed out of the nest, while his brothers and sisters told him to stop, to come back, that what he was doing was crazy. He dragged his fake wings as he made his way out onto a tree limb. The wind was getting stronger and the sky was starting to get dark.

"He started flapping his wings and praying, 'Great Eagle in the Sky, make these wings work, make me fly!' But no matter how hard he flapped the leaves and sticks he'd tied to himself, he stayed right where he was. Rain started to fall, and Ernie started feeling very hungry and tired from flapping his fake wings.

"The rain got harder and harder and before long it had washed away all the leaves from Ernie's fake wings. Ernie looked back at the nest where his brothers and sisters were resting comfortably, then looked down at the long-long distance between himself and the forest floor. He thought of going back to the nest, but then remembered how being pushed around all the time was no fun.

"He stood out on that limb with just sticks tied to himself, flapping them in the air trying to fly, and praying, 'Great Eagle in the Sky, please, please, please, help me to fly, I'm starting to get scared out here.'

"Just then the wind got stronger, so that now there was a little rain still falling and there was a strong wind, almost blowing Ernie off the branch. The wind blew so hard that the sticks tied to Ernie started coming loose. After about a minute of leaning into the hard wind, and trying not to get blown off the branch, all of the stick and twigs had fallen off Ernie. It was just Ernie leaning into the wind, wet, cold, and scared.

"Ernie looked back at his brothers and sisters in the nest and screeched, 'Help!' but there was nothing they could do to help him—the wind was blowing too hard for them to move. Ernie, feeling exhausted, prayed desperately, 'Great Eagle in the Sky, why are you trying to kill me? Why didn't you help me fly? Please help me, stop this wind!'

"But the wind only got stronger, and in an instant Ernie was blown off the branch and sent spinning and falling out, into the cold, wet, open air. Feeling terrified, Ernie stuck out his wings and froze in that position, frozen in terror.

"He started noticing that he wasn't so much falling anymore, but drifting, and the wind was pushing up into his little wings. As the wind pushed into his wings, he started pushing back by flapping his wings. Ernie had no sense of falling or flying, no sense of ground or sky, just the feeling of pushing against the wind with his wings: it felt amazing.

"Before he knew it, the wind had grown calm and the rain had stopped, and he was flying thirty feet above the ground. He looked for the great tree where his nest was and flew toward it. He flew up higher and higher until he found his nest where his brothers and sisters were poking their heads out of the top.

"They watched as he flew past them, and they heard him

screech, 'I'm flying!'"

The last page has an illustration of a single bird in the middle of a blue sky.

When the story ends Mindy looks at Elle and asks, "Could that really happen?"

"That's a good question Mindy. How do you think eagles learn to fly?"

Mindy smiles. Dollar and Elle can see that she is thinking about the question, but she doesn't have anything to answer. She looks down shyly and Elle reaches across Dollar to tickle her, then says, "Let's go out for a walk. We can go along the road and look at the mountain and smell all of the flowering trees." The three of them begin their walk.

As they are walking, Dollar asks Elle, "Did you bring your twenty sentence essay for Swordsmith's class?"

"Yeah, I worked on it last night and I've got it right here in my pocket. How about you?"

"Yep, mine's here too." He smiles at her and says, "So who's going first?"

"You first." She looks at Mindy, "These are papers we've been working on for class. You might find them interesting, and they're only twenty sentences long. Here, take my hand." Mindy's small hand feels light to Elle.

Dollar unfolds the paper in his pocket and begins reading his essay:

"The Bald Eagle—powerful and graceful—is not bound by the earth. It flies high above the earth, free. The eagle flies over a garden. The garden—rooted and earthy—is a place of fecund transformation. From seed and mud it creates beautiful flowers and delicious vegetables. What does the eagle know of the garden; the garden, of the eagle? What does the spirit know of the body; the body, of the spirit? They inspire and sustain each other. An eagle is constantly scanning the ground, hunting, in order to fill its need for energy and activity. The ground is the eagle's focal zone; though he is soaring in the sky, the eagle's thoughts are scanning the terrain below. Just as the eagle looks at the ground from the sky, the garden looks at the sky from below. The garden is soaking in the sun and rain from the sky; it is breathing in the carbon dioxide the sky provides: it relies on the sky for its energy and activity. As the plants grow they reach for the sky, stretching toward the sun. A relationship. Eagle and garden, sky and ground, spirit and body, these pairs need each other. Tending toward obsession and decay, the body looks to the spirit for motivation. From above, easily lost in abstraction, the spirit is bound to the body so that it won't fly away—like a balloon on a string. The string that holds them together is what is called 'being alive.' It is this string that keeps the eagle flying and keeps the garden growing. When the string is cut we call it death."

Dollar looks up from the paper when he finishes. To his left there is a row of flowering pink bushes in the front yard of someone's house.

Elle says to him, "Nice job Dollar. I didn't know you were going to write about the body and the spirit. I like it. I had thought of the body and spirit being tied to each other before, but I hadn't thought of them as drawing on one another for inspiration and support. That's an interesting way of looking at it. And . . . funny . . . . I wrote about a string too—but in a different way." She squeezes Mindy's hand, "What did you think Mindy?"

"I saw an eagle once when me and Mommy were picnicking. He was big and flew really high when he flew away." Mindy walks in the gravel by the side of the road. Her steps are less predictable than Dollar and Elle's. Her footsteps fall at different angles and the pace changes, unlike the regular, straight paths of Dollar and Elle.

Dollar says, "Mindy, did you know that I want to have an eagle of my own someday?"

"Really! Where would you keep him?" Mindy asks.

"Well, I'd build a cage. Have you ever seen a chicken coop? It would look something like that."

"Wow, that sounds cool!"

Elle says to Dollar, "I didn't know you were thinking of actually keeping one yourself."

Dollar answers, "Well, it's not going to be for a while. Definitely not until I finish school and have some connections through work. They're pretty tough to get legally."

Elle replies, "I think it sounds great. I bet living with an eagle would be really inspiring."

"It's a dream I've had for a while, and I don't know if I've told you this, but I didn't think it was actually possible until recently, after doing some research in the library. Anyway, let's hear your essay on the circle and the square."

She answers, "Okay, but it's a bit less grounded than yours, so Mindy (she squeezes Mindy's hand), just try to follow it and don't worry if you can't. I'm still working on making it clearer. When you take geometry later in school you might find this more interesting." She takes her hand-written, graph-paper, folded essay out of the pocket of her jeans and starts reading:

"If you start with a loop of string you can make it into a circle or a square. Well, you can make it into an approximation of a circle or square. Even more correctly, you can make an approximation of a representation of a circle or square. A true circle or square is two-dimensional, and therefore can only be represented in our three dimensional world—even a line drawn with lead on a paper is too thick to be a true circle or square. Where do they exist? They exist in our minds. In our minds we store the perfect archetypes that unlock the messy gate—the messy gate we must pass through to make sense of the world, the messy gate where cookies never finish baking at exactly fifteen minutes. Ding!, back to the loop of string. When that loop of string is made into a perfect hoop it is all about movement. Like a cat chasing a string, your eyes can fly around that loop of string without stopping, forever and ever amen. This is how the perfect blue iris is formed in the eyeball of an embryo. The stem-cells, cat-like, chase a looping string until the optic nerve is satisfied. In the chase they pass through the messy gate and a beautiful baby-blue eye ensues. The eye is nothing, if not movement. On the other hand, when that loop of string is drawn taught by four equal forces a square is formed. In the perfect balance of the corners the string becomes perfectly self-aware. As such the square is conscious of every single edge and angle—extremely conscious, to the point of paranoia. In passing through the messy gate the square becomes a mirror for the bust of a man who wonders whether his mind will ever evaporate. A circle and an iris, a square and self-awareness, a string tied end to end: the way it works is based in geometry, based in philosophy, based in theoretical topology. The picture of a spinning square is a circle."

When Elle finishes reading she looks up at Dollar and then at Mindy. Neither of them say anything. For about thirty seconds they continue to walk in silence. Finally Mindy says, "There, I see a circle on that sign."

Elle answers, "Good eye Mindy, that's small—you've got a good eye for detail."

They walk a few more steps along the road then Dollar says, "Elle, I like what you wrote. I'm not sure I really get it after hearing it just once. Did you make some of that stuff up?"

She replies, "Yeah, I made most of it up. I'm not sure it's finished. I think it might need to be more grounded somehow. It feels like the ideas are good, but I don't think they come out as well as they could—right now they're sort of like a nice dinner that is spread out in a mess all over the table."

"Are you going to make changes before class tomorrow?"

"I think I will probably rewrite it tonight. By the way, did you have a good time with Creek this weekend?"

Dollar yawns, quickly covering his mouth, then answers Elle, "I had fun watching his game on Saturday morning, but I can't really say I had fun on Friday night. We went to this party where there was a lot of drinking, and this really big football player got mad at me, and Mary left the party because she wasn't feeling well."

"Oh, that doesn't sound like a good time at all."

"I think Creek had fun though. It seems like he's made a lot of friends."

Elle says, "It sounds like they aren't that nice though. Was the party wierd?"

Dollar replies, "I mostly stood to the side and watched other people."

"Did Mary's crazy friends flirt with you the whole night, like last time?"

"Just one this time, and she wasn't too bad. I hope things are okay with Mary and Creek. After the game on Saturday he tried to get in touch with her and she wouldn't return his call. Usually they see each other after a game."

In fact, that evening Creek is in his dorm room lying face down on his bed with his head in his hands. He has tried to reach Mary by phone four times during the day and left a message on her answering machine three of those times. When he drove to her house to talk to her, her roommate stopped him at the front door and told him she wasn't home. A sickening feeling has begun to rise inside of him, though he doesn't understand it. This new feeling—confusion blended with attachment—is carrying him like a wave. Why won't she return his calls? What did he do wrong? The events of the last week are replaying themselves in his mind. Bent neck, twisting side, tightened jaw—contortions of the body become involuntary. He lies in bed. Bruised is the blue bird on his shoulder.

In the middle of his mind he knows that something has gone really wrong—but he has no idea what it is. It is a very real dark-ness that is settling on him, yet it is impossible to pin-point or cap-ture the cause, like punching at a dense fog. Obliged, or required, or bound, surely Mary owes him some good explanation for the sudden break in communication: does she not feel his dedication to her?

In her sorority house on Sunday evening, Mary and her roommate are sitting on Mary's bed talking. Mary is not thinking of her psychology test, or her biology lab write-up, or her art sur-vey reading, she is remembering the smell of the clinic. It had the beguiling fragrance of the candy factory next door to it. Just as she had waited for her period two weeks ago, yesterday she waited at the clinic for the results of her pregnancy test. The people sitting in the waiting room avoided eye-contact. A radio plugged into the wall played pop-music. Each of these times of waiting pulls her further away from Creek, pulls her away from the world. Within this waiting, she insulates herself. She builds up the protective walls around her with a false self-confidence. It can be seen in the way she sits on the bed, in her actual posture and in the con-trolled self-consciousness of her movements. Self captive in self;

unable to improvise in the world.

In their dorm room, Mary's roommate asks with genuine concern, "So, Mary, I know you've been feeling sick, and you've been staying at home in the room doing nothing but sitting and listening to music. When Creek stopped by I told him you weren't here. What's going on?"

"Oh, I don't know. I guess I'm just feeling overwhelmed by school and stuff."

"Have you talked to anyone about it?"

"Umm, I don't think it's really a big deal, and I don't want to bug other people with my problems. I should be able to figure out how to deal with them: after all, I'm not a child—I'm in college."

"Mary, you can talk to me."

"I know. . . . it's all about love and positivity. If I can keep a good attitude and stay strong then I won't hurt other people and I'll be doing the right thing."

"Mary, what's going on with you?"

Mary answers, "How are you? Did you have fun at the party you went to last night?" She refuses to share about her trip to the clinic.

Her roommate gives up trying to connect and starts telling Mary a story about the party she went to. She wants to at least be comforting to Mary by spending time with her.

That her mind gradually gains in downhill momentum, Mary is unconcerned. Harnessed to a circumstantial storm, she has relinquished her leading role in this dance: she is following with her eyes closed, pretending she is in control.

Creek is still alone in his room on Sunday night. Nothing is good. He tries watching TV, but his mind thinks of Mary. He takes out a bag of tortilla chips and they taste bland—they are his favorite food and they taste bland. His hunger is gone. He thinks of calling Mom, Dad, Lorne, Dollar. Yet none of these ideas lasts. In his mind he can quickly predict how each of the conversations would go, so much so that the phone calls seem unnecessary. He hungers to talk with someone, but he is annoyed by the idea of having any conversation. There is an odd tension in Creek's desires, something like being dehydrated in a boat on the ocean, where water is all around but none of it is good for drinking. The world is all around him, there are people who will talk to him, and he knows it's exactly what he needs, but he also finds the idea of talking to someone repulsive and repetitious. What could be said that would soothe the pain of Mary's turning a cold shoulder to him? What could possibly fill the hole in his heart, the hole with exactly her shape, the hole implacable in his memory? No, talking would only temporarily dull the pain; it would only distract him from the elephant in the room.

Every sound that he hears, each voice in the air outside, each car door closing—these fraudsters are mocking him with anticipation and implication of Mary's presence. He sees her and hears her in everything. Obsession is obsessive. It comes on quickly and strikes the hardest where it is unexpected. To the person that is unprepared, or overconfident, it can be heavier and harder than anything else. This is the case for Creek. His whole relationship with Mary was based on trusting that she wanted to be with him. It allowed him to see bright and good things in her amid the darker zones. Only because he believed they would go on together, figuring out how to care for each other, did he allow himself to become emotionally and physically invested in her. Now, faced with the reality of her rejection, he longs for the time of trust—misguided as it may have been—because it was good to believe in someone. He knows that it is gone, yet each of his thoughts is tempted to believe that it still exists.

He pushes himself up on his arms in bed, and punches the pillow with his right fist. Slipping his hands under the pillow he pushes his head into it, then screams into it. A picture of Mary, sitting on his lap and turning to kiss him flashes through his mind. Its getting dark outside and the thought of long sleepless hours of night is disquieting for Creek.

At eleven Creek cannot stand to stay in his room alone anymore, so he puts on a sweatshirt and shoes and walks out the front of the dorm, into the campus sidewalks and fields at night.

"But he himself went on a day's journey into the wilderness, and came and sat down under a solitary broom tree. He asked that he might die: 'It is enough; now, O Lord, take away my life, for I am no better than my ancestors.' then he lay down under the broom tree and fell asleep. Suddenly and angel touched him and said to him, 'Get up and eat.' He looked, and there at his head was a cake baked on hot stones, and a jar of water. He ate and drank, and lay down again. The angel of the Lord came a second time, touched him, and said, 'Get up and eat, otherwise the journey will be too much for you.' He got up, and ate and drank; then he went in the strength of that food forty days and forty nights to Horeb the mount of God. At that place he came to a cave, and spent the night there" (1 Kings 19: 4-9).

There are not very many people outside at eleven o'clock. It's dark, without a moon. Stars are absent because clouds cover them. Creek makes his way across a grass gathering field, around a brick building and at the edge of campus crosses a street that takes him into a residential area consisting of blocks of old houses. Every time Creek turns a corner to walk in a new direction, he thinks of turning back, but when he thinks of turning back it

makes him feel sick to his stomach. So he goes on walking aimlessly along the sidewalks and sometimes in the street, passing
from streetlight to darkness to streetlight.

Across a parkway, down a curb, he steps onto the paved
street and notices a dark stain on the road—it looks almost like a
shadow, but it is totally still and there is nothing there to cast the
shadow. Creek is standing above this dark spot realizing that it is
the silhouette of a bird. It reminds him of a time when he and his
brothers took photo paper outside and put leaves on it. When the
paper developed, the silhouettes of where the leaves had blocked
the sunlight remained. This is a similar type of impression, though
a stain, made on the road by a dead bird—judging from its size it
was a blue jay or starling.

With the streetlight to his left, Creek stretches out his toe,
rubbing the edge of the shape to see if it will rub off. The light
casts his shadow onto the road. There is something eerie about the
shadows made by streetlights at night. Perhaps it is the artificiality.
The shadows don't move. It's like a mini train set world and one is
shrunken so that he can walk beneath the plastic trees.

His toe on the edge of the bird's greasy silhouette, Creek
looks down and imagines the dead bird that was once there. Then
he backs up further and imagines the cause of death; possibly the
bird flew under a passing car then lay dead on the street for several days. In his mind he backs up further and imagines the bird
sitting on a tree limb, flying to land on a birdfeeder, pecking some
birdseed out from a hole in the side of the feeder.

There is a sound of muted laughter down the street. To his
left, past the streetlight, Creek sees a white car parked under the
shadow of a large oak tree. Through the front window he can see
movement in the back seat. It's dark out and the car is far enough
away that he can't make out any details, but he's fairly sure he

sees two people making-out in the back seat. The light catches the
bare skin of the small of a back as it rises up above the seat tops,
and it catches a glint of shiny hair near the side of the car. He's
fairly sure this is not Mary's car, but it is a similarly shaped white
car, and he cannot get the idea out of his head that it is Mary in
the backseat with another guy. He keeps looking and alternating
in his mind whether he thinks it is or isn't Mary's car. It is just far
enough and dark enough that he can't really say for sure either
way. Part of him wants to believe that it is Mary because part of
him hungers to see her regardless of the circumstances.

Creek crosses to the opposite side of the street from the car
and begins walking toward it. At this point he is oscillating back
and forth between being convinced that it is Mary and wondering
if he's losing his mind. Yet he cannot stop looking and wondering.
If he were in his right mind he would walk away, or he might even
walk to the rear of the car and look for the butterfly sticker in the
window to confirm whether it is Mary's car. But even if it is Mary's
car the best thing for him to do would be to walk away, to remove
her from his mind. Impossible. He is now walking toward the car,
peering into the side window, trying to make out the forms of the
two people in the back seat, in the dark, through a somewhat
fogged window. He is within ten feet, then five, then he is leaning over with his face only a foot away from the window, close
enough to hear their soft talking inside the car. Convinced that it
could be Mary, Creek stands there watching for at least ten long
and tense seconds.

A car alarm goes off randomly down the street. The two
heads in the car separate. First the man, on top, looks up and
with eyes widened by surprise sees Creek. Then the woman leans
her head back to look. Creek can see clearly that it isn't Mary. By
the time the man gets out the words, "What the hell!" Creek has

already turned and started running. He doesn't recognize either of the people, but he does recognize the look of anger on the man's face.

Creek runs down a driveway between two houses as he hears a car door slam and a man yelling, "Hey, what's wrong with you, pervert!" He can hear footsteps starting to run after him, but once he is in the back yards of the houses he finds a thick low bush in the dark corner of a yard and lies on the ground, hiding behind it. He stays there for about half-an-hour, listening to every sound, but undiscovered by the man from the car. After he is sure things have quieted again Creek walks through the yards and comes out on the other side of the block, walking quickly back to his dorm, looking over his shoulder and listening for the sound of cars the whole time.

Back in his room, he checks the answering machine—no messages from Mary. His roommate is in bed. Creek sits on the floor and watches TV with the volume off for a few hours until he falls asleep on the floor around 4am.

On Monday morning Mary parks her car on the street in front of the candy factory next door to the clinic, about a mile away from campus, and walks up the sidewalk for her ten-o'clock appointment. In her tight fitting jeans and t-shirt she looks like every young waitress and college student in town. One could easily walk past her without realizing she is pregnant. Her left arm is resting in the sling created by her large, brown-leather purse.

There is a young girl in a pink shirt that nearly matches Mary's pink shirt drawing with chalk on the sidewalk ahead of her. The girl is so involved in her drawing that she doesn't see Mary coming. Mary walks on the grass, around the girl and her drawing. Looking over her shoulder Mary sees a colorful line drawing of a square house with a pointed roof, one door, two windows, a sun in the sky, and a bird flying over the peak of the house. The young girl's hands are covered with chalk and her bare knees are pressing into the concrete sidewalk.

Mary has made a quick decision to have an abortion. Three days ago the Dr. had told her that she could take two weeks to decide—in fact, he had encouraged her to do so. However, Mary is certain that she is doing what needs to be done. Other than the Dr. and a few nurses, there is no one else in the world that knows Mary's situation. As she walks through the front door of the clinic, she is alone, so alone that she can almost imagine the person walking through those doors is not even her, alone to the point of losing herself—as if all the connections and ties that held her to herself were cut and now she is floating freely without a past or a future, with no memories, no gravity, no weight.

The doctor's face—mask, banner, front-door—is as unemotional as a road sign. Beyond professional, his demeanor communicates something like anesthesia. Not only is he stoic and humor free, but he also maintains a slight smile the whole time he is preparing Mary for her procedure. A smooth passage into the appointed plan of action, not any sudden revelation or amendment, is his goal. Order, quiet, cleanliness—such climate controls make him function efficiently. Before dinner-time, Mary is back in her sorority house, studying for biology class.

"O purblind race of miserable men,/ How many among us at this very hour/ Do forge a lifelong trouble for ourselves,/ By taking true for false, or false for true;/ Here, thro' the feeble twilight of this world/ Groping, how many, until we pass and reach/ That other where we see as we are seen!" (Alfred, Lord Tennyson, Idylls of the King, 73).

Around 10:15 on Monday evening the phone rings in the Moore house. Dollar's Mom and Dad have gone to bed and Dollar is still lying on the couch reading. He reaches behind his head to the coffee table, picking up the phone quickly so the ringing doesn't disturb his parents.

"Dollar, it's Elle," is the whispering voice on the other end of the line.

"Hi Elle, are you okay?" Dollar worries because Elle doesn't normally call—she usually just stops by—also he's surprised she's calling this late . . . and she's whispering.

Elle's voice is quiet and there is hesitation in between the syllables, "I'm okay, but I don't know about my mom. I'm sorry for calling—It's just that I'm scared and I don't know what to do."

"What's going on Elle? Should I come over there?"

"Wait. I was lying here in bed and I heard Mom and her boyfriend starting to argue. They were yelling at each other about money. I couldn't really understand what the money was for, but he started cussing at her, and she started yelling at him to get out. Then there was a thud, and the door slammed, and it was quiet. The door opened again. There were some heavy footsteps and he said, 'keep the goddamned boots.' Then I heard his truck driving away, and it has been quiet since. I'm afraid to go downstairs."

Directly below Elle, the front door of the house is half-open to the dark, rainy night. At the foot of the door are two empty, wet, work boots, with a trail of muddy prints behind them in a ten foot circle around the living room carpet. To the right of the door Elle's mom is crouching with her head hanging between her knees. She is crying. The left side of her face is hot and sore from his right hand.

Elle's mom and dad were divorced when she was three years

old. Elle has never been told the real reason why. Since the divorce her mom has had a few different boyfriends, but Elle hasn't really liked any of them yet. This latest guy had only been around for about a month. He and Elle's mom had been talking about saving up some money to help Elle buy a used car. He had taken the first bit of money and bought himself a new pair of work boots. It was especially vexing to Elle's mom because he isn't currently working. The argument ensued, and eventually he used his right hook to hit her with an open palm on the side of her face, and end the argument. He slammed the front door behind him, in his new boots, and stepped into the mud beside his truck. Changing his mind, he walked back into the house, around the living room once, and took the boots off at the door saying, "keep the goddamned boots." This time he left the door half-open behind him, walked through the mud in his socks, and drove away. Elle's mom was left crouching by the door.

Dollar says to Elle, "Elle, it's gonna be okay. Listen, don't hang up the phone; just leave it on the bed. Go down and just look to see if your Mom is alright. Then come back up and tell me what you saw."

"Okay, I'll be back in a minute."

Elle walks down the stairs, stopping at the base of the stairs, looking at her mom. Her mom does not turn to look at her. After watching her mom cry quietly for about ten seconds Elle goes back to her room and the phone.

"Dollar, I think she's okay. She's crouching by the door and crying. She's not moving, but I think she's okay. And the guy is gone."

"Alright, you should probably go down there and just give her a gentle hug and then sit with her. It's gonna be okay. Your mom will know what to do. I'll talk to you tomorrow on the way to school. Okay, bye."

Elle hangs up the phone and lies there in bed. She knew there was something about her mom's boyfriend she didn't like. She can remember a few other times when her mom was upset because of him, but she's not sure if he'd ever hit her mom before. Elle slowly gets out of her bed and walks quietly down the stairs. Pausing at the bottom, she can see her mom still crouching and crying.

"Mom," when she hears Elle's voice her mom turns to look at her and sinks into a sitting position on the floor. "Mom, are you okay?"

"Elle, how much of that did you see?"

"I didn't see anything, I heard the arguing though."

"Oh, honey, I'm okay. Come here."

Elle walks over and instinctively they wrap their arms around each other. Elle leans over her sitting Mother; they are both crying. Elle presses the side of her face against her mom's and their tears mix on the hot cheek where she had been hit.

"Honey, will you shut and lock the door? And, will you get me the ice-pack from the freezer?"

Peace at the house restored, Elle sits on a chair and her Mom lies on the couch with the ice-pack against her face. They breathe. As a wasp leaves its stinger under the skin, so her boyfriend has left his handprint on her face. Oddly, her hot face is a welcome distraction in that moment. It allows her to think about a symptom instead of its cause. A wounded face, so near the eyes, nose, mouth, ears, and brain, can have this wonderful all-encompassing effect. Because it makes everything look slightly red, because everything smells acrid, because there is a ringing in the ears, because the pulse of blood throbs, this head wound takes precedence above all else. Anger, argument, rationalization, revenge—

these activities are all set aside for the moment, in the singular awareness of the wound. Ironically, there is a crowning blessing with the injury: she falls asleep.

When she sees her Mom asleep, Elle puts the muddy boots away in the closet, then starts scrubbing the footprints out of the carpet. Her Mom's short, dyed-blonde hair is pushed up into a wedge by the couch pillow. In the quick onset of deep sleep there is evidence of exhaustion.

Elle and her Mom share the same broad smile and pro-nounced cheekbones. For thirty-eight-years-old her Mom has a surprisingly youthful appearance. Somehow the busyness of being a single mom has kept her young. Perhaps taking care of Elle has kept her from wallowing in her own stress. It doesn't always hap-pen this way. Sometimes busyness will turn a person into a raisin before their time. Yet in this case, Marika Crane has retained a youthful countenance.

Back at the Moore house, Dollar has fallen asleep on the couch, next to the phone.

In his dorm room at June College, Creek has also just fallen asleep. While Dollar is keeping close to the phone in case Elle needs help, Creek has a phone near him because he still thinks Mary might call him. In a twisted way, he wants her to be desper-ate and lonely enough to call him. Urges rise like waves, like the sound of waves against the boat of his mind. Creek dreams he is on a large sailboat.

At this moment, in his dream, Creek looks down at the boat from above, and he can see himself standing on the bow. In front of him, Coach Motto holds a rope and shows Creek how to tie a simple knot. Watching carefully, Creek holds a smaller piece of rope and tries to imitate the knot. But for some reason he can't get it to work. No matter what he does, his knot falls apart. Creek can see that Coach is getting frustrated with him. Oddly, Coach remains with his back to Creek for no apparent reason, making Creek look over and around his shoulder at the knot. From his dreaming crow's nest above it looks difficult, keeping his balance while trying not to be frustrated while leaning to look around Coach.

From above, he can see a woman's pair of athletic, tan legs, sitting in a skirt. Unable to see who the woman is because the sail is in the way, Creek is about ninety percent sure it is Mary. He recognizes the legs and suspects that it probably is her, yet because he isn't sure, he is tempted to keep looking for further clues. Close next to her are a pair of man's legs in white khaki pants. Their legs are too close together. Creek angrily senses that the man has his arm around her.

Across from the suspicious pair of legs Dollar and Elle are sitting and reading a shared book. They are not blocked from view by the sail, and they look happy. Toward the stern, a few of Creek's friends from the soccer team are goofing around, punching each other, splashing water over the side of the boat, standing to lean against the tilt of the boat. At the very back of the boat Lorne is controlling the rudder with one hand and fishing off the back with a pole in his other hand.

Creek and his coach, Mary and the unknown man, Dollar and Elle, Lorne fishing, the teammates—they all ride the waves, powered by the wind. What they are all doing together is a mystery to Creek. Not only is he overwhelmed by his inability to follow Coach's knot-tying instructions, not only is he unnerved by the pair of tan legs in a skirt that looks like Mary's, not only does he feel left out of Dollar's life and friendship with Elle, not only does he feel left out of the camaraderie of his soccer teammates, not only does he wish he could be content like Lorne fishing from the back of the boat, but also he feels a deep sense of meaninglessness in the whole dream. "What's the point? Why is everything thing I do ridiculous and empty?" His dreaming brain is now creating metaphors for emptiness as the sound and light of the boating scene fade away and he finds himself sinking in the dark green water beneath the boat.

1966

Hail

Four years later Creek wakes from sleep in his small rental house in the town of Chehalis, just South of Centralia on Interstate 5. It's 10:30 am on Wednesday. Creek works as a house painter and has the day off because it has been raining all morning and the rain is expected to continue for the rest of the day. He hates his job. On a day like this he usually will keep the sheets over the windows, sit on the couch, watch TV, and take random naps. If there's beer stocked in the fridge, he'll start having a drink every hour-and-a-half after lunch. At night he'll switch to the cheap whiskey he keeps in its plastic bottle above the refrigerator. Then around dinner time he'll find a fast food place to get drive through, and bring it home to eat in front of the TV.

His rental house is small, old, and unadorned. The main color is mustard yellow, with a brown trim. Oddly, the lowest five feet of the house, all the way around, slopes slightly outward, like a skirt. This was an intentional part of the design, but Creek can't figure out why anyone would build a house like that; it doesn't appear to have any practical purpose. The walls resume near verticality at the level of the porch and ground floor. There is no landscaping anywhere around the house. Some people would call it ugly, but Creek doesn't really think of aesthetics when it comes to houses. Anyway, he's just renting, so he doesn't care what the house looks like. The homeowners, Mark and Maddie, live next door. Never having children of their own, they see the rental house as a chance to help young adults transition out of college. Had Creek known they would be such a watchful eye, he probably wouldn't have rented the place. But it was the only rental he could find in his price range, and he liked the idea of having a whole house (albeit a very small one) to himself.

The blinds of the windows of Mark and Maddie's house facing the side of his living room are almost always open. Their house is larger, and the windows of their living room and kitchen look down at Creek's house. Maddie spends much of her days at home and running errands. Because of this Creek keeps his sheets pulled over the windows on that side of the house. Maybe he's ashamed that while her husband is at work, he is sitting in his living room watching TV all day; maybe he's just ashamed that he doesn't have anything better to do. In any case, he feels like an unhealthy fish in a small fishbowl and his impulse is to hide behind a rock.

The following day Creek is back at work, painting a house on the hill on the East side of town. His co-worker, Stan, tells crass jokes throughout the morning. Though he doesn't think the jokes are funny, Creek is tired of listening to the radio, and Stan's jokes are at least better than silence. Stan starts a joke, "So this hot chick is rollerskating in a bikini on the sidewalk along the beach. She passes an old man who is walking a poodle . . ."

"Stan, it's your turn to fill the paint." Creek interrupts. He is in charge of the crew and since there are only two of them on the crew, and Stan neither wants to lead nor is capable of it, they don't have too many problems with Creek being in charge. Though Stan is older, he has also grown comfortable with doing basic physical work without having to think—without responsibility.

"Fine, man, I guess you don't get to hear the punch-line to that one." Stan drops his large disheveled brush into the nearly empty five-gallon bucket. At 5'7" Stan is shorter than Creek; at 205 pounds he is heavier; and at 28-years-old he is four years older. With a paint-covered hand Stan rubs his left eye, then puts his hand to his behind and says, "Man, it's not even lunch time yet and I'm already sweating through my pants."

Creek shakes his head, "Go get more paint, Stan."

At lunchtime Creek and Stan sit in the grass on the parkway in front of the house they are painting. They are both wearing their blue work T-shirts that say "MEL'S" in yellow on the front. Creek wears his navy-blue baseball hat that is covered in flecks of paint. Stan takes his hat off and puts it on his knee, revealing the top of his bald head and the sweaty blond curls at the sides and back. Stan also takes off his shoes to let his feet breathe. His shoes are old basketball shoes, covered with paint, and they lie in the grass on either side of his small lunch cooler. The grass is a little bit wet with dew still, but neither of them care. Their white painting pants have become so covered with paint and caulk that they are basically impermeable to water from the outside. Unfortunately this also makes the pants get really hot because they don't breathe.

In his right hand Stan holds out a small white pamphlet, saying, "Hey man, have you ever heard of this church, the Knights of Reason?" Creek looks down at the cover of the pamphlet with a red logo that looks like the letter "D," except the curve and the line are not connected. Stan sees Creek looking at the logo, "It stands for the two ways to approach the unknown. You can approach it in a straight line, directly, or you can arc toward it by means of other exploration that eventually leads to truth. They say the important thing is that both paths start and end in the same place, and this search for truth is the most important thing you can do."

"That actually sounds sort of interesting," Creek answers. He thinks to himself, I know a lot of people, like my family, who seem to just sort of follow their church leaders without even thinking. I don't even feel like I can talk to them, because they already have an answer figured out for everything. I like the sound of a place that believes in the investigation. That's more like me. I love my family: they're great people. But, I just think they are sometimes too quick to act like they know what the answers are. My younger brother, Dollar, is that way. He's really nice, but he always has the same sorts of answers to things.

Stan interrupts Creek's inner thoughts, seeming to read his mind and speaking with surprising coherence, "This isn't like my youth-group in high school. Man, that was a messed up group. Everyone was in love with the leader, and they would just repeat back to him whatever he wanted them to say. My church, the Knights, we see the usefulness in the idea of God, we just don't have the arrogance to think we could ever comprehend or even picture a God—so we simply live with the evidence we are given. We also think that wisdom chooses to speak to us in metaphor and riddle in a lot of ways, including the Koran, the Bible, the Sutras, because we desire to use our brains to figure things out for ourselves. So, the talks are mostly questions and recollections of current world events. We're really interested in being environmentally responsible, so we compost all our bulletins after the meeting. We also are strongly against anger, and other strong emotions. The intellect is more important than emotions, and emotions should be released to the past, so that we are free in each new moment to think with a clear mind. Man, you should come sometime. We meet on Saturday nights in the gym, in the civic center, downtown."

"Okay, I'm interested, I'll go sometime."

Stan changes the subject, "Man, my sandwich is so soggy, it always gets like this. It's like eating stale chips."

"Well, maybe you should get different bread, or use less jelly. Anyway, lunch break's over. Let's get back to it."

Creek tilts his bottle of coke all the way back and shakes it to get every last drop. Stan takes twice as long to get up, then even longer to tie his shoes back onto his feet.

On Saturday afternoon Dollar and Elle are sitting in the TV room of Dollar's parent's house; both are reading books for their college classes. Elle brought her cousin, Mindy (now ten-years-old) to Dollar's house. It is an overcast day with occasional mists of rain, but Dollar's dad and Mindy are outside. Mr. Moore is working on building a composting bin.

In the backyard Mindy is sitting on a cinderblock. On three other cinderblocks Mr. Moore has laid out fence posts. He is standing and calculating what his next move should be. He leans against his post-hole shovel. Between Mindy and Mr. Moore, Sam, the Bergamasco Sheepdog, is lying in the grass. Sam is about three years old and her hair has started matting into dreadlocks. Her eyes are no longer visible beneath her bangs. She looks like a big, rolled-up ball of gray wool.

This scene, perfect and peaceful, possesses a timelessness.

Beautiful and still for a moment. Then, into the yard rushes a contradictory breeze, warm and wet pushing up the cool and dry. Mr. Moore lifts his head. Inquisitive. The dog's eyes, hidden behind a veil of fur, shift to watch the girl. She is looking at the boundaries of her life—the surrounding blue green hills, covered with fir trees. The earth is groaning silently—silently mourning over the impermanence of their momentary utopia. Regardless, Mr. Moore and Mindy drink in the passing contentedness.

The yard has a wonderful view of the valley to the East. Seeing to the North is more difficult because of trees on the property next to the Moore's. But they can see the sky to the North, and can see the dark clouds accumulating there. There are some days in Centralia when the weather and sky seem to stand still. On these days time itself appears to have slowed down. Other days though, the sky moves quickly and low clouds bring rain and wind with them. Mr. Moore and Mindy are about to experience a shift from one kind of day to the other, the sort of shift that often results in hail. Sam the Sheepdog starts becoming restless. She walks in a circle around the cinderblocks and two people, as though she is trying to keep them huddled together in one place. When the sky grows dark and the first flecks of rain can be felt against his face, Mr. Moore says, "We better head in side."

Sam insists on being the last one into the garage, protecting her flock instinctively. After they take off their shoes and walk through the garage into the kitchen they begin to hear the drumming of hail against the roof. The sound interrupts the focus of Dollar and Elle's reading, and they move to the kitchen to watch the hail with Mr. Moore and Mindy.

When the valley is dark, when the weather is tumultuous, when large storms pass over the house, they feel as though they are in a boat at sea, surrounded, like Noah, by floods. Their imaginations soar to places where litter and lost balloons fly. In the house, they are physically safe, though the sound and sight of the hail-storm is overpowering, all-encompassing. Attempting to re-assure one another with half-smiles, they steal glances around the room. The hail looks like popcorn popping in the grass.

It stops. Quiet. Breathing a sigh of relief, Dollar says, "That was awesome." Bright and glittering, the sun shines again on half of the valley.

They all stand looking out the window at the valley.

In her mind Elle is thinking of the night she called Dollar from her room, when her Mom's boyfriend was downstairs argu-ing with and hitting her Mom. She is remembering the feeling after the boyfriend had gone, when she stood at the bottom of the stairs, stunned, assessing the damage, overtaken by the silence. Peaceful, cathartic, drained—it is an odd mix of feelings. There is something like silent electricity buzzing in the air.

All of them sense it in their own way. Mindy recalls the feel-ing of being let out from the closet where she had so many times been locked-up. It is a mixture of relief and release. Yet in an odd way, there is also some fear of returning back to the unpredictable world. Dollar thinks of the moment of scoring a goal in a soccer game. It was such a rare occurrence for him when he played, but it was the only time on the field when he could relax and see the event for what it really was. When he scored a goal he could look around and see kids dressed in two colors of shirt, running in a rectangle of nicely kept grass, with others standing around the side yelling. Mr. Moore recalls the time he was in a car accident as a boy. His mother had been reaching beneath her seat for a loose tomato, and spun off the road into a ditch. He remembers the absolute quiet of the car, motionless in the ditch, as his moth-er leaned, unconscious, forward against the steering wheel. The dog feels no impulse to be anywhere other than where she is.

These reflective moments are built into the rhythm of life. Important discoveries are made during this time--this city-wide exhale of the psyche. One realizes what has been there before him all the while. A person is moved to see that the balance is precarious, that safety is not guaranteed, that every once in a while he should thank his lucky stars; that the speed of his pulse is parlous, that water stays liquid within only a few degrees, that when magnolias are the first to bloom it is a gift not to be taken for granted, that garbage goes somewhere, that his parents had parents too, that fences look thin from above, that much of life is about letting go of one thing and grabbing hold of another. Who knows what will be discovered in these moments? Sometimes the person who has discovered it doesn't even know it. This moment of reset is long and short, empty and full, quiet and loud. As they stand in the kitchen, as the quiet cessation of hail sets in, Dollar, Elle, Mindy, Mr. Moore, even Sam the Sheepdog to some degree, all experience this kind of moment.

The following weekend, on a Saturday night in Chehalis, Creek and Stan walk up the front steps of the city's civic center. Entering the old brick building, and the smell of cleaning products, floor wax, mustiness, they pass a bulletin board on the wall inside the entryway. Hanging by a green thumb-tack on the bulletin board is a yellow flyer with the Knights of Reason logo printed large in the middle—like a letter "D" with the curve and line separated. The flyer says, "Come Seek Truth With Us, Free Your Mind, 8 pm, Saturdays, Main Gym."

The building is quiet, the parking lot mostly empty, but down at the other end of the hallway, standing near the doorway to the gym is an old man in a button-up sweater. Beside him is a cardboard box with a handwritten sign taped to its front, "Compost." Creek and Stan walk past the old man, who greets them not with any words, but only a slow, gentle, handshake, and a minimum of eye contact. Half of the fluorescent lights in the gym are turned on, giving it the feeling of being regrettably lit, of being lit from past events, as though the space was actually inside the hippocampus of an old man's brain, turned on when thinking of stale coffee and the smell of floor wax.

There are about fifteen people sitting around six foldable round tables on red stackable chairs. To one side of the tables there is a screen on a self-supporting stand with an overhead projector aimed at it. At the other side of the tables is a long foldable table with a coffee urn and two paper plates with imitation Oreo cookies. Creek and Stan sit at a table with a middle aged man, wearing a non-descript ball-cap and thick glasses, who is resistant to noticing anything, including the fact that they just sat at the same table as him. In the next five minutes, four more people enter the gym. They are: a 50-year-old woman wearing a green sweat suit with curly-red, balding hair; an Asian man in black pants and an old, white, button-down shirt; a stocky young man in cut-off sleeves with tattoos all over his arms; and an extremely skinny young woman with hunched shoulders and pale skin.

"Welcome fellow seekers," the voice of a woman addresses the room. She is about 55-years-old, and wearing a black pantsuit, with a bright teal blouse. Around her neck hangs a silver necklace that is the shape of the Knights of Reason logo. Her face is too bright, as though any flaw in the brightness might cause the whole person to collapse, just as a dam is in some ways too impermeable and a small crack in it might lead to complete collapse. She has an indomitable spirit about her, like a dog in a dog-fight; it is clear that she fully intends to control the room and make her point, and that getting in her way would be futile at best. Yet she only stands about five-feet-tall. There is a purplish-red tint to the dark dye she uses in her short, curly hair.

She raises her left arm and puts a fist straight out in front of her, "This arm is like your life. You are in control of how it goes out into the world. Would you approach with determination? Or would you limply exchange your life for experience?" She keeps her arm in front of her but relaxes the fist and allows her arm to bend, "Would you aim towards an idealistic goal?" here she points her finger straight out, "Or would you make your life all about yourself?" and she points the finger back toward herself. "I'd like to suggest that your way of experiencing life should be none of these, but instead, a simple gesture. I suggest that this mental image, this gesture, if you take on this posture, it will transform your life. What I'm about to show you is the way to ask questions and the way to give answers, the way to both approach and retreat, to both win and lose, to laugh and cry, to buy and sell. If you can master this way of being, your pursuit of truth will be genuine and your receptivity pure." She extends her arm straight out in front of her, straight as a baseball bat, and also locks her eyes on a target straight ahead.

Sitting attentively at a round table Creek finds this woman mesmerizing. Whether it is something in her spirit, or simply in her voice and body, he is drawn to the confidence and fearlessness she possesses.

"Now," she sharply draws all eyes to herself, "look at the double purpose of my hand. The fingers are straight out and aggressive, searching. The palm is up and open, ready to receive. Here is the tricky part: I'm not actually telling you to walk around like this with your arms out, am I?" She walks between two of the tables and still holding out her arm she makes eye contact with several of the people sitting there. After a few seconds of rhetorical silence, she continues, "Of course not. I'm talking about a posture for your life; I'm giving you a metaphor. You search and you listen, you approach and you process, you drive and you wait, and you are tired at first, but you get stronger the longer you sustain this posture.

"And this is the what you need to take from my words tonight. Many of you come from a place in life where you've been taught to rely on certain truths, and you've been told these truths come from God. These things, like wearing bonnets and cowboy hats, are cultural interpretations and pragmatic solutions to social problems. Is there a God who has given us specific rules for how we are to live? Think about it. Why would a God want to create needy little creatures that spit and bleed? Why would a God create a whole world and then watch people destroy it and each other? What purpose could this possibly serve for God? Is it simply for his own sick entertainment? If so, this is not a God to follow, but one against whom to revolt!" She is becoming more animated and is walking along the outside of the group of tables, walking more quickly than before.

"Let me ask you this: have any of those truths you've tried so hard to follow stopped the headaches, have they fed starving children, have they brought an end to war, have they equalized the socioeconomic disparities plaguing most of the people on our planet? No. No. No, they haven't. Those truths, and that God you pray to, are inventions, invented by the highly intelligent, highly motivated, emotional, needy creature called Human Being. You can pray. In fact prayer is an excellent way for you to psychologically vent some of your deepest desires. But know this, when you are exhaling your last breath, there will be no God there ready to embrace you; your last breath is the conclusion of your search:

that is all. After that, well, there is some sense in which your energy and actions will continue to have an impact. And there is a sense in which your soul will have resonance in the larger story of time. But you won't be eating cookies and drinking coffee in the clouds.

She spins 180 degrees, facing the opposite direction, "Even so, it is of vital importance that we, the human race, continue to pursue excellence in every way. Most importantly we should pursue that excellence which we uniquely posses. I'm talking about our intelligence, our ability to reason, and our ability to reflect on ourselves. Because of this the pursuit of intelligent discourse in all realms of understanding is vital. Those disciplines that can be especially pursued are philosophy, and theology, as they reveal some of Mankind's most unique intellectual capabilities."

As she walks behind the table where Creek sits, the leader raises both hands in the air saying, "Everyone up. Stand up and move to a new table, so that you are sitting with a totally new group of people." The people slowly and quietly rearrange themselves. "Here's what I'd like you to do. Everyone put your two hands on the table in front of you."

Hands rest on the tables around the room as she turns on the overhead projector. There are four people at Creek's table. To his right is the 50-year-old woman wearing a green sweat-suit with curly-red, balding hair. Her hands are plump and purplish; her fingers, interlaced. Across from Creek is the Asian man whose hands are on the table, and he is fidgeting with his keys. Large, knobby knuckles are slowly working one of the keys off the ring, then putting it back on—over and over. The skinny young-woman with hunched shoulders and pale skin is to Creek's left. He can see long, almost invisible blonde hairs on her forearms. Shyly, her eyes have yet to look up at the others at the table.

The leader slides a transparency onto the overhead projector. It is an outline of a hand, a simple line drawing. She directs them, "Look at the hands of the person to your left. We are going to have silence for thirty seconds, and I want you to stare at that person's hands. For now, try not to think, but just look; allow your eyes to travel over the surface of their fingers and knuckles; move your eyes into the wrinkles and across the larger spaces; observe the overall shape of their hands, and allow yourself to feel that shape.

"Think about the emotions you felt. Did you feel connected to the person? Did you lose track of your thoughts? For our purposes, whatever you were feeling, however you were feeling, you'll want to remember that and try to avoid it in the future."

She draws the logo of the Knights of Reason on the hand on the overhead projector. "Look at our symbol. It follows the real, indisputable logic of nature, not the fickle up and down of skin. Our symbol shows that there is a road to follow when experiencing life—or maybe there is more than one road—but it is important to see that the roads begin and end at the same place. The most important thing is the journey. As you journey through this life you will have many decisions to make. Question them; analyze them: but make sure you are making your analysis based on vigorous logical argument—either with yourselves or with others."

The people at the tables stop looking at their neighbor's hands, and now look at their own hands. Creek tries to piece together the ideas she has just given and apply them to his own life. Not getting anywhere, he fears looking up and letting his eyes meet the leader, falling under her intimidating scrutiny.

To the left of his hands lies a small paper plate with crumbs from the imitation Oreo cookies he ate. Back and forth between the plate and his hands, a small black fly excitedly hovers. Creek tries to ignore the fly, but when it touches the back of his fingers it tickles. Either on his hands, or on the cookie crumbs, the fly becomes Creek's center of attention. Fortunately, the leader is looking at the other side of the room as she talks, so Creek is not under her direct watch. She talks about the ideal mind and the path to enlightened reasoning. On Creek's sleeve, in fits and starts, the fly moves toward his shoulder. The leader shifts her gaze back toward Creek's side of the room. He sits perfectly still, tormented at the same moment by her attention and by the fly moving toward his shoulder, just barely in his peripheral vision. Everyone around him is quiet and still, making any movement from Creek impossible without drawing further attention to himself. The leader continues to elaborate on the intricacies of logical decision making, while Creek focuses almost entirely on the fly. He feels it crawling on his face, up his cheek, toward his eye. He can't resist it any more! The quick movement of his hand and the slapping noise against his face cause everyone in the room to look at him. As far as everyone else can tell, he has just slapped himself in the face. The pesky fly disappears under the lip of the paper plate.

"Did you have a question young man? Do you need to excuse yourself?" the leader asks as she takes a few steps closer to him.

"Umm, I'm sorry, I uh, didn't mean to interrupt, but, um, what was the last part you were saying?" From the way he asks, it is obvious to everyone Creek is not focusing on the lecture.

"I was elucidating the misconceptions many people have regarding their intuitive interactions with the world, as they relate to the misuse of emotional cues in decision making. Now let's move forward and have a volunteer close tonight's meeting for us. Do we have any volunteers?"

To Creek's right, the woman with the plump, purplish fingers raises her hand, then timidly makes her closing ceremonial remarks, "With the conclusion of tonight's meeting we endeavor to go into the world with attentive minds, conscientious actions, and unquenchable searching for truth. Goodnight." Most of the others respond by saying goodnight in return.

On the drive home Creek listens to one of the local radio stations. A popular song about a high school break up plays. It is a melodramatic song yet somehow it doesn't make him sad, but instead, nostalgic. His small navy-blue Toyota, which can just barely pull the trailer they take to job sites for house painting, smells like plastic. He is glad to not be pulling that trailer tonight as he coasts along the 30 mph road with the windows down, in the cool night air. Whether the Knights of Reason meeting was a hoax or whether it contained the secret of life, Creek thinks it is probably good to have this place of deeper questions in his life being addressed. Though he felt uncomfortable at times in the meeting, he thinks, "At least they're not just going with the flow."

He hasn't decided what to do with the rest of the night, so he heads in the general direction of home. Sitting yet moving, calm yet volatile, satisfied but yearning, the contradictory within Creek is stirring. Blue stripes, dark-green herring-bown, brown-pink polka-dots—the color of his mood is evasive. This emotional state of unrest is familiar. As he drives through the small Chehalis downtown the illuminated signs catch his attention. Not working the next day, he has no reason for returning to his little rental house so early in the night. He parks in front of a bar. Noise. From the sidewalk the folks inside look merry: once inside their particular merriment looses its charm, but the frenzy has a magnetic power to detain.

Creek leans his left side into a small gap between two men

at the bar and waits for the bartender's attention. Once he has acquired a beer he moves down to the far end of the bar where there is more space, and takes a stool next to a man who also looks to be by himself. The man doesn't say anything as Creek sits down, but he raises his glass toward Creek and they give each other a wordless clink of glasses—the sort of respectful reticence some men find most meaningful. This man seems a bit out of place in this bar. To begin with, he's not wearing blue-jeans and a ball-cap; nor does he have any facial hair. He looks more like the type of man to stay at home sipping merlot in a leather chair with a hard-cover Dostoyevsky novel in his hands. His skin, though aged, is relatively smooth and blemish free. There is a sharpness to his eyes, as though he knows more about the scene than anyone else. Around his temples, gray hair has delicately made an appearance, in a haircut that looks timelessly accurate in the company of his face. And he is just slightly underweight; his weight and posture a projection of his competent self-discipline.

When Creek orders his second beer, the man turns for the first time and looks at him, saying, "Did you see that rainbow tonight, to the East of the highway?"

Creek realizes he could take the simple yes or no route with this question and leave it up to the man to continue the dialogue, but he feels comfortable and so tries to embellish his otherwise simple answer, "No, I was in a meeting earlier, but I've seen them out there over the hills before. Sometimes they double up—that's pretty cool."

The man waits a few seconds, then says, "Yes. I've seen those, but this was just one solid rainbow. What sort of meeting were you at on a Saturday night?"

Creek, still feeling comfortable, decides to answer the somewhat more invasive question honestly, "Oh, I was at this group that meets in the Civic Center downtown. We talk about philosophy and theology, and how to best go at life. It's called the Knights of Reason. It's left me pretty confused tonight though."

"Well, I hear that. I've certainly felt confused often enough. I'll tell you what though, that rainbow tonight got me thinking about Noah. You know, Noah and the Ark."

"Oh yeah, I know it," this time Creek keeps his answer short because he can sense some sort of sermon coming on. The man has been really polite and easy to sit next to so far, and Creek doesn't want the bar experience to be ruined by an unwanted sermon he feels obliged to sit through.

"What a guy," is all the man has to say. This comment reminds Creek of the way they clinked glasses when he first sat down. The man is obviously aware of himself and Creek and doesn't want to make the conversation burdensome for either.

Relieved, Creek leans forward onto the bar, puts his left elbow down and rubs his eyes with his left hand.

"I'm not so sure I could be like Noah," Creek says while still rubbing his eyes. "How many years did he supposedly spend building his boat, while everyone else thought he was off his rocker?"

The polite man answers, "I think it was somewhere around 100 years."

"Man, slaving away like that for 100 years, building something no-one else needs or wants to help with—the guy sure had determination." Creek and the man raise their beers to drink at the same time. The man places his hands on the bar and with his right fingertips around his left ring finger turns his left hand back and forth, as though turning a wedding band. Creek makes sure to take a second look, because the movement is so convincing: but there is no wedding band there.

The man makes a hand motion like he's removing the wedding band and gently putting it on the bar with his right hand, face down. He looks at his right hand, positioned on the bar, then looks at Creek, "It's interesting that you used the phrase, 'slaving away.' I wonder about Noah. It seems like he was either incredibly restricted, and enslaved, working without a reasonable goal or reasonable compensation, or he was amazingly free, capable of working with conviction despite a lack of support, capable of building something no one else thought worthwhile."

"Well, I'd say he was free if he could do whatever he wanted, but it seems like he couldn't: I mean, he had to build that boat," Creek replies.

The man sounds surprised, "So you don't think he could have stopped? I wonder what would have happened if he would have stopped? Also, if he didn't build the boat, he would in some ways be a slave to other people's opinions and a slave to his own lack of knowledge of the future flood. I suppose he inevitably would have to follow some guiding belief, whether himself, or God, or culture, or he could just make decisions in the moment and call it chaos—but even then he'd sort of be a slave to chaos."

"That's a depressing outlook. It makes me think there is no freedom." As Creek says this his mind is darting back through the last few days, to the house-painting job-site, and then to the Knights of Reason meeting. It seems just about right to him; life doesn't hold much freedom, just the freedom to be frustrated.

The easygoing stranger continues, "Well, you look like a smart guy: I'm sure you'll figure it out. I think there's a lot more to life than frustration and disappointment, but maybe there were times when Noah himself would have disagreed with me on that point. Have a good night—get home safe. The drinks are on me. I'm going for a walk." The man leaves a twenty-dollar bill under his empty glass as he smoothly and quietly stands and walks out the front door. Creek finishes his beer and a few minutes later decides he too will take a walk outside in the relatively quiet streets of downtown at night.

"Many years you were patient with them, and warned them by your spirit through your prophets; yet they would not listen. Therefore you handed them over to the peoples of the lands. Nevertheless, in your great mercies you did not make an end of them or forsake them, for you are a gracious and merciful God" (Nehemiah 9:30-31).

On a summer night in downtown Chehalis you can hear crickets.

Creek walks under a streetlamp, past a park bench, slightly uphill. He knows the alcohol has had some effect because his brain feels light, a helium balloon on a string.

Creek hears in the distance a car door being closed and then a girl's short laugh that reminds him of Mary. The sound of Mary's laugh and then the shape of her belly—magnetically smooth and tantalizingly curved—light up like flares in his mind. Without lifting his head to look, he turns and walks five steps in the direction of the laugh, then thinks better of it, turns and recovers his route. He hasn't talked to Mary in years, not since she mysteriously dropped out of his life in college. It's not as though he misses her company, or her conversation; it's more like his body misses her. The physical memories are still occupying a part of his brain and emotions. There are times when he's lying in bed at night when he is certain she is there next to him, but when he moves to touch her she disappears.

His brain slips and slides into dark places.

He subconsciously jumps the track, escaping by looking down at the cement sidewalk, and finds himself attempting to connect the dots. There is a pattern of dark spots made from air bubbles that must have popped on the surface of the cement as it was drying. It's not as though they are arranged in a regular pattern (their placement seems random) but it is also somehow predictable, in the sense that they are spread fairly evenly. Then too, there are little pieces of rock in the cement that stick up from the surface, catching the streetlight and making tiny shadows. Patterned, but random, these protrusions happen in about the same number per square foot as the popped air bubbles. Creek is unconsciously making triangles of one type, and then triangles of the other type, overlapping the first. The sizes of his triangles are increasing and decreasing at his whim. Finding concentric triangles is more difficult. Within this slab of concrete he experiences an odd sense of depth. No longer connecting spots, he now pushes forward into the concrete in his mind. Two inches, three, four, he moves about six inches in before his concentration is broken and he looks around him into the mostly vacant downtown streets.

He decides to walk home instead of walking off the beer and then trying to drive. The several-block walk goes by quickly and before he knows it, he's in his bed asleep in his clothes.

In the nighttime, in his dreams, Creek unconsciously experiences a miraculous event in which patterns of lights fill the sky. At first it is subtle, and there is some doubt about what the lights are. One light grows stronger in the black space of the universe, appearing to come closer. Then it moves quickly over the expanse of the sky, from one horizon to the other, and stops low on the horizon, hovering. People begin to come out of their houses, and there is a general sense of anxiety with this never-before-seen movement of light in the night sky. Then three other lights appear alongside the first, and the group of four lights begins to slowly move, curving gently over the broad dome of the atmosphere.

Within minutes there is panic among the people on the ground. In the distance a warehouse goes up in fire. Clouds are moving through the sky too, temporarily obscuring the strange colored lights. Another group of lights, larger, and farther away, consisting of at least fifteen yellow lights in the shape of an elongated diamond, moves toward earth. In Creek's dream he is soaring up into the night sky, watching the lights, keeping an eye on them so he can tell people on earth what to do. But Creek is caught up amongst the lights, and soon finds himself far from Earth, cruising into space in the light formations. Then the odd and uncanny occurs; he has the sense that he has left the system of time behind, and that he is no longer in a body, but that his body consists of lights. He cruises into distant space, outside of time, without a body. There is a feeling of adventure combined with anxiety as he tries to keep an eye on the other lights that are also moving around him.

Creek wakes in warm sweat, and shifts under his comforter allowing some cold air in. Though he feels the need to get up and go to the bathroom, the cold air deters him, and he rolls onto his other side, under a cooler, dry area of comforter, and falls back into sleep.

He dreams again. This time he is in the grocery store on Main Street in Centralia, where he grew up shopping with his family. He is in the pharmacy section of the store, near the check-out counter. Looking down the isle, through the cards that are for sale, he sees Mary. There is an immediate sense of urgency that comes over him, like he needs to get her alone and talk to her, but the reason for the urgency is not very clear. It looks like Mary has seen him a few times, but he's not really sure, and she hasn't acknowledged his presence. Her friends are talking to her, surrounding her, as though she is in the middle of a circle they have formed. When he walks toward the group of girls they move over an isle and they're out of view. Desperately, he hurries to the end of the isle and turns with expectation, but they're not there. To his right he hears girl's voices, and looks around the corner of the next isle. Empty. He backs away from the ends of the isles and looks right and left but the whole store now appears to be empty. The music has stopped and the lights overhead turn off one by one. In his mind he wants to shout, "Hello! Is there anybody here?" but when he opens his mouth to speak his breath is simply not there and no sound comes out. Fear fills him. The idea of being locked in the dark, empty grocery store is terrifying.

Creek wakes up again in a warm sweat, the heat of his comforter too hot for the summer nighttime room temperature. His alarm clock reads 3:17 am. The deep of night. In the blackness of his room he begins to worry that he is actually in the grocery store, and is relieved when he reaches over to turn on his bedside lamp and sees the familiar walls of his bedroom.

On the same evening that Creek has these disturbing dreams, Dollar and Elle have a life-changing experience. They have spent the day in their separate classes and then in the library, across a large table from each other, studying. Now they are taking the long walk from the community college back to their homes. They are like two trees that grew from sapling to maturity side-by-side. Wind, rain, and sun have been shared by them. Always having the other there, neither can imagine the possibility of anything else.

On the walk home they stop under the shade of a crabapple tree. Their first kiss is like the evening sun kissing the top of a tree as it sets; it is like the conclusion of a full day, and the beginning of a restful night; it is like the chorus of your favorite song.

The next day, Dollar finds out from a letter in his school mailbox that he has won the Bob Turner Wildlife Preservation prize, for his research paper on bald eagles. As usual, Dollar and Elle meet in the cafeteria for lunch.

As he looks across the plastic table at Elle, Dollar courses with excitement. He sees her as she was in the moment before their kiss. Soft lips. Dollar does not notice how there is something different in her demeanor. She holds back from full engagement. "I have good news Elle," he says without looking up from his lunch tray, as he handles his sandwich preparing to bite into it. "I won the Robert Turner Prize for Best Nature Essay! I guess they liked what I had to say about bald eagles! Here's the best part: the prize includes going to the State Wildlife Rehabilitation Center and choosing an animal to take care of, and I know they have at least one eagle they can't release back into the wild. I might have my very own eagle Elle!"

Elle replies with checked enthusiasm, "Dollar, that's awesome. Congratulations on the prize, I know you worked really hard on your paper."

Dollar continues, "Oh man, I can't believe all this good stuff is happening!"

"Um, I wanted to talk to you about that," Elle's hesitation has yet to effect Dollar; he does not see what's coming. "About last night, and the kiss: we're good friends Dollar; I think you're a great person. But that's all this can be. Friends. Last night was a mistake. I don't know what is coming in my future. I do know that I want to be challenged and probably to move to a city where I can write for a newspaper. And you're happy here, in the country, and you seem happy in general. I need something more though. I'm sorry. It was a mistake."

Dollar puts his sandwich down and stares blankly at the space over Elle's shoulder. He can't believe what he's hearing. He doesn't understand how his excitement about the relationship could not extend to her. His feelings are so strong and clear. She must be lying to herself, afraid of the feelings.

Dollar stands from the table, leaving his food, and walks out of the cafeteria.

He goes home and lies on his bed. The bedroom door is shut, and no one else is home; his room is quiet. In the evening when his dad knocks on the door, Dollar gets up and calmly answers it. "Oh, hi Dollar, didn't know if you were in there. We're going to eat some dinner if you want to join us."

"Okay, thanks, I'll be right there," Dollar answers with the slow words of someone who's just taken a nap.

At dinner, when asked how his day has been, Dollar responds, "Oh, fine. I got an award for my paper on eagles, so I'm probably going to bring home a new pet as my prize. Probably keep it in the back shed if that's okay." His tone is matter of fact.

His parents are a little surprised that he's not more excited about the prize. "That's great! Congratulations on your paper. I know you worked really hard on it," his mom tries in vain to add some enthusiasm to the moment. Dollar has not an ounce of enthusiasm to show.

Dollar brings home a three-year-old, male bald eagle from the State Rehabilitation Center. The eagle has a cracked beak and was taken in because it couldn't catch its own food. Apparently it missed a critical period of learning how to hunt and will never be able to survive in the wild. Dollar names the eagle Isaiah and puts him in an old dog cage in the shed while he works on building a larger cage in the back of the shed, taking up about half of the total space.

A few months later Dollar sits on a stool in the shed next to the chicken-wire that keeps Isaiah in. His back is against the wall and the door is open to let in light. Isaiah is perched behind the wire, diagonally across from him, on an old wooden chair Dollar found in the dumpster at school. Dollar talks to Isaiah, "I don't know man. I don't understand why she suddenly shut down like that. I thought we were really close, and I thought she really liked me. How can we go from spending so much time together, to now, not even talking for months? I'm angry at her, but I also know that if she showed up right now and said she wanted to be with me, I'd say yes in a second. Isaiah, I'm glad I have you. Look, I'm not going to abandon you. I care about you. You and me, we're soul mates."

Dollar's dad calls to him from the back door of the house, "Dollar, phone call for you, it's Elle."

Surprised, Dollar gets up and walks quickly across the yard and into the house to take the call.

"Hi Dollar, how's it going? So, I'm going to be transferring to Portland University next semester; I got into their writing program. I leave in two weeks and I was wondering if you'd like to get together to say goodbye this Saturday?"

Dollar's answer is slow, "Okay." They've arranged to meet at the ice-cream shop downtown on Saturday.

Dollar has already found a booth and is waiting when Elle walks into the ice-cream shop on Saturday to join him. In their hello's Elle smiles momentarily but Dollar keeps a straight face.

He makes eye contact once when they first greet, but after that he mostly looks down at the table or off to the side.

"How are you?" Elle asks with nothing but sweetness and care in her voice. Her kindness and interest in connecting with him is all the more frustrating. For Dollar it is somewhat like looking into the sun; it hurts. It's hurts for him to let her be kind to him but to not have her as a girlfriend. If he is kind in return, then she is getting everything she wants, and he is not getting what he wants. She wants his attention but will not return affection. Before, it felt like there was a mutual interest, but now he feels used by Elle. All of these thoughts wash over him in the first minute of their meeting.

Elle goes on to tell him about her courses for the next semester and says that she'll miss him. Dollar sits, mostly without talking, and feels his mood spiraling down. He is feeling angry at Elle and disappointed in himself. Without finishing his ice cream, and without allowing the conversation to naturally close, Dollar gets up and says, "Well, have a good time; I have to go home now to feed Isaiah." He walks out the front door without waiting for a reply.

Upon arrival at home Dollar does not go into the house but instead goes immediately to the shed and sits on the stool against the wall, sits outside the wire cage keeping Isaiah in. Isaiah is perched on the chair diagonally opposite him; he was perched there when Dollar opened the door and walked in.

In a low mumble with closed eyes, Dollar talks to Isaiah, "Well, I guess we're in for a nice week of weather my friend. Mom said she could hear you from her bedroom, pecking at the wall of the shed last night. What's up with that? Oh, you were just having a bad dream. I hope you were still able to get some sleep. So, Elle's leaving to go to school in Portland. . . . I know, but she wants to experience something other than this town. Well, my friend, we'll just have to make do." Dollar's words are getting slower and quieter as he carries on his conversation with Isaiah. He is falling asleep.

In his dream Dollar waits in line behind the counter in a deli. The shop is very busy, with at least fifteen people in line and seven or eight behind the counter. From the moment the dream begins, Dollar feels confused. He doesn't know whether the people around him in the end of the line are still looking at menus waiting to order, or waiting to pick up their finished orders. The line snakes around to finish where it starts, and the space is crowded and small, and there is no physical partition between the two directions of the line. Behind the counter, the people fixing the sandwiches keep switching their positions, so that the person starting a new sandwich has to ask who's next, resulting in awkward exchanges between the customers in an attempt to both get the order placed quickly and not offend someone by cutting in line. To make matters even more confusing there are sandwich types listed on a hanging sign on the back wall, and some listed on a paper taped to the inside of the glass over the food, and a hand-held menu; the different menus don't seem to agree on sandwich names, sizes, or prices—and they each have different combination deals to offer.

After placing his order Dollar moves to a new spot near the center of the line. "Cheese?" He hears the question asked from behind the counter. "Hey, buddy, you want cheese or not?"

"Yes, please," Dollar answers apologetically.

"Well, what kind of cheese would you like your highness?"

"Ummm . . . provolone." Dollar is feeling small and out of place.

"American-o, Swiss, Cheddar-ino, but we got no Provolone-y, what'll it be pal?"

"Oh, um, Cheddar." Dollar is relieved the questioning is over, and he no longer cares what type of cheese he gets.

Dollar looks down toward the three registers. One of them hands out condiments, the next looks to be ringing up drink orders, and the final one takes cash from a customer. There are also white paper tickets being passed back and forth. Dollar has no idea where the tickets are coming from, or what their purpose is. He shyly says to the person in front of him, who is holding one of these tickets, "was I supposed to pick up a ticket?"

"You a club member?" The man's reply is quick and no nonsense.

"Oh, no." Dollar decides to leave it at that and not pursue what becoming a club member involves or what the benefits might be.

A different person behind the counter, without making eye contact with anyone, says, "what d'ya want on it?" When no one answers he looks up and at Dollar, saying, "would you like some condiments buddy?"

Dollar looks at the six or seven unlabeled plastic squeeze bottles, and in a defeated tone, replies, "no thanks." Though he really wants mustard and mayonnaise, the thought of getting that accomplished is too much. On top of that, he has no idea how they have kept track of his sandwich. There didn't appear to be any communication between them, and at least three different people have taken orders from him—and there are probably ten different sandwiches being made. Like many of the deli's he's experienced in real life the employees have devoloped a system of working efficiently that appears baffling to a person stepping in off the street.

When he gets to the end of the line the woman at the first register asks him if he wants any to-go toppings. While she's showing him the options, the woman at the second register says, "Honey, you want fries and a drink with that?" At the same time the woman at the third register says, "you eatin' in or out?"

As he walks to his table Dollar passes a newspaper with a headline, "Vietnam War Claims More Local Lives." There are several black and white photos of young men under the title. They look clean and healthy, not like men during war. He searches the faces for people he knows, friends or classmates who were drafted. All of the faces look familiar but he cannot specifically put a name to any of them.

1968

George Washington

Two years later, Dollar wakes from a dream feeling hungry. He is twenty-four-years-old, lying on the couch in his parents' den on a Saturday afternoon.

His job working for the city isn't physically tiring, but something about the long days spent mostly inside, sitting at a desk, makes this Saturday afternoon nap a necessity. The job really isn't that difficult; he's basically a secretary for a low-key bureaucratic organization. Yet somehow, the stress in his life is increasing. It is not the sort of stress that comes from real pressure applied by people who need things done. Instead it's an internally based stress, like heartburn. For example; he hasn't pursued a job involving work with wildlife, instead he's working for the city as a sort-of errand boy; he hasn't found his own place to live, he still lives at home with his parents; he doesn't have a girlfriend, he hasn't dated anyone since Elle left over two years ago. As a result of these missing pieces he feels inadequate, underused, incomplete, like a failure. This creates a constant source of internal burn.

In the bathroom Dollar rinses his face with water to wake it from the nap. Leaning forward he rubs his eyes while looking in the mirror. There is still some ink on his left finger from a pen he was trying to fix the day before. He is twelve inches away from his own reflection. There are the two eyes, alert, though muffled. The shoulders need to be adjusted so they are level. The light scar under his eye, like a dent, reminds him of Creek.

Creek works as a Mail Carrier for the Chehalis Postal Service. He has just finished his work route and returned home to his apartment when he gets a phone call from his mom. She sounds more resolute than normal, quicker to get to the point, "Hi Creek, how are you? Look, I'd really like it if you could come for dinner tomorrow night. I won't get into it now, but there's something I'd like to talk to the family about together, in person. Well, of course Lorne won't be there, but I'd really appreciate it if both you and Dollar could be there with me and Dad for dinner."

Lorne lives in Florida with his wife and two kids, so it is no surprise that he won't be there. His family has only been to visit twice in the last four years. Not having a busy social schedule, Creek is quick to reply yes. The truth is he looks forward to the free meal and the company.

Most of Susan Moore's life has been devoted to her three boys. From their earliest days she was the one in charge of planning their schedules, doing their laundry, cleaning their bedrooms and bathrooms, making their meals, driving them to various events and classes, and giving them emotional support. This is not to say Jacob has been absent; he has played a role in all of these things, and has been important in other ways: but Susan was always the day-to-day workhorse in the children's lives.

In some ways this has kept Susan from becoming really in

touch with her own needs and personhood. She hasn't had hob-
bies, or even her own passion in life—apart from her family. In
other ways her devotion to her family has determined who she is.
It has become the defining element of her personhood.

A similar sort of paradox can be applied to how raising
children has effected her relationship with Jacob. On one hand,
their shared mission of raising the boys has brought them together.
They have joined in a difficult and rewarding task. It has given
them more than enough to do and talk about, and has united
them with similar goals. On the other hand, as the boys became
the center of her focus, Susan's relationship to Jacob suffered.
He lost the number one place in her heart. Though he shared the
same mission in raising the kids, he could sense the distance between them widening. Her interest in him didn't disappear, but it
lost some of the enthusiasm given to a number one interest.

Jacob is setting the table and talking to Susan about one of
the classes he's teaching. He describes how one of his students
has a tendency to take over the class by attempting to answer
every question with lines from popular movies. Jacob is express-
ing frustration with the student's lack of awareness in letting other
students talk, and with the student's distraction invoking movie
quotes. Susan is trying to listen and respond to Jacob, but she's
really thinking about Dollar and Creek. She wonders what sort
of mood Creek will be in for dinner tonight. She tries to think of
ways to get the boys more involved in positive ways in each other's lives. She wishes Creek would invite Dollar over to his place
more. This would get Dollar out of the house and give Creek more
company. She hopes Creek and Dollar will stay friends all of their
lives. Somehow it's different with Lorne. She doesn't worry about
him, or imagine the future for him.

Dollar has left an unfinished glass of orange juice on the

counter. Susan walks by it three times, each time conflicted about whether or not she should clean up after him. He's an adult now, he should know how to pick up after himself. If she does this now, how will he ever learn. But, he's going through a rough patch in life, and having his Mom harp on him about cleaning up will only accentuate the awkwardness of their Mother and Adult Son cohabitation. It's only one glass, a tiny drop in the huge ocean of cleaning she's done as a mother. She picks it up, rinses it in the sink and places it near the back of the top shelf of dishwasher; in an almost unnoticed internal flash she thinks of how it would be un-rinsed and placed near the front if he had ever gotten to it.

There is poignancy in the way an adult enters his parents' house without knocking. For the parents it is unexpected, yet it reminds them of the days when they only barely noticed their children come and go with regularity. Creek enters his parents' house and says hello to his mom and dad who are working on dinner in the kitchen. They tell him dinner will be ready soon, and that Dollar is in the TV room.

The brothers greet in the TV room without any outward signs of greeting. It is their brotherly way. They are so comfortable with each other and have spent so much time together that to be in the same room again is not something new, but rather a continuation of the way things are.

After a few minutes Dollar says without turning his head from the TV, "Wanna come feed Isaiah with me?"

Creek doesn't need to reply, but is close behind Dollar as they walk out the back door toward the shed. Inside, Dollar sits on his stool and tosses little chunks of dried fish through the chicken wire. Isaiah gracefully bends and snags each piece off the straw floor with his once broken, now naturally fused, beak.

Creek, crouching across from Dollar and watching Isaiah eat, says, "He's looking great. Energetic. Shiny."

Dollar answers, "He wouldn't eat for a couple of days, but now he's back on track."

They remain in the shed for a while, without talking, watching Isaiah eat. Their mom's voice is heard from the house, "Food's ready guys."

The dining room is modest. Four wooden chairs are around a medium sized rectangular wooden table, centered in the room. There are cloth placemats and two white candles in the center of the table. Mom and Dad bring chicken, green beans, mashed potatoes, gravy, and a salad to the table. Mom's glass is half-full with milk, Dad's with water, no ice, Creek's has ice-water, and Dollar has poured a can of soda into his glass of ice.

After all of them are seated Mom reaches her hands out and they join hands on the sides of their plates. She prays, "Lord, we are grateful for this moment of being together. Thank you for your grace, mercy, and ever-flowing river of life. Thank you that Creek and Dollar can be here. We ask you to bless this food to our bodies. Amen." When the prayer has finished, Creek reaches for the chicken, Dollar takes a sip of his soda, their Dad pulls his napkin from under his fork and places it on his lap, and Mom gets up from the table, coming back with the salt and pepper. The conversation is mostly small talk about their jobs.

When they have all finished eating and the plates are cleared Dad pours everyone a cup of decaf coffee. Mom brings out a plate of homemade molasses cookies and sets it in the middle of the table. She addresses Creek and Dollar as she sits down, "Boys there is something I need to talk to you about." She is looking alternately in each of their eyes as she talks, but there is also a distant aspect to her gaze. It is as though she is comprehending much of the past, present, and future as she talks—it is a look of knowing and it is full of sadness. Her eyes become wet.

She leans forward, interlacing her fingers on the table in front of her, and glancing up briefly before returning to eye contact with Creek, then Dollar. "I have breast cancer. I was diagnosed yesterday with an aggressive malignancy and they want to start treatment immediately." Tears have begun to run from her eyes but she continues talking, now looking down at her hands. "The prognosis is not good. The lump is in my left breast," she places her right hand flat against the center of her chest, "and they haven't found a consistently successful treatment for my type of cancer, so they will be approaching treatment from several angles at once, which will be especially difficult on my body." She reaches her hands across the table to each of them and they place their hands in hers. "I love you so much." Tears begin to stream from her eyes and she is unable to speak more.

As they look at each other and hold hands, the lump in her breast slowly grows. It is completely oblivious to the situation, but strikes ahead in chaos, disorder, and destruction. The nacreous lump is black and blue and red and green. It moves and twitches imperceptibly. It is hard and soft, wild, putrid, diabolical. An invader in her extraordinarily complex biological systems, it strengthens itself while planning its crazy mutiny. This darkness within her dampens the joy of all her moments.

Dad speaks in a soft voice from across the table, "Mom and I will both be taking the week off from work, and probably spending most of our time at the hospital. Dollar, some folks from church will be bringing meals to the house, and we might need your help with shuffling things back and forth from the hospital, and maybe with communicating updates to some people.

Neither of the boys have spoken yet. Creek gets up from his seat and hugs his Mother, saying, "Mom, I'm so sorry. This is terrible." He squeezes her and lays his forehead against the top of her head.

From underneath his hug, from the midst of tears she says, "Thank you Creek. We will fight this, and God is good."

Dollar is looking down at the table when he says, "I can't believe it. Are they sure they've diagnosed it correctly? Is there any possibility they're wrong."

Mom looks at Dollar and says, "Honey, the doctor I saw is a specialist. He's a good doctor."

After a few minutes Dad breaks the silence, "Well, you both have work tomorrow, so why don't we say goodnight so everyone can get some rest. This is going to be a difficult week." He gets up from the table, taking his and Creek's half-empty coffee cups into the kitchen.

Creek leaves for his home in Chehalis and Dollar goes to his bedroom. The house feels especially quiet. Susan is still sitting at the dining room table while Jacob loads the dishwasher.

The city of Centralia, Washington, sits on a line halfway between Portland and Seattle. The line was once a railroad; it is now Interstate 5. It is a tightrope—when you fall off it you land in the open country, in the Wild West, on an Indian Reservation, in the Appalachia of the Northwest. The city of Centralia sits on the line like the line traversing the center of a yin-yang symbol. Mountains rise up in the distance like the little circles of opposition within each side of the symbol. The line negotiates a path between the heaven and hell of Seattle and Portland. Centralia is a depiction like Michelangelo's last judgment, live, in real time. The blessed are carried North to the city on the Sound, the city floating in a heavenly dale surrounded by crystal seas and majestic mountains. The cursed fall down to the South, to the city nestled deep in the fog of rolling mole-hills, always aflame, confused, darkly seeping into the river that drains their nightly dreams, and they crawl upside-down across the bellies of bridges that grip from one side to another, refusing to let go. And Centralia is that ripple between the two, it is the diagonal dividing heaven and hell, resting under the bottom of the staff Christ holds. When he strikes his staff against the ground it lands on Centralia.

It is said that one half of the world knows not how the other half lives. In Centralia neither half exists, for all dwell in a deep purgatorial in-between. The quality of life is thus dispersive in its shadowy form under the staff of the creator. And the city, inflexible to all entreaty, impassive as a statue, emits a perfect riot of color with a foggy mind of guessing. It is a place where a series of singular perplexities is daily met by a draft of heavenly pleasure. And it is impossible to look with insensitivity upon its people, who skate over thin ice, whether they glide like a sunbeam on a winter's day or grate under the pressure of calamity.

Benjamin Franklin wrote in his autobiography, "Human felicity is produc'd not so much by great pieces of good fortune that seldom happen, as by little advantages that occur every day." Centralia is the place where these little advantages and their counterparts are continually wrestling. In Centralia the lonely way of isolation wrestles with the milk of human kindness.

Hub City. So Centralia is named, as the hub of a wheel, the fulcrum in the scales of justice.

"I know, O Lord, that the way of human beings is not in their control, that mortals as they walk cannot direct their steps. Correct me, O Lord, but in just measure; not in your anger, or you will bring me to nothing" (Jeremiah 10:23-24).

In the town next-door to Centralia, in Chehalis, Creek's old co-worker, Stan, comes home from the bar to the room he rents in a disheveled old house, and watches a movie about a tough-guy detective. Stan lounges back, letting his buzz settle and eating left-over frozen pizza.

In downtown Seattle, Creek's old girlfriend Mary works as a sales associate at a spa. She lives in a small studio apartment in the Capitol Hill area. She has access to a grocery store, a Laundromat, and a bar, all within two blocks.

At his quiet home on the outskirts of Centralia Mr. Swordsmith sits in a chair, reading a book about the history of China. Classical music sounds softly from the record player.

In downtown Centralia, Raspberry, the old school bully, closes the storefront gate to the video store where he has just finished his first shift as manager. A tattoo of raspberries marks his neck, showing just above the collar of his shirt.

Cyril the eagle keeper sleeps in bed. He sleeps at dusk and wakes at dawn. There are four different tan work uniforms hanging in the closet beside his bed.

In a restaurant one exit South of downtown, Miss Goodrich and five of her fellow teachers close out the week with happy hour and appetizers. She listens with active eyes to a story one of the others tells about a rowdy detention group earlier in the week.

Dollar's friend Kevin works late to finish designs for one of his company's architectural projects. He drank a coffee at six in the evening to maintain his focus.

Creek and Dollar's dad sits in a chair beside the bed in Mom's hospital room. He holds her hand as she sleeps after one of her chemotherapy treatments.

Somewhere in Portland Elle laughs as she sits across from a

classmate, flirting, playing a game that involves choosing random sentences from random books and mixing them together. Her hair is cut above her shoulders and for the first time since she was twelve, she has bangs.

Isaiah stands on the chair in his cage, wings folded, watching the recesses of the dark interior of the shed.

Late on a Thursday night, during her first week of treatments, Dollar sits by his Mom's bed in the hospital. She sleeps. Dad has gone home to get some rest for the night and plans on coming back again after work on Friday when she'll hopefully be more awake. Everything about the place makes the situation feel cold. The floors and walls are unadorned and cold. The colors of the sheets are cold. There is a cold look in the eyes of the nurses passing by the door and occasionally entering the room. Even his Mom seems cold to Dollar. He doesn't often see her sleeping, but now her rigid posture in the bed is unknown to him; it is hard to believe it is a restful position. The bed is elevated under her head and upper body, and she is on her back with her arms straight down at her sides and her head pointed straight forward—eyes closed and mouth open. Maybe it is the fluorescent light, but even her skin looks cold, slightly bluish-green, and he didn't realize she had so much gray hair.

He hasn't been praying very much in the last year or two, but Dollar feels compelled in this moment to plead with God—there is nowhere else to turn. The doctors are not hopeful, and he very much senses his Mom's life is in the hands of fate. He leans forward, putting his closed eyes against his palms, with his elbows on his knees.

"Dear God, I know I haven't been praying very much lately. But please listen to me now. I'm falling apart, and I can't lose my

Mom. I need her here. Please God, please, please, please don't let her die. I know I lost Elle, probably because you probably weren't happy with me. Maybe I'm too selfish, or I haven't been as nice as you want, but please don't take my Mom." Dollar starts to cry as he prays. His words are slightly audible, but he is alone in the room with two sleeping patients. "Please God, I'll do anything. I'll change anything. I'll give up anything. Please God, you can even take Isaiah, but let my Mom live."

Dollar looks up when he hears noise coming from his Mom's bed. Her hand opens and moves toward him as though she wants to take his hand. Her eyes are still closed, but he can hear her voice clearly now, as she talks without moving her head. "Dollar, is that you? I just woke up with a warm feeling all through my body, and I heard you talking."

"Oh, Mom, I'm sorry to wake you. Yes, it's me, Dollar. I was just praying for you. How are you? Are you feeling rested?"

"Honey, thanks for coming, but shouldn't you be getting some sleep. I can tell it's late." Her eyes close, then re-open, "I'm feeling very good right now, very rested, and peaceful. Now you go on home, and tell your Dad that I'm looking forward to seeing him tomorrow."

"Okay Mom. I'm glad you're feeling good. Get some more sleep and I'll see you tomorrow night." He leans forward and kisses her on the forehead. As he walks out of the room Dollar is really happy to have talked with his Mom. He thought she might sleep through his whole visit. He has totally forgotten the prayer he just said.

When Dollar walks out of his mom's hospital room, she does not immediately fall back asleep, but is instead preoccupied by two strange and simultaneous feelings. First, she feels good; for her it is similar to feeling like she did when she was young. Her body is rested, strong, and taut, though also relaxed as she lies on her back in the hospital bed. Only an hour ago her body felt broken, discombobulated, tense. This new feeling has come suddenly and spontaneously, and makes her wonder if the feeling is all in her imagination.

The second feeling is also experienced as qualitatively good, however the way it is good does not avail itself at first. It is a feeling of absolute smallness and unknowing. She reflects on the complete lack of control and knowledge she has had in the last several days. She has not been able to actively participate in this fight for her life, and she has known next to nothing about the procedures that have been applied to her body. She has been tossed like a boat in a storm, and yet, here she is feeling good and breathing real air.

"For surely I know the plans I have for you, says the Lord, plans for your welfare and not for harm, to give you a future with hope. Then when you call upon me and come and pray to me, I will hear you. When you search for me, you will find me; if you seek me with all your heart, I will let you find me, says the Lord, and I will restore your fortunes and gather you from all the nations and all the places where I have driven you, says the Lord, and I will bring you back to the place from which I sent you into exile" (Jeremiah 29: 11-14).

On that same Thursday evening, Creek walks between Iron and Rock Streets, on West Locust, in downtown Centralia. He's used to walking in Chehalis for his postal routes but this is the start of a new habit for him. In the evenings, for the last few weeks, he has been watching the stars and learning the constellations. With the passing of sidewalk squares beneath his feet, he feels as though he passes back into time. A book with a map of the constellations remains open in his hand at his side while he walks. Vast, communal, ageless, the stars spin around the Northern Star at an imperceptible speed—they sneak across the sky throughout the night.

Low on the horizon to the North the big dipper moves left to right, and up to the right is Cassiopeia, moving up higher in the sky. He finds Cepheus between Cassiopeia and the North Star. Following King Cepheus's raised left arm he finds the bright star Deneb in the tail of Cygnus the flying swan, also known as the Northern Cross. From Deneb, through the bright star in the swan's left wing, he finds Vega, the bright star in the neck of Lyra, the charming singer Orpheus's lyre. From Deneb to Vega, to the bright star Altair is the summer triangle, high in the sky toward the West. And Altair lies in the neck of Aquila the eagle, Creek's favorite constellation. In Greek legend, Aquila was the thunderbird of Zeus, carrying and retrieving the thunderbolts he wielded against his enemies.

Dollar's love of eagles has inspired Creek's choice of Aquila as his favorite constellation. The celestial eagle watches over Creek. Looking at the constellation he thinks about the tenuous nature of his astronomical eagle. His eagle is just a few dots connected by lines with an imaginary drawing of a bird over it; just a story made up by another culture thousands of years ago; just a chance arrangement of bright lights in three-dimensions taking this two dimensional shape because of the Earth's position in the galaxy; just a group of stars as far away from each other as they are from him, spinning in the disk of the galaxy much like the Sun does. And yet there is something incredibly permanent and concrete about his eagle. 365 nights a year his eagle soars across the sky somewhere, and it has been doing this for many thousands of years. Many people through the history of humankind have looked up into the night and found this same grouping of stars. They have told stories about it, wondered about how far away it is, and they have used it to guide them in navigation.

Creek doesn't pray often, but as he looks at the hugeness above him, at the drama of stars around his constellation Aquila, he too is inspired to pray. While looking up, without closing his eyes, he prays, "Great God, bigger than I can possibly imagine, please send your gentle hand of healing to my Mom. I know I haven't done anything to deserve your attention, probably it's just the opposite, but please God, give her more time." Creek's prayer, like Dollar's, mixes nebulous guilt with desperation.

He hears the low rumble of a truck on the interstate. By this time Interstate 5, built during the Eisenhower administration during nation-wide freeway construction, is about eight-years-old.

In that same spot on the streets of Centralia, long before the noise of the highway (ninety-years before Creek stands there pondering the stars), the frontiersman George Washington likely stood outside his fourth home with his son Stacey, looking at the stars. He was the African-American founder of this city, originally called "Centerville" because of its location halfway between Tacoma to the North and Kalama to the South.

Creek is only vaguely aware of George Washington's history. Born in 1817, George Washington grew up in Missouri with adopted parents. He was black; they were white. As a gifted young man he learned to sing hymns, he taught himself to read (because blacks weren't allowed to attend school) and he became quite skilled with a rifle and broad axe. He could draw an "X" on a sheet of paper, tack it to a stump forty yards away, and hit the crossing on the "X" eleven out of twelve times with his rifle. His skill with the rifle would earn him respect and bring in game from hunting throughout his life. With the broad axe he could chop and assemble a wooden floor that was leak tight and smooth enough for children to walk on. For much of his life he earned an honest living cutting timber, working with his hands.

As a young man Washington attempted to build and establish a distillery in Illinois only to find out, after his business was set-up, that Illinois had just passed a law that didn't allow blacks to make or sell liquor. So he set off for the freedom and adventure of Oregon Country.

On the journey, Washington and his family mostly ate corn-bread. When they did eat biscuits, they called them "seldom," because they were seldom available to eat as a substitute for cornbread.

In 1852, he staked a squatter's claim where the Chehalis River joined the Skookumchuck River. His cabin was made out of wood he chopped, with a fireplace made from mud he packed. Oat, wheat, and garden foods were farmed on about twelve acres of his land. He had two cows. His own cooking, hunting, tailoring; he did it all. He and the Native Americans shared peacefully as they passed through on fishing expeditions. They continued to use their burial ground, located on some of the land he claimed.

Amazingly, this African American, who wasn't even allowed to sell liquor in Illinois, began a city by parceling off his land for sale. Within a few decades he was wealthy and well respected. The kids in town called him Uncle George. In 1875 a Baptist church was built on the corner of Main and Gold Streets. His wife named it Gold Street after the golden streets of the New Jerusalem. Nearby was Pearl Street, named after the pearly gates. Uncle George could be heard singing hymns while plowing a mile away from town. He was an extremely honest businessman and a generous friend to the needy.

Creek doesn't know the whole story of George Washington, but he does think about his own story, and what the stars looking down require of him. The life of George Washington makes an unfair comparison to the life of Creek. Times have changed and they were born into very different situations. As a young man Washington had a tangible sense of his own worth as it related to his very survival. He could see the piles of wood he cut with his own hands. He could feel his hunger when the farm's production was low. He knew the adventure of entering an untamed place and building something worthwhile there. Washington even knew the feeling of taking care of his parents, wife, and children by the time he was Creek's age. Despite all of the excuses he could have made for simply lying down and giving up, Washington rose above his circumstances, and did so without guile, but with generosity.

One might say they don't make men like they used to. Perhaps that's true. In the more tame and nurturing environment of his youth Creek has not faced the types of challenges Washington faced. It could be that not having these challenges made Creek soft, indecisive, and confused about his own role and worth. His high school and college years passed like the run of a successful television sitcom. After college he found himself quite unsure of who he was and what he was supposed to do. For Creek, this question, "who am I and what am I supposed to do" has existential overtones. For Washington, the same question would have seemed silly. He might have replied, "What sort of question is that? Look at me. This is who I am and what I'm doing."

On Friday evening of the same week, Dollar and Creek's dad stops at the college to pick up some books from his office and check his phone messages. Jacob is a literature professor specializing in early British Literature, particularly Chaucer. His classes have been cancelled all week because of his wife's cancer treatments, and his needing to be at the hospital with her. One of his students, Tara, is waiting for him in the lobby.

Young women in college are a conundrum; they are cripplingly self-aware, and at the same time completely unaware of themselves—like a twelve-year-old boy dressed-up in army gear holding a real AK-47. They are overly aware of what they're doing, and at the same time they do so much more. While Tara waits in the lobby for her professor amidst all the mayhem comprising her life (the boyfriends, the drinking, the self-image complications) one concern occupies the front of her mind—her grade in Mr. Moore's Intro to Literature class is dangerously close to failing. His lectures, polished by years of practice, endow him with a tantalizing charisma in the eyes of most young women. In her imagination, his mind comprehends the mysteries of the world. She would do anything for the approval of this powerful man, and a better grade .

The rain falling outside, Tara dressed in her pajama pants and a tight t-shirt, the other faculty gone home for the day—the stage awaits the deviants. Jacob has so much on his mind that he doesn't think to leave the door to his office open, that he doesn't hesitate to ask Tara how her week has been, that he allows his eyes to circle around her waist along her waist-band as she describes her latest tragedies and leans to pull a late paper out of her backpack. She is excited, accelerated, ignited by the attention he is paying her. Uninhibited ego.

He reaches for a pen; she, for a tissue. Gently her hand

brushes against the top of his. Bolstered by broad scruples, she allows her hand to rest on his; his hand does not retreat but waits. Lust's momentum is aroused. They kiss unannounced by words; kissing over the desk between them, more active than he remembers kissing to be. Bad man. He, with the strength of his hormones, lifts her over the desk and into his arms, her pajama legs around his waist. In a matter of minutes he forgets his wife and her cancer, his job and his morals. Something about Tara's movement—quick, aggressive, perfunctory, unresponsive—makes the sex feel dry. Just like that, he escapes his troubles, she improves her grade. The deviants exit the stage.

This is not the first time Jacob has cheated on his wife. When he was younger, when the Dollar was crawling and Lorne was in elementary school, when Jacob was working towards a full-time position at the college, he had an affair with one of his Senior Seminar students. He was less than ten years older than her, and they truly connected intellectually. It continued for almost a year until she wanted to rent a room in the house next door to his family. Too close. He ended it.

In Jacob's mind, his actions were not so much treachery, but more of a pragmatic diversion. Back then, with the boys rolling all over the place, it was actually helpful for him to be away and relieve some tension elsewhere. Also, Susan was so tired from dealing with the kids; she didn't have that sort of energy for him at the end of the day.

His recent dalliance cries out unpremeditated from within the pain of his wife's cancer. Who wouldn't understand this? An escape from the pain. A leap off the gravitational mound of reality. It isn't a question of his love for his wife. What she can't know shouldn't hurt her, he imagines.

On Friday night by her side, she vigorously recalls to him the events of her day with clarity. Susan talks about the events surrounding the new patient in the room with her, the changing of the bed, the patient's noisy visiting family. Her voice clear, her body refreshed, her eyes darting about the room, Jacob is struck by fear. Afraid of her movement, afraid she will see what he has done. Despite his care for her, he now fears her recovery. An oscillating ambivalence towards her paralyzes his interaction. At once he pities her weakness and fears her strength—back and forth. She looks at him, "Jacob, what's wrong, there is a distant look in your eyes?"

His reply, "Oh Susan, I'm so glad you're feeling better. What do you think has changed? Have the doctors said anything about it?"

"Not yet, they're going to do some tests tomorrow morning, but at this point they don't know what is happening."

Without leaning forward he stretches out his hand and takes hold of hers. They sit hand-in-hand without eye contact, without speaking. At midnight she sleeps and Jacob leaves without waking her.

On Saturday morning Dollar sits in the shed with Isaiah. There are scraps of food all over the floor on Isaiah's side of the cage; he's not eating. Dollar leans back in his chair and lets his eyes wander up toward the dark roof of the shed.

Thoughts of Elle enter his mind. At first they trickle down from the dark roof through a small space in his consciousness. There is the sound of her voice saying, "Dollar, I just don't know about that" with a knowing smile. Then he remembers playing tennis and not caring who wins. In a matter of seconds the trickle has become a flow of memories and longing for Elle. The softness of her lips when they first kissed strikes at his heart. And then he is in the cafeteria hearing her tell him she doesn't want to be in a relationship. Voices inside Dollar are telling him he is no good. No wonder she doesn't want to be with someone who lives with his parents and doesn't even want to get out of this town. Mercifully, the reality of Isaiah's shed asserts itself through the smell of his uneaten food scraps. Dollar's thoughts are brought back to the present by the acrid smell.

About 100 years after Centralia's George Washington was born, in 1919, there was a town tragedy. In the U.S.A. fear of communism combined with a growing patriotism from WWI. Tensions between labor forces and big business mounted, and those fighting for labor rights were often seen as dangerously Marxist. It was the time of the "Red Scare" and the "Industrial Workers of the World," also called "Wobblies," were endowed with sinister anti-patriot attributes by their adversaries.

As he continues looking into the darkness of the shed's roof, Dollar talks to Isaiah about his visits to the hospital to see his Mom, "Isaiah, you should have seen it. In the last two days mom's face has totally changed. She has brightened and looks normal again. It's amazing. The doctors are calling it a miracle. They've never seen such a quick recovery, and don't know exactly why it has come about."

In a photograph taken in 1919 an 18 year-old woman stands with her 36 fifth through seventh graders. She would walk several miles to school early in the morning to sweep and put coal in the stove before the students arrived at their one-room schoolhouse. Six of the students have slight smiles on their faces in the photograph; the rest stare straight into the camera with little expression. It was a time when photographs were not yet expected to capture such ephemeral emotions as a smile.

Dollar puts his fingers through the wire in an effort to comfort

Isaiah. But the sick eagle does not respond.

In November of 1919 tensions between those wanting labor rights and those against organized labor unions rose to a boiling point. Buildings were vandalized; people were assaulted. Then, during a parade honoring Centralia war veterans, three veterans were shot as they passed the Wobblies' hall on North Tower St. A mob responded by chasing the Wobblies and throwing them in jail. In the chase one of the Wobblies shot one of his pursuers. Later that night, in the dark of night, the town's power went out, setting the stage for revenge. Several men went to the jail, took one of the Wobblies, and hung him from the Mellen St. Bridge— filling his body with bullets. The National Guard came to town to restore order.

The area once explored by Lewis and Clark, the city started by an African-American frontiersman, the land of the Native Americans, struggled through a bloody worker's rights battle. The bruised torch of exploration for a life and a place of freedom passes from generation to generation.

When Dollar looks down into the cage he sees Isaiah limp and lifeless on the floor.

Isaiah dies.

"It is not for your sake, O house of Israel, that I am about to act, but for the sake of my holy name, which you have profaned among the nations to which you came. I will sanctify my great name, which has been profaned among the nations, and which you have profaned among them; and the nations shall know that I am the Lord, says the Lord God, when through you I display my holiness before their eyes" (Ezekiel 36: 22-23).

Dollar buries his body in the backyard, but lacks the emotional energy required to clean out the shed.

Dollar and Creek's Mom comes home from the hospital, miraculously healed.

Their Dad, Jacob, spends several evenings a week "working" late at school. Actually, he spends these evenings driving with his student Tara to a motel in a small town ten miles north of Centralia.

At 8pm Creek walks the streets of Centralia, passing the time and looking at the stars. The November sky is dark and moonless. Venus shines brightest in the heavens, toward the South, near the horizon. By 9pm the Pleiades, which form a tiny dipper, and the Hyades, a slightly larger cluster containing the bright star Aldebaran of the constellation Taurus, rise above the Eastern horizon. Creek follows the path from the Pleiades through the Hyades down toward the horizon, looking for the bright star Betelgeuse and the three-starred belt of The Giant Hunter, Orion. There are a few clouds near the horizon, and the sky is a little lighter there, so he is not sure if he's found Orion. In fact, he has not yet seen Orion this year and he's excited for his first definitive sighting of the whole constellation. In the recesses of his memory are times when Orion shone brightly overhead, so he knows it is just a matter of waiting for winter to set in. Orion, the Adonis of the heavens, will chase the doves of the Pleiades, with a lion's skin held aloft in his right hand and a club in his left, only to encounter the great bull Taurus along the way. When winter is closing and Orion has shifted toward the western horizon, Scorpius will begin to rise in the east. Orion will flee to the western horizon to hide from this stinging foe who alone can defeat him.

Creek stops walking and sits on a bench near the sidewalk on

Pearl Street. The air is crisp. He feels content. This new sensation has grown in him in the last several months. Despite his mom's cancer, despite his brother's eagle dying, he feels at home in the moment—as though he can rest assured in the validity of each bit of news and each new interaction. The postal route becomes an enjoyable daily excursion. Legs, arms, turning neck, bending waist, his very body assimilates into the mechanisms of his environment so that he feels and thinks with an awareness fully in tune with the moment. The whole experience is odd, refreshing, and new.

Returning to his little house in Chehalis, Creek heads directly for the bathroom and specifically to the dental floss. The satisfaction of a clean bathroom. Earlier in the evening he'd cleaned the kitchen and bathroom, and done some laundry. As he flosses he enjoys the feeling of a freshly cleaned bathroom and spotless mirror. The uniform shine of the sink cradles a faint lemon smell in the air. Between his lower right wisdom tooth and the next one forward he flosses with special attention. This gap was very tight until his last dental appointment, when a filling was needed. In the process of doing the filling they must have pulled hard enough on the tooth to shift it slightly forward. Now it is easy to floss there and usually rewarding too—in the form of trapped, sinewy food. Just like cleaning the bathroom, there is satisfaction in cleaning his teeth.

Tired, content, peaceful, Creek falls asleep quickly. In his dream he is waking up on the morning of a wedding. He's not sure who's wedding it is, but he definitely feels like he is an important part of the wedding party. His head feels fuzzy; his vision is blurred, almost to the point of blindness. In the dream he climbs out of the bed he shared with his brother Dollar and feels his way to the bathroom. Dollar is asleep, undisturbed in the bed.

Outside, the sun begins to lighten the sky, but has not yet broken the horizon. Creek stands in front of the bathroom mirror, struggling to get a clear view of his reflection. Pulling his right eyelids open with his fingers, he can see that his eyes are red and swollen. There is a fleck of white near the corner that he is able to dig out with his pinky finger. As he rolls his eye to the side he sees another bit of white in the opposite corner. The more he looks to the side the more of this white thing he can see. It looks like a wad of chewed up paper, soaking wet in the recess between his eyeball and its socket.

By pulling on the front corner of it he is able to extract a one-inch long paper wad. His vision gets clearer. There are similar bits of paper near the front of his left eye also and he cleans them out with his hands, rinsing his eyes with handfuls of water as he cleans. His vision is slightly better, but there is still a fuzziness. He closes his eyes and looks down for about thirty seconds, then opens them and looks up, leaning in toward the mirror. A bit of white clings near the very bottom of the right eye. Pulling gently on its tip, so as not to separate it from the rest, he slowly extracts it from behind the bottom of his eyeball. It is two inches long and as thick as his index finger. Almost immediately his vision clears and his head feels better.

In the next half-hour of the dream the wedding morning continues as Dollar and Jacob wake in the same hotel room. Creek still stands in front of the mirror, now leaning forward and looking at his forehead. He pinches a blackhead on his forehead with his two index fingers. As he squeezes the dark point coming out gets thicker and longer. It is as thick as a ball-point pen, and continues lengthening and extruding: it is a ball point pen. Removing it from his head feels so good, but Creek can't understand how there was space in his head, in his brain, for a whole pen to be in there.

He squeezes several more pens and pencils from various spots on his forehead. Dollar sees him doing this but is unimpressed and looks more interested in getting his own clothes together and cleaning himself up. Creek asks his father, Jacob, if he's ever seen something like this before. Jacob tells him that he does remember doing that once or twice a long time ago, but not recently. Jacob tells Creek he thinks it is a good thing, and probably not harmful. Creek's head is feeling better and better.

1970

Metal Box

Two years later, on a Saturday morning in 1970, Creek wakes in his Chehalis rental house. He has the day off from work at the Chehalis Post Office and plans on spending it building a sort-of greenhouse in the spare room of his house. This will involve a few hours of planning, a trip to the hardware store, and several hours of construction. His old friend Stan has volunteered to come by and help in the afternoon.

Repetitive actions like making coffee comfort him Creek. He goes through the same motions each time, emptying yesterday's grounds, putting in a new filter, rinsing out the pot, filling the reservoir with water, grinding new coffee, pushing the On button, pushing the coffee pot back below the cabinet. With a piece of typing paper and a pencil in front of him, he begins sketching the shelves and lighting he has imagined for his greenhouse. He plans to build three shelves on one wall, stacked vertically, about six feet long and one foot deep, and strong enough to hold several plants, pots, and their wet soil. There will also be two supports coming off the wall on either side for clamp lights, four lights total.

Creek's newfound interest in gardening has taken him by surprise. Perhaps it's a desire to be in touch with the seasons, or an interest in seeing things grow, or an urge to be a caretaker. Whatever the reason, this year as winter approaches he eagerly anticipates the prospect of planting his own seedlings in his own garden when spring fully arrives. Also, as he's walking through town, and looking at other people's gardens, he subconsciously fosters a desire to garden. With his stargazing skills encouraging him to pay attention to seasonal changes in the night sky he can't help but desire a daytime counterbalance. He plans to have a row of vegetables, a row of herbs, and a row of flowers starting their growth in his spare-room/greenhouse over the winter.

With some coffee in a plastic to-go mug, and his drawing and list of materials to buy folded up in his coat pocket, he wipes the condensation off his car windows and drives to the hardware store.

Creek loves popcorn. But for some reason the popcorn they give away for free in the hardware store is not at all appealing to him. As he walks into the store he wonders why the local auto shops and hardware stores offer free coffee and popcorn, and why he never wants it. Would it be different if they were offering free cookies, or apples, or hotdogs? Maybe what bothers him is the idea of eating something with your hands and having to lick your fingers in a store where lots of people have touched things. Or maybe it is the idea of free food being distributed by a store that doesn't sell food—there are all sorts of unknowns, and a lot of trust is involved. And the coffee and popcorn usually don't taste good anyway.

As he walks toward the isle with bolts, nails, and nuts, he hears an oddly familiar voice, "Is this the illustrious Creek Moore before my very eyes?"

Turning toward his left he sees an older man in a tweed coat looking at him and smiling. It takes him a few seconds, then Creek recognizes his old English teacher from high school. "Mr. Swordsmith, I almost didn't recognize you. It's been a long time." He'd been a student of Mr. Swordsmith for one English class as a freshman. He's surprised the teacher remembers him because he mostly sat in the back and didn't talk much at all. "How are you Creek? What's keeping you busy these days?" Mr. Swordsmith looks at Creek with real care and openness in his eyes, giving him his full attention, as if he's looking at a portrait painting in a museum. Creek does remember Dollar having several classes with Mr. Swordsmith, and remembers Dollar really liking him.

Creek at first feels slightly awkward, but then is calmed by the tone and expression coming from Swordsmith, one of real interest. He wonders if the old teacher has confused him with Dollar. But Mr. Swordsmith definitely got his name right, and recognized him—and he doesn't look much like Dollar. "I'm doing alright . . . working for the post office in Chehalis, living in a little rental house downtown. I'm here to buy stuff for a little greenhouse I'm building in my spare room," Creek feels safe talking, and tells him plainly about his life.

"Oh, good for you. You know, I remember when you were in my class, years ago." Swordsmith remembers how Creek sat in the back, and didn't contribute much, but always possessed a certain unique attentiveness, one not even Creek himself could stifle. He could see the wheels in Creek's mind turning back there, and knew Creek was participating in his own way. Creek and his soccer buddies acted like they didn't care about anything in class, but

Swordsmith could tell Creek connected with some of the literature they read. In fact, he distinctly remembers one day when they were discussing *Lord of the Flies*. As Swordsmith described the meaning behind Simon's discovery of the Pig's head and his discovery that the dead parachutist was mistaken for a beast, Creek alone in the room was smiling.

Swordsmith asks him if he remembers reading the book.

"Wow, I can just barely remember that story now," replies Creek, still surprised Swordsmith remembers him.

A woman's voice sounds closely, "Perseus, I've found them, oh, who is this?" She doesn't recognize Creek, but Creek immediately recognizes Miss Goodrich's big eyes and musical voice.

Perseus Swordsmith replies, "My dear, this is Creek Moore. Perhaps you remember him, or his younger brother Dollar Moore? Creek, I'm sorry, I should tell you that Diana and I were married a few years ago."

A big smile grows on Diana Goodrich-Swordsmith's face. "Yes, yes, of course I remember! Perseus, the Moore boys were some of my favorite students." She reaches out and lightly pinches Creek's cheek between her thumb and bent forefinger.

Mr. Swordsmith says, "Creek was just telling me that he's building a winter greenroom, so he can plant seedlings in the spring."

"Oh, Creek, that's wonderful! We do the same thing. In fact, you should come over and see what we do, and eat dinner with us. Wouldn't that be fun Perseus?"

"Yes, yes, great idea my dear. Here Creek, write your phone number on this box I'm buying." Swordsmith hands Creek a pen from his pocket and the box of nails he's holding.

"Creek, you must come by. We'll call you to arrange a time, maybe next weekend."

"Okay, thanks," Creek says as he hands the pen and box back to Mr. Swordsmith. The two teachers walk to the check-out counter and Creek goes into the isle, to find his own nails.

When Creek gets back to his house with his hardware store purchases, Stan sits on the front porch waiting. Stan sits there as Creek carries the purchases from the car in through the front door. Stan has changed a little in the last few years. He's lost some weight, and he no longer works as a house painter: his general appearance is less scruffy. But he hasn't lost the ability to sit and relax in the middle of anything—work, activity, the bustle of the moment. For him life is a parade, an opportunity to sit in a lawn chair on the sideline and watch.

"Hey Stan, thanks for coming by," Creek says as he passes Stan with the last load of supplies from his car, "Can you shut the door."

"Yeah, no problem. So what's going on, man? How's Chehalis's greatest postman-astronomer doing?," Stan replies, as he enters the house without shutting the door.

"Well, the mail is still flowing, and the stars are still spinning in the sky. What's going on with you?"

"Umm, not much. I've been going to this new church. Man, it is so funny to remember the days when we were going to the Knights of Reason. That place was strange! This new place is totally different. They have music and the lectures aren't as harsh. I don't know if I'll keep going, but it seems decent so far. It's a late Sunday morning thing. You can come sometime if you want. There are quite a few ladies there too. Oh, and you remember that weirdo teacher, Mr. Swordsmith, from high school? He married Miss Goodrich, and they go there."

"Hey, I just saw them at the hardware store—what a coincidence." Creek let's the church comment go unanswered. He is still skeptical after his Knights of Reason experience. Looking down at his drawing and he grabs a box of nails as he finishes his sentence.

Stan is not the best working partner to have around, but Creek could use the company and he hasn't seen Stan in a while. The problem is that Stan likes to talk, and he likes to make jokes. This would all be fine if he could keep working while he talked, but he doesn't. Creek remembers how he dealt with it when they used to paint houses together; so Creek's appeals wouldn't sound like a broken record, he made up at least five ways to ask Stan to get back to work.

Regardless, they do eventually get the shelves up, and the supports for the clamp lights. As the work is coming to a close and it is getting later in the afternoon, Creek keeps wondering when Stan is going to call it quits. Instead of leaving, Stan is basically following Creek around, even when Creek begins putting soil in his little pots and dropping seeds in. While Creek brings the potted seeds into the greenroom, sets them on their shelves, and turns on the light, Stan sits on the floor with his back against the wall.

Stan asks Creek, "So how's your family doing? I haven't seen Dollar or your parents in a long time."

Creek really does not want to get into the details of his mom's new health kick, his dad's constant busyness with work, and Dollar's less than energetic life. Instead he answers, "Uh, they're alright. Hey, do you want to go pick up some pizza for us?"

Stan could have no way of knowing that at the same time he asks Creek about his family they are experiencing a momentous change. Their tectonic plates shift irreversibly. Lava flows, and nothing will stop it. That Saturday evening in the Moore house Dollar watches a football game on TV. He snacks on a plate of tortilla chips covered with melted cheese. He has yet to notice the shifting tectonic plates right there in the house.

Upstairs, Jacob stands on one side of the bed looking at Susan, who sits with her back to him on the other side of the bed. Jacob started the conversation about divorce calmly, but after half-an-hour of argument, he now speaks with the energy of anger. Susan, on the other hand, tried passionately from the beginning to convince him that she didn't understand and that the marriage can survive. Now she has given up on speaking, and sits in a state of silent shock.

Somehow, Jacob went into the conversation thinking he would not have to tell her about the affairs. In his self-centered world, that sort of information was peripheral to the main point— that the love between them had dwindled. But now, with her refusal to even speak, with her unwillingness to acknowledge the rift between them, the truth of his affairs slides slowly toward the tip of his tongue.

In the TV room, Dollar itches the scar under his eye. He does not hear the argument taking place above him.

Jacob's passionate anger turns vitriolic. His voice is not loud but it is heavily punctuated with spear-like points spitting across the bed at his wife's back. "You just sit there, fine! That's all you ever did anyway. Your disinterest is what made me have to look in other places, turn to my college students just to feel loved! And I finally found a girl who makes me feel like a man, not some machine created to turn off the lights and lock the door at night so you won't have to move from your cozy little spot in the bed. And no matter what I did, you never moved from it anyway. There might as well have been a ravine running down the middle of this bed." Jacob gives up on getting a response from her—by the end of this torrent his words hiss at the walls of the room and he paces in a circle by the side of the bed.

Susan feels the weight of the news of his affairs like the weight of an announcement of birth or death. It hits her with a singular profundity. Permanent. Never can this be undone. It reminds her of hearing of her father's death and her realization that his strength, resilience, life, were gone, never to return. What she knows of Marriage as an ideal, and of her own specific marriage, is now changing forever. As she listens to her husband's angry voice, she is surprised by how quickly the man she thought she knew disappears. She hears the voice of a different man, one she doesn't really care about. This new man seems strange and unknown to her. She turns on the bed and says in a calm voice, "you should leave now."

"Though the fig tree does not blossom, and no fruit is on the vines; though the produce of the olive fails and the fields yield no food; though the flock is cut off from the fold and there is no herd in the stalls, yet I will rejoice in the Lord; I will exult in the God of my salvation" (Habakkuk 3:17-18).

When Jacob moves out of the house, into a small apartment downtown, it is only Dollar and his mother who remain in the house. Their relationship has not changed much since Dollar was a boy. She still worries about him when he drives somewhere at night, and wonders where he's been when he comes home late. But they don't talk about it. Their conversations are limited to the practicalities of the day. Safe, comfortable, predictable, they have learned to interact in the most non-confrontational ways possible.

Susan Moore struggles to hold on to a sense of purpose in her life. Her husband has left her, all three of her sons have grown, and she does not have a job or a hobby to occupy her time. Fortunately, she received the house and some monthly income from Jacob in the divorce settlement. Financially she is stable, but emotionally she is empty.

As a result of the city's budget being cut, Dollar is laid off from his job with the city. For about a week he looks through the jobs section of the newspaper, and makes calls to possible leads. At first he wakes up at 8am, takes a shower, dresses as if he was going to work, and gets right to the newspaper and making job inquiry phone calls early in the morning. However, as the days pass he wakes up later, his showers shift to the afternoon, and he doesn't change out of his slippers, sweatpants, and sweatshirt all day. So far he's avoided taking a minimum wage job, but his bank account is quite low, and soon he will take any job he can get.

The spirit of Isaiah the eagle is dense and descending. Though his body decays no more than four feet deep in the soil in the backyard, his spirit moves through layers of soil, then rock, then caverns of water, then many, many miles of rock, to arrive at the molten core in the center of the earth. When it arrives in the core it is not burned up in the heat, because it is a spirit. There are other spirits there. In fact it is the energy of their animal spirits that makes the core of the earth hot enough to liquefy. Isaiah's spirit radiates heat the color of blue flame, amidst an ocean of flaming animal spirits all radiating heat in a multitude of colors from purplish-blue to blue to green to yellow to orange to red to reddish-purple. In the heart of the molten core is a purplish sphere Isaiah can only barely see. It is the beginning and the end, where the color starts and finishes. It is the silence quieter than the softest noise and the clammer louder than the harshest sound. It is the place where laughter and tears are exactly the same. Isaiah's spirit gradually shifts colors as it moves around the central purple sphere.

Mary moves back to Centralia. Exhausted by the speed and force of the many quickly turning gears of cosmopolitinalia, she swallows her pride and returns to her grandparent's home northwest of downtown. Does her past haunt her? Of course it does. Every day in the years since she left Centralia, she has relived her lonely trip to the hospital. Though her time in the city has trained her to dress and pose with panache, inside she is frail and crumbling.

Her grandparents have been retired for a few years, but they have by no means slowed down. Her grandma is part of at least seven different clubs—as Grandma says, "one for each of the six work days, and two for Tuesday." There are cooking, sewing, book, bingo, tea, prayer, and walking clubs. Grandpa doesn't have clubs: he has projects. He is rebuilding the church organ, creating a model train village in the basement, crafting a new set of dining room chairs in his woodshop, repainting all the ceilings in the house, and creating a large Japanese rock garden in the backyard. In fact, her grandparents are so busy that Mary's return to Centralia to live with them has had little impact on their lives. They love her and are happy to have her around, but she is not even close to being the center of attention.

Mary sleeps on the second floor, in the bedroom at the end of the hallway. Once upon a time it was her mother's bedroom—before she became pregnant with Mary at age seventeen and left home for the city. Her mom's junior high yearbooks, and yearbooks from her first two years of high school are on the bookshelves above the desk. Pinned to the vanity mirror are dried flowers from school dances her mom attended. For the first time Mary can clearly see the tiny grain of sand representing herself in the hourglass of time.

Grocery stores are in some ways like the anteroom to heaven. It is impossible to avoid people there. Everyday-shoppers never get to see it, but all the knots from their personal history are stored in the rear of the store, behind those swinging plastic doors with the little windows at the tops and the metal kick plates at the bottom. Filling that mysterious back space from floor to ceiling are spool upon spool of knotted history, mangy, greasy, frayed, like a giant clogged drain, like a barn full of shoelaces, like fishing lines hanging from a tree over a muddy river.

In this small town it is no surprise that Mary and Creek would happen to be picking out produce in the same grocery store, on the same afternoon. They are standing on either side of a bin, one holding apples and the other bananas. But when Creek looks up to see the face connected to the hand across from him, he is not prepared. He is not prepared for the blow. The blow is like turning on a hundred televisions at once. It is too much information, too mixed, too fast, too loud. But he remains quiet on the outside and in a few seconds he is saying hello. His rational mind blows a fuse and their conversation is relegated to reflex. "How are you?" and "what have you been up to?" sound almost natural as he battles through the initial surprise and awkwardness.

Mary talks about the job she left in the city and how she really wanted to be around family more. Now she works at the shoe store in the mall. Creek tells her about his job with the post office. As the adrenaline of surprise begins to wear off, they both sense the awkwardness of deep emotions unaddressed. Yet, at the same time, they both feel a sense of change in the other, and are curious to understand the change. They agree to exchange phone numbers and get together for a cup of coffee in the coming week.

Back at his house and unpacking groceries, Creek pulls the bananas out of the bag and sets them on the counter, as a wave of anger passes through him. He recalls the months of hurt and confusion he experienced when Mary mysteriously dumped him and cut off all communication. Oddly, barking at the heels of this frustration is a feeling of gratitude. Creek is happy to be where he is in life, happy to be delivering post, happy to be planting seedlings in his greenhouse. The old anger with Mary blows away like a curious gnat in a this larger breeze of gratitude.

In the town next-door, Creek's dad and his college-student girlfriend, Tara, don't often go out together in public. They have become aware of other people's darting glances and curious shifting eyes. People see an older man being affectionate with a woman who's young enough to be his daughter and they are curious. Despite this awkwardness, Jacob makes a point of repeatedly inviting Dollar to breakfast with them on Saturday mornings. These breakfasts are difficult for Dollar, in so many ways. He has the logistical problem of getting out of the house without having to tell his mother where he's going. And there is the emotional challenge of betraying his own mother to appease his father. Then there is the uncomfortable tension between him and his dad's girlfriend because they are about the same age, and because she exudes a flirtatious sexuality that makes him feel slightly sick to his stomach.

Yet Dollar always joins them when he's invited. He ignores the other people in the restaurant though he can sense their repeated inquisitive looks. Dollar can't say no to these breakfasts because he feels sorry for his dad. Though Jacob has clearly been a scoundrel, Dollar has always been close to him, and he sympathizes with his dad's loneliness and desires to assuage the feeling. It's like his own loneliness after losing Elle, a crushing loss. But Dollar does not have an answer to the pain; he does not anticipate revival. Because he has given up on the natural, or supernatural, workings of justice, he simply wants every moment to be peaceful and without confrontation. Since he does not find himself in a world where good and evil, just and unjust, fair and unfair, have distinct courses and outcomes, he wants nothing but the numbness of tepid congeniality. He joins his lascivious dad and the trollop Tara because he feels sorry for them, and he is afraid of rocking the boat: he's afraid of saying no.

Dollar sits across from the two of them in a booth in a break-fast restaurant downtown. She orders a small bowl of fruit. Jacob orders oatmeal, a side of sausage links, and a coffee. Dollar as-sumes that his dad will pick up the tab and orders a combination platter with eggs, bacon, hash browns, and toast. There is a slight fuzziness in Dollar's head. When he turns his head quickly, it feels like his brain and eyes take a moment to catch up. Focusing on anything more than ten feet away is difficult and unsustainable. The waitress walks away from their table. Slow and lifeless, the waitress's attitude is not rude, but simply defeated. All the while, Jacob's girlfriend is talking about her new running program that al-lows her to eat four meals a day. A flash of reckless interest flickers in Dollar's eyes as he imagines calling this girl "Mom." He laughs inside. The flicker of interest comes from a moment of absurdity, recognized as such by Dollar, common for those who have given up keeping track of life's ups and downs.

She pokes Jacob playfully in the ribs, simultaneously winking at Dollar.

"Dollar, how are things at home?" Jacob asks his son this question intending not to upset him, only to make small talk. But it is not a small talk question when asked in this context, by the father who has left the home. Jacob believes that Dollar is a grown man and so his leaving should have little impact. However, though he doesn't express it, Dollar is very angry with his father. The anger in Dollar, not finding an outlet, travels up and down the length of his body like an electrical current looking for an exit. Unlike an electrical current the anger doesn't emit energy but instead it draws energy into itself.

"Fine, Dad, fine. We think there are raccoons living in the attic again." Jacob has obviously heard Dollar's statement about the raccoons, but he completely ignores it, as if it had never been spoken, as if Dollar had said nothing.

Instead, his dad reveals the real reason for the start of conversation. "Well, I thought I'd let you know what I read in the paper this morning." Jacob cuts off an inch-length of sausage and puts it in his mouth as he finishes his sentence. Dollar is looking at him expressionless, as if to say, "yeah, go ahead, tell me." He has no idea what his dad might say. It could be anything from "there was flooding on the West side of town," to "the President has declared war on the Soviet Union." Jacob glances up at Dollar, then looks back down at his plate as he begins cutting another length of the sausage and says, "I'm sorry Son, but your old friend Elle Crane was in the obituary this morning, she died of heart complications in Portland."

At first Dollar wonders if maybe this is a joke, that his Dad in some sick way thinks it is a funny thing to say. But as he looks across the booth at Jacob and Tara he notices that for the first time all morning Tara sits still, not fidgeting, and looks at a blank spot in the middle of the table. Jacob continues, "Tara noticed it in the paper this morning. Tara's sister used to be a classmate of yours and Elle's." Dollar wishes that his Dad would just stop talking. Everything he says is maddening. Dollar tries to picture Elle; for the first time in a long time he actively conjures her likeness in his mind: he had spent several years doing everything he could to forget her.

Dollar asks them, "Did you bring the newspaper with you?" In a moment of want, he hopes to see a picture of Elle in the obituary.

"No, we don't have it. But you should consider going to see her mom. I think the funeral will be here in town, and I'm sure her mom would like to see you." Jacob reaches across the table, extending his arm to Dollar. Instinctively, Dollar puts his hand above the table where it can meet his dad's. Instead of taking Dollar's hand Jacob's hand passes over Dollar's and lands on Dollar's forearm, giving it a gentle squeeze. "I'm sorry Dollar. I know you were close to her."

After a few minutes of sitting in silence, though his food is unfinished, Dollar tells his dad and Tara that he needs to leave. It is only about forty degrees outside but Dollar drives home with his windows down. He thinks about leaving—about getting on the highway and driving to Idaho—about sleeping in the back of his car in some small town in the middle of nowhere. But he lacks the energy to turn onto the highway. Instead he returns to the home where he lives with his mom, where Isaiah is buried, where he and Elle had shared so much time together.

When he arrives at home, Dollar's mom is at the kitchen table working on a crossword puzzle. She says, "Dollar, where were you? Are you alright? You don't look too good."

"I'm fine Mom. Everything is fine." He walks past her, goes to his bedroom and shuts the door.

Lying in his bed, Dollar still cannot picture Elle's face. It is difficult to believe she is gone, especially considering her absence from his life for the last few years; nothing has immediately changed for him. He searches for things to remind him of her, in his closet, in his drawers. Shutting the top drawer of his dresser he remembers his lockbox. At the back of his bottom dresser drawer is a small metal box with a locking lid. If he remembers correctly the key should be taped to the bottom of the drawer above the box. After pulling the box out of the drawer he reaches with his left hand and finds the key where he remembered it.

It has been a long time since he's opened this box. No one else in the world knows about it. He bought the empty metal lockbox at a resale store when he was in junior high. The feel of the metal in his hands is so unique that it immediately triggers memories of Elle. When he opens the lid the first thing that strikes him is the smell. There were a few years in high school when Elle put some of her perfume on every note she sent him. Stored in the airtight box, the smell is distinct and sends Dollar back in time through his memories, washing over him like a wave.

Under the notes is a larger folded sheet—it's her essay on circles and squares she had him proof read. He remembers listening to her read the essay in Swordsmith's class. She was so precise in her enunciation. At the bottom of the box is an eagle feather she found while out walking and gave to Dollar for one of his birthdays. Dollar slowly picks up the feather and runs it through his fingers. Kneeling on the floor of his bedroom, kneeling over the metal box, Dollar prays in a whisper, "God, if you are God, this doesn't make sense. Make it make sense! How can you do this? What is the point? God . . . if you are God, why have you left me for dead? I don't like this. I don't agree with what you've done!"

Dollar puts his two fists to his forehead and rubs them both there stiffly, simultaneously.

He closes and locks the box, puts it back in the drawer, and walks out of his room. "Mom, I'm walking over to see Miss Crane. I'll be back in a little while." Dollar is out the door before his mom has time to respond. She still doesn't know about Elle's death, but she does know it has been years since Dollar last talked to Elle, so it's odd for him to be going to her mom's house. Concerned and confused, she can do nothing other than wait for Dollar's return.

When Elle's mom opens the door to Dollar, she immediately starts crying as she says, "Dollar, thank you for coming," and pulls him inside with a hug.

"Miss Crane, I'm . . . I'm so sorry." Dollar is at first taken aback by the intimacy she immediately shows him. But looking at her face he sees she is emotionally drained and he sympathizes with her.

He can see she is alone in the house. There are jackets and clothing strewn about the living room and the kitchen counter presents all sorts of clutter. Obviously she has been grieving. Her hair looks greasy and her eyes are red. "I haven't known how to let people know, Dollar, I'm sorry. I'm glad you found out. Thank you for stopping in." She sits on the end of the couch that is less cluttered and motions for him to sit in a chair across from her. Dollar remembers how the first thing she would always ask him when he'd come over with Elle was "Can I get you a snack, something to eat or drink?" It was an inviting welcome that made him feel taken care of and special. He always had the feeling she wanted him to be with Elle. This time however, there is no offer of food or drink.

Elle's mom begins talking, while looking down at her hands, "Did you know she'd become quite anorexic? That was the source of her heart trouble. I tried and tried to encourage her to get help but the more I pushed the more she backed away into her own world. I don't know what happened to her. When she left here she seemed excited about taking on new challenges and making a way for herself through journalism. Maybe I shouldn't have let her go."

Dollar had always known Elle to be slender, but she wasn't obsessive about it. Yet, hearing that she struggled with an eating disorder doesn't totally surprise him. He can see how she might use that to gain some control over her life, over her search for her identity, over her muddy family history. He cannot think of any-thing to say to Miss Crane, so he starts talking about a memory with Elle, "I remember one time we were walking home from school and she had just gotten an A- on a math test. She was so upset about it and complaining that the teacher hadn't prepared them for all of the questions. I was teasing her and saying that she should just be happy, that the best I'd done on a math test all year was a B."

Looking up at Miss Crane, Dollar can see that his story has taken her to another memory of her own, that it triggered a series of thoughts in her mind, and though she started by listening to what he was saying, she has now traveled to a place in the past all her own. He does not feel the need to ask her what she's thinking of.

"Miss Crane, I have to go."

"Oh Dollar, you were always her best friend, and we always thought of you as family. I'm sure you would have reconnected." She gives him a hug.

As he closes the door behind him Miss Crane's words stick in his heart—"I'm sure you would have reconnected. . . . We always thought of you as family. . . . You were always her best friend." These seem like kind things to say and surely Miss Crane meant no harm with them. However, as they sink in, as they coagulate around his heart, their soft, innocuous kindness cures into a fossilized titanium cage.

When someone important to someone else dies they leave their beloved in a state of permanent suspension. Though the one who lives on may spend an entire life attempting to resolve the conflicts and play out the dynamics of that relationship, in reality, for all earthly purposes, the conflicts and dynamics are frozen. The exact moment of freeze varies depending on the situation. Had the freeze occurred for Dollar just before going to visit Miss Crane, perhaps his life would be different. But for him, seeing Miss Crane was precisely the key required to lock him up, immobilized. Had the freeze occurred for Dollar just before going to visit Miss Crane, perhaps Elle would have slowly faded in his heart like a crumpled paper letter weathering on the forest floor somewhere. Yet, because of her words, and because of his receptivity, her letters will not fade but will be preserved in the titanium cage around his heart.

Miss Crane thought she was speaking a kind and hopeful truth to Dollar, telling him that she and Elle thought of him as family, that she thought they would reconnect. But really it was cruel and precisely timed. It sparked a fresh fire of absurd hope about Elle in Dollar, and as soon as the fire grew, Dollar's moment of permanence set in leaving him with an unquenchable thirst. Sometimes the changing nature of life, emotions, relationships, can be tiring—but even worse is rigidity.

Elle's body weighs 92 pounds at the coroner's lab. After her life left, her body gradually cooled to room temperature. Though actually room temperature her body feels cold to the touch because of expectations of warmth. Her body is so thin and lifeless that the skeletal structure is already dominant. In the embalming process her flesh is opened and the insides are visible. Her organs, muscle, tissues, nerves look nothing like the illustrations in a medical book. They are all packed together, intertwining, gray, pink, white, blue-gray. For an amateur, navigating her insides would be like riding a bicycle through Manhattan; there does appear to be some order, but the overwhelming feeling is confusion. Yet, she is dead, void of energy. "She," is not really even Elle anymore, depending who you ask. Some would say that this is merely a dead body, and the spirit of Elle has departed. Others would say that this is Elle. Elle is dead. End of story.

Knobby knees, prominent ribs, closed eyes, shoulders pushing forward, the body is bird-like. Why are the elbows so large? The hands alone, like anyone's hands, are worth many lifetimes of mechanical investigation. But the hands are now stiff and resist anything but a slightly closed posture. The toes are as clean and well groomed as the hands. There is elegance to the young thin body, elegance like the elegance of a long crack in the ice of a frozen lake.

None of the friends or family will see the body, except her mom. For her mom seeing the dead body once is enough.

Elle, though immature, you were a noble princess; you were a sincere explorer; you were an oboe solo; you were a cat-tail in the winter; you were vanilla ice-cream; you were venetian blinds; you were Imagist Poetry; you were string; you were the eastern shore; you were helium; you were a wooden music-box playing Doctor Zhivago; you were a porcelain cherub in a cloudy snow-globe; you were the square-root of two; you were a democratic caucus; you were an Arabian sword; you were the star Rigel in Orion; you were a stalemate in chess; you were the one who could have warned Lincoln about Booth, had you known, and had you been there. Goodbye Elle.

But not Dollar. And not a goodbye from Dollar. Let this be clear: Dollar's eyes look but do not see Elle's casket, and Dollar's heart does not abide her death.

On a February evening in Centralia, in the Northern Hemisphere, around 46 degrees, 43.5 minutes North Latitude, the king of the stars, Sirius, shines in the evening, in the Southern sky. The Moon is almost full, and approaching its zenith before midnight. Sirius and the moon dance in the sky, moving at arms length together, but not at exactly the same pace.

The full Moon is thought to call out the canine in man, and Sirius is the great Dog Star, the shining wonder in the mouth of the constellation Canis Major. Canis Major is Orion's hunting dog, sitting attentively with an eye on Lepus, the hare, at Orion's feet. To the ancient Egyptians Sirius was the star associated, among other gods, with their god Annubis, who had a dog's head on a man's body. They built massive temples aligned so that Sirius would shine though a gap in the stone at the desired ritual moment of the year and illuminate the room with its cool light. In late July the sun was aligned with Leo and Sirius began to rise in the East in the morning. The star's rising, watchful and faithful like a dog, warned the Egyptians that the flooding season was beginning. As the star and the sun proceed up to the noon zenith together during the summer, we have acquired the phrase, "dog days of summer." But in late winter, the king of stars and the sun are well into opposition, and Sirius rises visible in the dark sky, after the sun has set.

It is thought that the Moon may have been born in an early planetary collision, when some other planet hit the Earth and the resulting debris spun into orbit like Saturn's rings. Over time this debris coalesced and became a low orbiting moon. In its yout the moon may have looked from earth as large as an outstretched palm in the sky. The tides would have been huge and the effect of the tides has been gradually distancing the orbit of the Moon from the Earth—like hips pushing out on a hula-hoop.

All things orbit. Everything orbits something.

Creek and Mary meet for coffee on a Thursday evening that is surprisingly clear and warm for February. Clouds and rain settled in Centralia over the past two weeks, without a break. Finally, in an unpredictable act of grace, the winter skies have temporarily cleared. The smell in the air is infectiously spring-like, tempting even the most rusty bicycles to make a break for the outdoors. Creek and Mary both bike to the coffee shop under a nearly full moon. As he rides north from Chehalis to Centralia the bright winter star Sirius sits low above the hills in the south behind him. They are both nervous.

From the outside they don't have much in common. She is a disillusioned city girl returning to her hometown. He has been living and working in his hometown since college. Creek has found contentment in a low-key life as a postal worker. Mary has found discontent and is fleeing its sugary grasp. The great similarity between them is a shared sense of urgency to disrobe the pain of the past. Ironically the pain they would like to disrobe is a shared one and their meeting again has the effect of resurrecting this pain.

The pain, though related, is not exactly the same for them. Creek's pain has to do with Mary's unexplained desertion when they were in college together. Mary's pain has to do with their aborted child, a secret she has kept to herself all this time.

When they sit down together at the table in the downtown Centralia coffee shop they are like children around a summer swimming pool, eagerly desiring to escape the heat and jump in. After years of burning in the ultraviolet of a broken relationship they crave swimming unhindered in the cool truths between them.

"Creek we need to talk about our past, in college: we need to talk about the elephant in the room."

"Yeah, it's been a while." He feels awkward; he wants to talk but he's not really comfortable sharing yet.

"I know, but I think we've both changed since then, and we're more able to listen to each other now."

He answers Mary between tiny sips from his extremely hot coffee, "Well, I think you're probably right." He struggles for the right words, "Look, a lot of time has passed, yet somehow thinking about our relationship and you ending it without explanation, then disappearing, still makes me angry."

"I know; I can tell you're trying to be nice, but you're still angry. I think I can see it in your eyes, when you look away from me. Look, Creek, I don't know what's going on with my life. It feels like I'm in a boat being carried around by the currents of the ocean. Living with my Grandparents isn't as easy as I thought it was going to be . . . but I'm getting off the topic. What I'm trying to say is, it's really good to see you, and even though some things are hard, I think there are reasons why we end up doing what we do. I mean, we were so young in college and didn't really know what we were getting involved in. You had that accident in the soccer game, and I was only showing up to half of my classes. It's amazing how distracted and immature we were, but somehow here we are and we're okay." Mary still wears her hair in carefully designed curls but her clothing is much more modest than it used to be.

"Yeah, immature, without a doubt," Creek replies.

"But that's what I'm saying," Mary's face is becoming more expressive as she allows herself to connect with feelings from the past, "we can't really be upset with each other, and we can't really be upset with ourselves. We were both trying to figure out who we were and learning how to make decisions. Anyway, I guess there are some decisions you can take back and some you can't. Did you ever feel like we were meant to be together?"

The question totally catches Creek off-guard. In the midst of his emotional confusion, anger mixed with memories of fondness, the last thing he is wanting or expecting is some sort of easily reached reunion. "Mary, I'm not sure I can answer that. We've given it a try and we can't ignore the real history between us. I spent a lot of time angry with you and having no idea why you broke it off."

She leans back in her seat, looking off to the side, "I know, I know, you're right. I'm sorry; I really am. I wish there would have been some way to make it easier. I'm sorry. I'm really sorry. I wish that I could have handled it better. Have you ever been faced with a difficult situation, where every possible option would be painful?"

Creek is still not ready to move on from his grievance. "Wait, Mary. You suddenly disappeared without telling me why, and have left me in the dark for years, wondering if it was another guy, or the way my breath smelled, or who knows what. That was painful for me. I'm the one who had no options; I simply had to take the pain of your decision."

"I know, I know, Creek, and I'm sorry. But wait, please, there is more that I have to tell you." She leans forward with her head angled slightly downward, looking up at him, meeting his eyes.

Folding her arms over her lap, Mary says, "Creek, I was pregnant, and had an abortion."

Stunned, Creek doesn't respond. There are competing signals inside of him. One of the signals is telling him everything is normal, this is not a big deal and it was a long time ago, there is nothing to be upset about. The other signal is shocked, jarred, confounded.

He is nauseous; he walks to the bathroom in the back of the coffee shop and throws up in a dirty toilet. When he comes back with a wet face Mary is still sitting there.

Neither of them looks at the other. Creek quietly asks, "The baby, it was mine?"

"Yes." Her one word reply is about all either of them can handle.

Mary's elbows are on the table and her face is in her hands. The more she thinks, the more she wants to get up and run out; she stops thinking and silently hums an old lullaby her mother used to sing to her. In Creek's hands rests the next move—whether they will reconcile or dispose of the reunion. A single thought, miraculous, lands gracefully like a canoe on a beach and rests in his mind. There is no other way to proceed: he must ease this woman's pain. That he must let go of years of pain he does not consider. He has a single goal: peace. Creek reaches across the table, he clings to the matter at hand, and gently squeezes her arm. From this precarious peak of clarity, he says to her, "Mary, it's okay."

The womb—dark, warm, quiet—once, once upon a shooting star. Timid yet powerful, delicate yet enduring, the beginning. Wait and see. Death. Forgiveness. The greatest truths cannot be proven, only proved when allowed to be true—hovering like humming birds, easily spooked. Truths are guarded by their frailty. Snuff. For man it is impossible, undoable, unimaginable, irrevocable. If there is no spring, if there is no scent of spring, if there is no memory of spring, then how can spring come again. Unrest signifies the struggle; rest, the end. This much, at least, is known; the wrongdoing can never be undone.

Of course there is no easy answer here; there is no easy action, only grace to be granted.

"Mary, it's okay," Creek says, and there is a clearing in the woods. Stargazer lilies grow on the forest floor. For years on end the words stood in the wind waiting to be heard in the space between Creek and Mary.

He is not saying her actions back then were okay. He is not saying she did the right thing. He is saying, "Mary, it's okay," meaning he is here with her now, sharing the weight of her pain.

It often rains at night in Centralia, and during the day. For half of the year the world turns in upon Centralia with cloudy wet skies like a morning glory at night; the other half of the year the town blooms in the glorious sunlight of late spring, summer, and early fall. The marvelously tactful morning glory opens during the day because the heat of day causes the inner surface of the petals to grow. During the night the inner surface stops growing but the outer surface continues, causing the flower to close. So too, the town is continually flexing then resting, singing then silent.

This is a good reason to be in Centralia. Bring a knot that cannot be untied. Allow the expansion and contraction of the place to work on the knot. Stay still and let the environment massage the knot, feeling out the tangles, working loose the ends, slowly doing what cannot be done with your own hands.

How can it be? Mysterious thing! Maybe this is why the town rises and falls. By remaining in perpetual reconstruction the town avoids the error of overdevelopment. This mechanism is built into the ecology of the place to keep it from aggrandizement of ambitions. There is just the right amount of moss, just enough to gently point out what has been standing unattended for too long, just enough to make it all look pretty anyway.

Creek and Mary have moved into a new season; their morning glory is opening again. In the coffee shop he holds her hand across the table, closes his eyes, and gently pulls her closer, placing the back of her hand against his closed right eye.

A week later they are together for a dinner at Swordsmith's. Around a table covered by a dark blue tablecloth (a tablecloth that is also a map of the stars spread out over the cloth in two large, slightly overlapping circles) sit Creek, Mary, Stan, Perseus Swordsmith, and Diana Goodrich-Swordsmith. Perseus sits at the head of the table near the constellation Hercules; Diana is across from him near Sagitarius; Creek and Mary sit on the side to Perseus's right near Leo and Virgo; Stan is across from them between the oceanic constellations Pisces and Cetus.

If instead of sitting around a flat table they were all really on the sphere represented by the two circles on the table cloth—the topological puzzle pieced back together—their seating arrangement would prove to be more than coincidence. Perseus and Diana would actually be close together, separated only by Ophiuchus. Creek and Mary would be right next to each other, not very far away from Perseus and Diana. Stan would be on the other side of the sphere from them in the area the ancients of the Mediterranean saw as a chaotic sea representing the unknown. On each of the celestial poles is placed a tall white candle in a silver candlestick; the Northern is on Swordsmith's end on the star Polaris; the Southern is by Diana near the constellation Octans.

On an actual sphere these two candles would be opposite each other. The planet Earth and its solar system are inside this sphere. As the Earth spins on its tilted axis and rotates around the Sun, as the Moon makes its 29-day trip around the Earth, the stars appear to spin around the slightly shifting candlesticks, and day and night as well as seasons pass in the form of time—days, months, years. Movement is time.

The group of diners sit around the heavens like celestial demi-gods dipping breads, meats, and vegetables into the melted cheese fondue pots near the celestial poles. Time passes for the melted cheese as it slowly rotates in its bowl from the heat beneath it and disappears with each demi-god's dip. The Milky Way sprawls across the length of the table in a gentle "S" curve.

As he often does, Perseus has moved his wine glass to his left hand. When he picks up the glass, Aquila the eagle and its star Altair are exposed. Holding his glass in front of him he makes a toast, "A toast, to the good people before me, may your hearts be softened my friends, may you ride through the night skies with glee, may there always be cheese in your pots for dipping, and don't forget to hold hands when you dance." They smile, clink glasses together, and drink.

After about a half-hour of light conversation, when a lull in the conversation occurs, Perseus addresses the whole group, "There has been something on my mind lately and I would really like to hear your thoughts on it. I've been thinking about the bigger picture of my life and what sort of impact my life is having on the world. I'm imagining myself as an anthropologist studying the person Perseus Swordsmith in a scientific way, assessing the impact this person has had on his environment, his society, his culture, future cultures. I'm trying to realize an outside and objective assessment of myself. And well, no, I'm sorry to disappoint, I'm

not asking each of you to dissect me right here and now. Instead
I'm wondering if each person would be willing to attempt a short
summary of their own life's impact. I'm really curious to hear how
you would approach the question."

Without much hesitation Stan jumps right in, "Well, for me
that's a fairly easy question. I see myself as basically a low impact
person. Most of my life has been spent working on fairly mean-
ingless jobs. I am part of a church now and I guess the church
on the whole has some impact but I'm not sure my being there
really makes a difference." Stan stops there with nothing more to
say. There is a moment of awkward silence because the others are
expecting him to say more.

Diana leans toward Stan, her bright red hair falling over
her right shoulder and onto the tablecloth, and says, "Stan, we
are very glad you are here tonight. And you are probably making much more of a difference in the world than you think." She
winks as she finishes her sentence, making Stan feel good about
himself and nearly forget the conversation all together. Then Diana continues, "To answer your question Perseus Hercules," she
winks across the table, "I would say my life has been like a song
in the world. I hope that my song makes other people's lives more
enjoyable, more live-able. I would like to think that I'm helping to
motivate with a song, sort of like the dwarfs in Snow White, whistling while they work."

Perseus answers her softly, "Thank you, my dear, for your
song."

Creek is the next to offer his thoughts as he leans forward
and runs the backs of his curled fingers across his forehead, "This
is a tough question for me. When I stop to assess my life, I've
really done more damage than I've done good. I was a bully in
high school. Most of my time was spent thinking of ways to pick

on other people and make myself look 'cool.' Then it didn't get any better in college. I basically gave my whole life to the soccer team and pretty much ignored studying and learning from classes. I didn't really even have any good friendships. An outside assessment would probably sum me up in one word, 'selfish.' I haven't even kept close to my family. My brother Dollar and I have become more and more distant. Now he lives with my Mom, only a ten-minute drive away, and I rarely see them. When I do see my Dad I spend most of the time getting frustrated with him. The thought that he's left my Mom and is 'dating' some girl my age makes me think of him as a joke. Then there's my older brother who I haven't seen in years. I just feel like I'm part of a voyage that has gone wrong and is coming off the rails."

Stan chimes in, "But what about me Creek? I'm glad you're around. You've been a good friend to me."

Perseus looks Creek in the eyes and says, "Creek, thank you so much for your honesty. I hope you are finding at least some cracks of light in the dark world you've described. From my perspective, the fact that you can see your dilapidated shell, means there is already a fair amount of light getting in. It's wonderful. I want to encourage you not to give up but to keep letting the shell be broken so more and more light can get in. You are a good man."

As he looks down shyly Creek does not have a response for Perseus. Slightly embarrassed, he is also warmed by Perseus's words and is quieted as a result.

Sensing that the others are now expecting a response from her Mary begins talking without much thought. She had been thinking about Creek. "Umm, this is hard, I don't really think about things like this too much. I guess I'd think that I'm not really making much of a impact, sort of like Stan. But I don't think I'm like Creek, I can't really say that I matter that much, to make such a negative impact. I don't know. I'm definitely not a song like Diana." Mary is fiddling with her fondue stick in her right hand, spinning it like a butterfly between her thumb and index finger. She says, "I guess I'm hopeful that I'll still have a chance to make a good impact. I don't know, does that make any sense?"

From the end of the milky way Diana answers, "Mary, I think it makes a lot of sense. Sometimes it's much better to be hopeful for the future than to dwell in the past. Well, Perseus," Diana holds up her wine glass, she pauses as some refill their glasses for the toast, then resumes, "I'd like to make a toast: to the beautiful honesty of our noble guests."

After they've toasted, Perseus stands but doesn't walk away from the table. He addresses the group as would a president, or the commander of an army, looking down at them, moving his eyes from person to person as he speaks, "There are few pleasures greater to me than sharing a meal and connecting with a group such as this. Thank you so much for attempting to answer my question. I have listened carefully and have learned from each of your responses. I have formulated my own response. If you will oblige me, here it is: Perseus has kept his heart soft and open. He has followed the path revealed to him to the best of his ability. Surely he is not without fault but he has contributed to the lives of his students, friends, and family. Perseus has been Perseus Swordsmith to as many as have allowed him. His impact on the world fulfils its small part in the design of a much greater work." He pauses to allow others to respond.

When there is no response, he continues, "Okay, okay, enough of this heavy stuff. If you're all up for it let's go outside for a lazy walk—under the real stars."

Further out of town under the same stars, up on the hill, Dollar and his Mother are both eating, both in the kitchen, but they are not eating together. They are both talking but they are not talking in cooperation. Instead their conversation is like a sword-fight—they fight against each other. This swordfight is character-ized by familiarity between opponents; they have fought each other many times and they both know the opponent well.

But they fight with words not swords. Their facial expressions are like the footwork between swordfighters being watched and interpreted in aid to anticipation.

When he sees the slightest dip in the point of her sword ac-companied by a small backward movement of her right elbow he knows she will thrust for his body. He can easily defend that thrust with a quick, though not deadly, chop to her right shoulder from the outside, forcing her to adjust and defend the chop. But when this chain of events occurs (she attempts the thrust then sees he is going for the chop disruption) she simply takes one step back and swings her sword counter-clockwise connecting with the motion of his chop from the outside and pushing his sword in front of her and across her, leaving her with the best attack position and him with a crossed arm and exposed shoulder. This is just one of the hundreds of ways the battle can play out.

She says to him with assertive eyes, "what does the day hold for you?"

Dollar can tell from her eyes, like footwork bringing her within striking distance, this question carries the weight of attack. She is obviously asking not out of simple casual conversation but because she sees that he's getting a slow start to the day and hasn't done his usual job-hunt through the paper. Not prepared with a counter attack, Dollar must simply defend against the subtle attack by making its intentions obvious, overburdening it with energy. "Well, I don't have a job yet, if that's what you're getting at. But maybe you have some great ideas for me today?" His sarcasm is like a wrist-lock on the end of a reversal.

Her only option is to either cry "mercy," or ignore the pain from the wrist-lock and manufacture a counter twist in the hope that he's left some other area vulnerable in his focus on the wrist-lock. She stays in the fight, "I have an idea, why don't you clean out the garage; I've only been asking you to do that for the last three weeks."

Caught by surprise, Dollar's only option is to retreat. He walks out of the kitchen, saying, "Oh, yeah, that's right—I had totally forgotten. I'll try to get to that at some point." But instead of walking to the garage he walks to his bedroom and shuts the door.

Dollar lies on his bed thinking about how the world has turned against him. He feels like he is a king who has been captured and forced to live like a slave. He flies a light airplane, alone, against a mighty storm.

When the pilot of a small airplane realizes his plane has failed and is going to crash he has a decision to make. Will he continue to attempt gaining control of plane or will he put on his parachute and jump out, leaving the plane to its destiny as a heap of scrap metal? If he doesn't face the fact that his plane is doomed he will continue trying to save it and eventually end up squashed inside the heap of metal on the ground. However, if he recognizes the problem and jumps out of the plane before it crashes he has some chance of surviving. In this case the question of when he decides to jump is important. Basically, if he waits too long he will be too close to the ground for the parachute to slow his descent and he will end up a lifeless heap of flesh and bones on the ground. Though generally speaking, there is an adequate amount of time for the pilot to assess the problem with the plane, put on the parachute, and jump before he risks the "splat on the ground" fate.

Dollar's airplane is still several thousand feet above the ground but it has been failing for quite some time; the time until it crashes is only getting shorter. The worst thing for him would be to pretend the plane is not even falling. The second worst thing would be to resign himself to the fall and take solace in the ever shortening time before he's dead. His habit is to escape reality, find something that will keep his mind off the plummeting plane. This is the same impulse as the one to jump from the top of a cliff, the impulse to fall in front of a speeding train, to let the car curl gently, head-on, into oncoming traffic. It is the second temptation of Christ in the desert, to throw himself from the temple and let the angels work it out. Christ quotes scripture to Satan in response, "Do not put your Lord your God to the test."

The problem is, Dollar believes he is a good person who has done right and deserves better than he's been given; he is an imprisoned king. Thus, he will not face the facts of his crashing plane: he will put the Lord to the test.

Oblivion. It is a scary place that feels lawless because of its adherence to law, merciless because of its adherence to justice. Oblivion is like a desert mirage, like a shower that spits out dry sand. It is lipstick on a dead pig, oinking in the electric chair.

Dollar takes the metal box out of his bottom dresser drawer and reads through some of Elle's old notes to him, mostly taking in the smell of her perfume.

The following morning, Creek and Mary are walking hand in hand along Tower Street in downtown Centralia.

Sometimes when a couple is walking together holding hands there is a slight awkwardness to the movement. It's hard to know what exactly is causing the awkwardness because it is an incredibly complex situation. First of all there is the emotional aspect, the relationship between the two people. It will inevitably affect their body language toward each other. If it's a young relationship there might be an unhindered magnetism. If it's an older relationship there might be the casual element of familiarity. If it's even older there might be some resentment, possibly boredom, but also an accompanying strength in the other's trust, reliability, and willingness to look beyond the negatives.

In addition to the nature of the relationship having an effect there are also the basic physics and mechanics of the two physically constructed figures in motion, joined at one point through the hands. The motion of one body alone is enough to beguile imitation. Each person's step-length, bodily-proportions, hip-twist, shoulder-swing, elbow-bend, head-movement, is slightly different, and in combination extremely unique. When two of these unique movers are joined together, hand in hand, in space, in time, the permutations are endless. Still yet to be considered is each individual's responsiveness to the other. If both are uncompromising with their movements there might be problems, and if both are overly compromising there might also be problems. There are at least three levels of analysis . . . of two complex systems attempting to harmonize. It's amazing anyone attempts to hold hands at all.

However, as Creek and Mary walk their harmony is so perfect it is almost heard as just one note. There is a natural synchronicity to their bodies and spirits in this moment. The flowerpots they pass have been in hibernation all winter but as Creek and Mary pass, the buds open ever so slightly, stirred to respond.

Dollar is not so lucky as he dreams, sleeping late into the morning in his bedroom. In the dream he is in an unfamiliar house. The architecture of the house is confusing with none of the rooms appearing to relate to each other spatially. There are frequent changes in the floor level, few windows, and many small hallways with turns at odd angles. He is trying to find his way back to the front door so he can get some fresh air. He is desperate for light, clean, open, fresh air, fresh air, fresh air. The hallways and rooms are getting smaller and there have been no windows for quite some time.

Occasionally he hears muffled voices through the walls. It's hard to tell if the voices are also inside the house or coming from outside in the fresh air. It's hard to tell who's voices he's hearing but he thinks it is probably Creek, Elle, and Lorne. There are objects on the floor he picks up every once in a while, a sock, a comb, some tissue paper. He can tell these are things his mom has dropped. Off to the left is a very narrow hallway with what appears to be some natural light. Dollar squeezes into the hallway holding the objects he has picked up against his chest. As he inches sideways towards what look like stairs leading up at the end of the hallway a few of the things he's holding begin to slip from his hands and nearly fall. There are about five stairs going up with a ceiling only four feet above them. Then the stairs continue up but there is a turn to the right so he can't yet see how far they go.

One of his mom's hair brushes has fallen from his hand onto the first step where his feet are now. He wants to retrieve it but at the same time he is finally able to peer up and around the corner. His urge to go back and retrieve the brush is equally as strong as his urge to continue upward. But the corner is incredibly narrow and the five stairs above it have only a two-foot ceiling overhead. Dollar can see a small sliver of blue sky in a narrow line above the last stair. He looks up, then turns his eyes, but not his cramped head, down to the brush on the steps below. He feels incredibly uncomfortable. He is trapped. Going forward appears nearly impossible. Maybe if his hands were empty and he could bend his legs to push, maybe he could inch his way upward and out.

A sound from outside trickles down to him reminding him of Elle laughing. He wants to move forward toward the sound but going back would immediately create more space and he'd be able to hold onto the things he's picked up. Though the hallways inside seems endless and confusing at least he'd be able to walk comfortably. He lies on the tight stairway clutching the loose objects to his chest with his head angled up toward the sliver of blue light.

1982

Soda and Crackers

Twelve years later Dollar wakes from a dream, wakes from a long night of sleep. He is thirty-eight years-old. It's 7 am and time for him to go to work at the lumber mill. He is not happy about opening his eyes, not happy about pulling on his work jeans, not happy about the pain in his lower back. As he takes the lunch he packed the night before from the refrigerator of this little house on Galvin Road he can see light from the television flashing in the living room: Mom is already awake, or maybe she never went to bed.

At work during their lunch break Dollar and two guys talk about old poker games they'd won big and this leads to Dollar inviting them to a game at his house. In the evening Dollar brings them home with him. Susan has scrap-booking supplies spread over the dining room table and is watching the television through the dining room into the living room. "Oh, hi Mom. These guys came over to play some poker. Um, do you mind if we use the table?"

One of the other men says, "Oh, no, she'd have to stop what she's working on. We can find something else."

Dollar answers, "Well, there's a card table in the garage, there's even a TV in there, but it's not hooked up."

The other man replies, "Doesn't your garage get cold?"

"Yeah, it gets cold, but listen, I've got an idea. Mom, how about we move the card table and TV into the basement, and you can work down there. It's not as cold down there as it is in the garage, and I think there's even that old armchair from the old house packed into one of the corners. The guys and I will set it up, it won't take more than a few minutes." She doesn't answer but Dollar directs them into the garage to get the little television and the card table.

Dollar gathers her scrap-booking materials into a pile and follows the men with the card table and TV into the basement. It's not a finished basement. There is a concrete floor and concrete walls. The stairs are simple platforms nailed between two side-pieces spanning the eight feet from ceiling to floor. In one corner is a water heater and a sump-pump with an exposed, two-foot in diameter, hole in the foundation dropping about six feet down. Next to these is a shop sink made of plastic with four metal legs. In the opposite corner there's a pile of furniture and appliances from the old house with a furniture blanket somewhat covering the top portion. They pull the armchair out of the pile. Visible in the ceiling are the supporting boards for the floor above as well as a lot of old wiring and a few pipes. There is one small window at the top of the wall on the side of the house. The smoked plate-glass can't be opened and doesn't allow any clarity of vision but does allow a little bit of natural light in. There'd be nothing to see through it anyway, as it sits in a window-well that is overgrown with weeds. Otherwise, the only light source is one exposed light-bulb in the ceiling by the base of the stairs. Dollar pulls on its two-inch chain with some effort, turning it on.

When they've set up the TV on a few cardboard boxes and pulled the chair in front of it with the card table at its side, Dollar's two co-workers head back up the stairs. Dollar walks to the base of the stairs and without turning around to face her, says, "I don't know how long we're gonna be playing, so just knock on the door and let me know if you need anything." He walks up the stairs and shuts the door behind him without waiting for a reply.

"Then Jesus said to the Jews who had believed in him, 'If you continue in my word, you are truly my disciples; and you will know the truth, and the truth will make you free. . . . Very truly, I tell you, everyone who commits sin is a slave to sin. The slave does not have a permanent place in the household; the son has a place there forever. So if the Son makes you free, you will be free indeed" (John 8: 31-36).

The poker game goes late into the night. Mrs. Moore falls asleep in the armchair with the TV quietly flickering in front of her.

That night Dollar dreams of a time when he was happy, strong, focused: he dreams of his childhood. The dream, more vivid than a movie, takes place in the woods behind his house. Dollar runs through the woods, Elle just behind him. Since Creek and his friend are faster, since Dollar and Elle are younger, they don't stand a chance of escaping from the older boys. Wild, ag-gressive, zealous, Creek and his friend bear down on the two spies who they've caught eavesdropping on their stick/sword-fight.

Overcome. Calmly Dollar turns to face the attackers. He is impressed by his own calm, calmness like a buoy at sea. Guided by confidence he stands between the two stick-wielding boys and Elle. Unexpectedly there is a throbbing—sharp and painful—beneath his eye. Putting his hand to the spot below his eye he turns to make sure Elle is at a safe distance, but she is gone: she had never been there. Judgment, wrath, cruelty, rage—when he turns back toward Creek the fury of the heavy stick lands just below his eye, tearing open the skin.

He wakes as an adult. Hurried and anxious, confused and frazzled, Dollar enters the kitchen and is surprised to see his mom at the table eating breakfast and reading the paper. Pouring himself a cup of coffee, the coffee she made an hour ago, he says, "Good morning Mom. Sorry, I totally forget to let you know when the guys left last night."

She answers without looking up from the paper, "That's okay honey; I fell asleep in the basement, in the chair, in front of the TV. I'm so glad you had guests to the house." There is a pause as she turns the page of the newspaper. "Now you better hurry or you'll be late for work." Dollar pours his coffee into a thermos and walks out the front door without saying goodbye.

When Dollar comes home from work that night he finds his mom, once again, working on a scrapbook at the table. She is assembling old photos of their family vacations from before the boys were teens. It's a Friday night, and Dollar's tradition on Friday nights is to watch a couple of movies with the lights off in the living room. Instead of greeting her he gets right to the point when he walks in the door, "Mom, I've got a couple of horror movies I'm gonna watch with the lights off in the living room."

Susan is visibly happy to have him back at the house and offers a smiling response, "Oh, that's nice honey. I wish I liked those movies."

Somewhat irked by her smile, because he's tired from work and because he doesn't like being the highlight of her day he responds, "So, I think you'll have to move somewhere else, because the lights should be off in here too."

"Okay sweetie, that's fine, I'll just go downstairs and watch some TV. I'll just grab a few crackers and a soda to snack on."

Dollar doesn't reply but goes to change out of his work clothes into a pair of well-worn sweatpants and matching sweatshirt. Excited about slipping into a distant world of imagination in his movies he returns to the living room in his slippers, turns off the lights, and settles in to the couch as his movie begins. Susan has already gone downstairs, shutting the door behind her. The night passes like a mist; arrives, obscures, departs.

Late on Saturday morning he wakes: returns to the daylight, and to the responsibilities of home ownership. Lawn-mowing, gutter-cleaning, bathroom-cleaning—each chore sounds in his ears like the rhythmic beeping of an alarm clock. He doesn't shower. Neither does he reflect on the evening before, nor does he plan out the day ahead. He pushes into the day with the obedience of a burdened ox.

Back and forth across the lawn he mows in parallel rows. The mower (loud, droning, constant, destructive) can be felt through his hands and arms, into his torso and head: he embraces the feeling. When he comes back into the house, Dollar washes his hands in the sink, but can't find a kitchen towel to dry them. "Hey Mom?" he says without turning from the sink. There is no answer so he turns around and aims his question down the hallway toward her bedroom, "Mom?" Again there is no reply. The basement. He walks to the basement door, opening it, and speaks down the stairs, "Mom, do you know where the hand-towels are?"

From the sharp light of a single bulb comes a cloying answer, "Look on the dryer honey, oh, and can you leave another can of soda and a pack of crackers there at the top of the stairs for me? I didn't want to come upstairs because of all the noise."

Dollar is frustrated that she seems to be complaining about the noise the mower makes—as if he could somehow make it quieter. By this point he has unconsciously dried his hands on his sweatpants, and forgotten about finding the hand-towels. He takes a can of soda and a packet of crackers out of the pantry and puts them on the top step of the basement stairs, then shuts the door again.

That evening Dollar again finds himself watching television in the living room with the lights off. He has two beers and a bowl of honey-roasted peanuts beside him as part of his Saturday night routine. Mist fills the night air.

In the morning when Dollar wakes on the couch the mist is still there. Sitting up, he looks toward the kitchen table expecting to see his mom but she is not there, and the smell of coffee is not in the air. The basement door is still closed. With a slight groan he slowly ambles into the kitchen and begins making his own coffee. The brewing coffee fills the air and Dollar remembers his coworker, Steve, is coming over to borrow his lawnmower. Steve and his young son live a few houses away. Dollar can vaguely remember the phone call from Steve last night—something about his lawnmower not starting and coming by around ten o'clock with his son because he can't leave him alone.

He opens the door to the basement and sees that the overhead light bulb is off though the TV is flickering light. "Mom, I just remembered that Steve and his kid are coming by this morning."

She answers as though the conversation had been going on for half-an-hour, as if within the normal flow of everyday exchange, "Oh, thanks for letting me know honey. Why don't you lock that door, I don't want to surprise anyone who might open it and wander down here. And can you put another pack of crackers and a soda at the top of the stairs. Thanks honey."

Dollar finds the key to the door among a drawer-full of random little tools, gadgets, rubber-bands, pens. He locks the door and decides to put the key in his bottom dresser drawer under the old metal lock-box where it will be easier to find. As he's putting the key under the box he's distracted because he forgot to get the crackers and soda for his mom. Leaving the drawer open he returns to the pantry for her food. With some frustration he realizes that he's already locked the door to the basement and left the key in his bedroom and now he's standing in front of the locked basement door with crackers in one hand and a soda in the other.

There is an air vent at his feet. Dollar gets down on his hands and knees, lifts up the grate to the vent and looks down a shallow dusty shaft to a narrow ledge that is open to the darkness of the basement. Placing the soda and crackers on the ledge he speaks into the vent, into the dusty opening, "Mom, the soda and crackers are here in the air vent."

After a pause of a few seconds he hears her unchanged voice, "Oh, thanks sweetie, I see them."

When Steve and his son, Derek, arrive, Dollar is watching a football game on TV, eating a bologna on white-bread, with mustard and mayonnaise, sandwich. Dollar offers Derek a soda and pours it into a glass with four ice cubes. When Dollar and Steve go to the garage to get the lawn-mower he says to Steve's kid, "You can watch the game for a few minutes if you want."

Derek sits down on the couch where Dollar had been sitting and sees the half-eaten sandwich on the coffee table. He's not really hungry but finds the sandwich enticing because it belongs to someone else and it will enter someone else's body through their mouth. Not hearing any voices nearby he carefully picks up the sandwich and takes a small bite, trying to make his bite marks fit in with those that were already there. The sandwich tastes salty and exciting. Derek picks up the remote control and focuses on the large, red, on/off button. He looks around the room then puts the remote near his mouth and licks the button with the tip of his tongue—and puts it back exactly where he found it. Sensing a swelling in his pants he gets up to look for the bathroom to pee. In the hallway he sees a closed door and tries its handle. There is some give in the locked door causing it to rattle back and forth as he turns the knob and pushes. He hears a woman's quiet voice through the door, "Who's there?"

Startled by the unexpected voice and the unknown person in the house he runs back to the couch where he was sitting and adjusts his pants to hide the bulge. Just as he sits down his Dad and Dollar come inside through the back door. He can hear his Dad's voice mid-sentence, " . . . just a little bit strange sometimes."

And then he hears Dollar's awkward reply, "Oh."

Steve and Dollar walk into the living room with their eyes on the TV. Dollar addresses Derek, "How's the game going?"

Derek can only return a shy reply, without looking away from the TV, "okay."

Steve says, "Well, thanks much, Dollar. I'll have the mower back by tomorrow night. Son, finish your drink now, say thank you to Mr. Moore, and let's get back home."

Derek struggles to finish the soda, as his bladder is full and his pants throbbing. He gets up awkwardly saying, "Thank you, Mr. Moore."

Each morning Dollar places a can of soda and a pack of

crackers in the vent before he goes to work.

Susan's sleep schedule is different now that she stays in the basement. She is generally on a cycle of three hours awake and five hours asleep. It's possible that checking various channels on the television could help her figure out what day of the week it is but she doesn't really care what day of the week it is. The hole in the concrete near the water pump makes for a toilet and the sink allows her to wash every few days. There is a faint rainbow that moves across the floor on sunny days as the light catches the angled edge of her one small window. However, Dollar's regular footsteps above her are her true interest. In the morning she wakes at the slightest sound and listens for the slow creaking of his steps moving from the bedroom side of the house to the kitchen. In the evening when she hears the front door closing she turns the volume down on the TV and listens to his steps moving into the house.

In the dim light of the basement's mid-day, Susan dreams; footsteps fill the dream. In the dream she is aware that the world is without order; it is a feeling pervading the dream like nausea. There is a single disquieting aspect to the footsteps she hears: they seem to move without pattern or rhythm. Her world (once lulled into calmness by the regularity of footstep sounds) is filled with confusion and anxiety. Once the sound of footsteps was clear; now, muffled and evasive. Whether stubbornness is inherent to the nature of dreams or whether this dream in particular allows no refutation, the comforting regularity of the rainbow moving across the floor is totally absent from her awareness. Cold and alone and exhausted, she desires only to know that there is some order in the sounds, some meaning—even if only revealed in pattern—in the dark concrete maze of her dream. Flat. Her hands press against a cool concrete wall. Difficult to discern, her own heartbeat flickers like a dying bulb. She tries to walk a straight line down the hall—to keep straight in the oddly crooked hallway. Surrendering, she crumples like a ball of newspaper in the corner of the dream.

1990

Historian

Eight years later, in the town next-door, Chehalis, Creek and Mary are sitting on either side of their eight-year-old boy Thomas, reading him a book in bed. Thomas has dark hair, a sharp nose, and a stocky build like his father. As far as eight-year-olds go he is relatively stable emotionally. His eyes are darker than his mother or father's; like still pools of water they make no superfluous movements. Creek and Mary decided to have only one child. It's one of those decisions they reached together silently, without discussion, similarly to how they decided to only allow folded clothes in the bedroom.

Though he's too young to categorize his passion, Thomas has shown an interest in historical accounts of America from the Civil War to the First World War. Remarkably for a boy his age, he watches and re-watches documentaries on these two wars and the time between them, documentaries on the building of the Panama

Canal, on Thomas Edison, on early electric cars. On this night his parents are reading him a book about Edison inventing the light-bulb.

Thomas asks his parents, "Did Thomas Edison ever go to Europe like Grandma?"

The question catches them by surprise. Creek answers, "That's a good question. I'm not sure, but I do know that his inventions made it to Europe. They have light-bulbs there, just like we do."

Susan wakes in her chair in Dollar's basement. She assumes it is night because there is no light coming in the little frosted glass window. In the dark corner behind her is a stack of nearly three-thousand empty soda cans, one from each day of the last eight years. Next to the cans is a tall pile of cracker wrappers. Her daily exercise consists of walking to the vent to retrieve the day's soda and cracker rations. On the couch upstairs, in front of the quiet television, Dollar is sleeping next to two empty beer bottles and a bowl of peanut crumbs. Under the metal lockbox in the bottom drawer of Dollar's dresser the key to the basement door has been untouched for eight years.

Eight years ago when Dollar first lied to Creek about their Mother it wasn't premeditated. Creek caught Dollar off-guard when he asked if he could come by and see her. Dollar didn't want Creek to find out about her living in the basement, much less to see the actual conditions of her living quarters. Caught by surprise he answered, "Oh, Creek, I'm so sorry. She left for Europe last week. She wanted to say goodbye to you, but everything with the plane ticket happened so quickly. She's gone to look for our long-lost relatives and said she might just stay there for good if she likes it."

For the last eight years Creek and his family have believed that Susan is in Europe and has severed communications with them. They don't know why, and they don't know if she will ever come back. Thomas hasn't met his grandmother but has heard a few stories about her from his parents. Most of the stories are about her fight against cancer. About once a year Dollar tells Creek a new story about how he's heard from her and she's doing fine, "staying with some relatives in England, not sure how much longer she'll stay."

Sitting on either side of Thomas after answering his question about Edison and Europe, Creek and Mary tell Thomas another short story about his grandmother. They tell him that she asks about him often, and that she loves him very much.

As Creek looks at the top of Thomas's head, he thinks about the life ahead of Thomas and the many twists and turns it will hold. Creek reflects on the rocky paths he and Mary traveled to get where they are. In some ways he wants everything to be perfect for Thomas. He wishes only happiness and success for him. But Creek knows how important all of the failures and sadness were in his own life. They pushed him in the right directions and helped him learn to love what is. Creek's love for Mary and for life in general has only gotten bigger and bigger over time, and it all started with some major failures and sadness. Over time, as he learned to love what is, the awareness of being loved right down to his core grew in Creek and became the foundation of a relationship with Jesus, his Lord and Savior. This relationship spread into the rest of Creek's life and family.

Warmth. Creek's family together on a twin bed, epitomizes cozy. Love, they share generously. Together they are a home. Peaceful and safe, comfortable and trusting, they fall asleep with their heads together in Thomas's room. Fast asleep. They dream together, the same dream, dreaming of a world saturated with color, where they are hiking toward a mountain, feeling more energy with each step.

2000

Our Family

Ten years later, in the same bedroom, young Thomas wakes next to his young wife Ellen. Thomas and Ellen are each eighteen-years-old; they have been best friends since they were 12. Creek and Mary are happy to have Thomas and Ellen living with them while the young couple attends the community college. Creek and Mary are especially excited about the little boy Ellen is expecting in about five months. Thomas and Ellen have decided to name him James after the civil war historian James G. Randall.

Thomas is studying late 19th and early 20th century American history. Ellen is working towards becoming a Nurse Practitioner.

Ellen's parents live down the street. Ellen and Thomas grew up exploring the neighborhood together—playing in sprinklers and selling lemonade, playing tag and reading comics, walking through backyards and riding bicycles—exploring life together. Though they are young their relationship embodies a sincerity and purity not often realized in relationships.

As Thomas eats a bowl of cereal in the kitchen, his Dad, Creek, tells him about an idea he has. "I'm going to call it, Our Family," Creek says with enthusiasm as he writes his idea on a scrap of paper. "People in the community will be able to recommend old-folks who they think would appreciate a visit from kids. Schools will make it a part of their after-school programs. There will be a coach and everything. Maybe they can even figure out a way to give credits and involve the old-folks in mentoring of some type."

Thomas says, "I like the idea, Dad. Definitely keep it simple though. I think you want to leave some of the outcome to chance. Using the schools and having a coach sounds like a great idea—like a sport where instead of competing you are helping people."

2001

Lint

"In that sense it will be true for those who have completed the journey (and for no others) to say that good is everything and Heaven everywhere. But we, at this end of the road, must not try to anticipate that retrospective vision. If we do, we are likely to embrace the false and disastrous converse and fancy that everything is good and everywhere is Heaven" (C.S. Lewis, Preface to The Great Divorce, IX).

About a year later, while Thomas and Ellen are in class, Creek drives his infant grandson, in a car-seat, west on Galvin Road. Creek wants to get out of the house for a little while, and he knows Jim likes riding in the car—it is a fail-proof way to keep him from crying.

And then there is Dollar, driving in the opposite direction, heading into town to re-stock soda and crackers for Susan. Dollar is still in a fog. He is momentarily distracted by a piece of lint on the dashboard. Dollar's car crosses the centerline. There is no time for Creek to swerve.

Dollar survives the crash with two broken ankles. Creek dies almost instantly. Baby Jim survives with no serious injuries.

When the ambulance arrives Dollar is sitting against the passenger side of Creek's car, passed-out, with Jim in his arms.

2010

Prayers

Nine years after the accident, Jim walks past the spot of the crash, picks a blue flower, and goes to visit Dollar as part of his participation in the Our Family program. Some of the insurance money from Creek's death was used to start the program and in nine years it has become successful, a great way for kids to contribute to the community.

From the basement Susan thinks she hears extra footsteps in the house as Jim walks into the kitchen and Dollar offers him a Coke. The extra footsteps are unusual, and she wonders if she is dreaming about the footsteps again. The floor above her is quiet for about 15 minutes while Dollar is showing Jim his irrigation system in the backyard. Then there are a few more minutes of extra footsteps as Jim walks back through the house and leaves through the front door, leaving his small blue flower on the railing of Dollar's front porch. Once Jim is gone, the sounds of the house return to normal for Susan.

Only momentarily distracted, Susan returns to her project. For the last decade or so, ever since the basement TV stopped working, she has been obsessed with her project. Hanging from the exposed boards in the low ceiling are hundreds of her prayer strands: sculptured aluminum cans tied together in strands of ten or so with plastic cracker wrappers. The basement has become like a forest and an ocean, a jungle and a metropolis, filled with the shimmering strands of cut up cans hanging from the ceiling. Thickened by scars, her hands have become tough like a farmer's. With each can she removes the tab on the top and uses it to cut into the body of the can. As she cuts she bends and folds the aluminum, shaping it sometimes into recognizable forms, sometimes geometric, sometimes totally abstract. During the first five or so years of doing this daily she would accidentally cut her hands almost every day. Whether because of the toughness of her scarred skin or because of her experience she cuts herself less now.

While she shapes the cans she prays; with each can she focuses her prayer on a single person or idea. Forgetful. Sometimes she forgets she is praying and as she talks to herself the words become like raindrops falling and landing on grass. And there are times when she simply cannot think of anything or anyone to pray for. When she is unable to come up with an idea, she makes something up. One of the cans, shaped like a starfish, was sculpted while praying for an imaginary woman name Anna who struggles with arthritis; another, like a rocket, while praying for the conflict between warring nations at the bottom of the Atlantic Ocean.

When she is not sleeping or sculpting she walks aimlessly amid the hanging prayers. Like a dance, these walks are an impromptu performance as she responds to each strand in the moment. She gets lost in her performance, lost in her shimmering jungle, lost in her prayers, lost in her 800 square feet of concrete.

Freedom and faith are unexpected guests in Susan's secret basement dungeon. There is so little space and so little possibility of leaving that to mention freedom sounds like a cruel joke. There is so little hope in change and so little desire for it that mentioning faith doesn't make sense. That great symbol of freedom, the eagle, represents power and swift flight in huge open spaces. This is no place for an eagle. In her isolation, the supporting help of faithful friends and family is absent. Even so, the glory and light that pushes through the great dark-blue tarp over the night sky, in stars, also amazingly finds ways to show in the most isolating and constricting places on Earth. Freedom and faith do visit this basement.

This is an external reality that cannot be stifled. They make their way into the darkest places.

2020

Emergence

Dollar is 76 and alone when he dies from a stroke in the middle of the night. Thomas is told that when the police came to the house and found Dollar's body in bed, he had a small Bible in his left hand, open to a page with a pressed and dried blue flower. They also found Susan's decayed body buried in the center of the backyard, with a ceramic eagle marking the grave.

Mary, Thomas, Ellen, Jim, and a handful of people from town are gathered around a two-foot cube of earth cut out of the ground in the cemetery. Dollar's ashes are in a silver urn sitting in the base of the empty cube. The folks standing in a small circle around the grave can just see the top of the urn. At the end of the short ceremony each person walks over to a white, plastic, ten-gallon bucket filled with dirt, takes a handful and walks over to drop it on the urn. As Jim drops dirt on the urn he thinks of his visits with Dollar, starting with that first visit ten years ago. Dollar became less and less communicative as time went on. In the last few visits, Dollar would let him in, and they would walk through the house to the back yard without any conversation. For a while they would sit on the back step of the house looking at the yard without speaking. At one visit Jim brought his pocket Bible and read from Revelation. After that, it became their routine. Dollar never said anything but just sat there looking at the yard. The last visit was at least a year ago and Jim remembers accidentally leaving his pocket Bible on Dollar's back steps. Jim wonders why Dollar hid his great-grandmother from him. With some anger he wishes he would have gotten to know her before she died.

When he's helping clean out the house Thomas finds the Bible and opens to the page with the flower where Revelation 4:2-6 are underlined in shaky blue pen, "At once I was in the spirit, and there in heaven stood a throne, with one seated on the throne! And the one seated there looks like jasper and carnelian, and around the throne is a rainbow that looks like an emerald. Around the throne are twenty-four thrones, and seated on the thrones are twenty-four elders, dressed in white robes, with golden crowns on their heads. Coming from the throne are flashes of lightning, and rumblings and peals of thunder, and in front of the throne burn seven flaming torches, which are the seven spirits of God; and in front of the throne there is something like a sea of glass, like crystal."

Later in the week Thomas and Jim are back cleaning out Dollar's old house. They open the tomb-like basement and discover the hundreds of strands of sculpted cans. Jim is the first to go down there. He yells up to Thomas, "Dad, you have to come down here and see this!" Thomas makes his way through the jungle of hanging cans and opens a rear cellar door that hasn't been opened in decades. Light floods into the basement. The thousands of cans catch the light, spinning gently in the flow of fresh air. Dust from the years of darkness is stirred, making thousands of beams of light visible in the gaps between the cans. It looks like a universe of uniquely shaped stars, spinning in space.

References

Research on the City of Centralia:

Centralia, The First Fifty Years, 1845 -1900, Compiled by Herndon
  Smith.
The Land Called Lewis: A History of Lewis County, Washington,
  by Sandra A. Crowell.

Bible Quotations:

The Holy Bible, New Revised Standard Version

Edition Reference for Page Citations:

Franklin, Benjamin, The Autobiography of Benjamin Franklin, Dover Thrift Editions, 1996.
Lewis, C.S., The Great Divorce, HarperOne, 2001.
Tennyson, Alfred Lord, Idylls of the King, Dover Thrift Editions,
  2004.